Also by Shane Peacock

Eye of the Crow
Death in the Air
Vanishing Girl
The Secret Fiend
The Dragon Turn
Becoming Holmes

The Dark Missions of Edgar Brim

SHANE PEACOCK

Tundra Books

Tundra Books, a division of Random House of Canada Limited,
a Penguin Random House Company

Library and Archives Canada Cataloguing in Publication

Peacock, Shane, author
The undead / Shane Peacock.

(The dark missions of Edgar Brim)
Issued in print and electronic formats.

ISBN 978-1-77049-698-9 (bound).—ISBN 978-1-77049-700-9 (epub)

I. Title.

PS8581.E234U54 2016   jC813'.54   C2015-903997-5
C2015-903998-3

Published simultaneously in the United States of America by Tundra Books of Northern New York, a division of Random House of Canada Limited, a Penguin Random House Company

Library of Congress Control Number: 2015947652

Edited by Tara Walker and Lara Hinchberger
Cover images: (boy) CP Photo Art/Getty Images; (x-ray) Yuji Susaki/Getty Images; (fog) © Deviney/Dreamstime.com; (hole) © Carlos Caetano/Dreamstime.com
Designed by Jennifer Lum
Printed and bound in the USA

www.penguinrandomhouse.ca

1 2 3 4 5 6   21 20 19 18 17 16

TUNDRA BOOKS

Penguin
Random
House

To the admirable Hadley Jane,
who has faced her fears

I

Preparation

I had a dream, which was not all a dream.

∞

"Darkness," George Gordon,
known as Lord Byron (summer 1816)

1

After the Demon

Edgar Brim can't breathe. An old woman is upon him. She digs her knees into his chest, her talon hands grip his throat and her vile breath assaults him. Only his brain is alive and it is on fire. He wants to scream but can't. He opens his mouth but no sound comes out.

"Edgar?"

It's Lucy's voice, distant.

"Master Brim?"

Jonathan is there too, in that realm between sleep and life.

The hag usually comes as Edgar rouses. But today is different. He isn't in his bed. He is a passenger on a locomotive heading north, a bleak landscape whizzing along on either side of the rails.

Is the world out there reality? Or is this thing on his chest?

This time the old crone may kill him. He is sure that one day she will. He tries to tell himself that she doesn't exist, but he knows better. The hag is as authentic as the moors around them.

Edgar imagines how he appears to his friends: his electric expression of fear, wild eyes like a horse's being led to slaughter. He must seem a lunatic, paralyzed on his seat.

Professor Lear barks something out like a gunshot and the old woman begins to fade. She loosens her grip and vanishes as she always has. So far. Edgar sits up.

"Yes?" His voice sounds weak and he hates that.

"Is everything all right?" asks Lucy.

Sounds are coming to him now in a rush: rhythmic chugging, voices and the blast of the train's whistle. He feels cold. Lucy is looking at him with sympathy, Jonathan with concern and the professor with interest.

"It was the hag," says Lear, matter-of-factly, turning back to his paper.

"I am fine," says Edgar.

"We shall tend to her someday," adds Lear, without lifting his eyes, "once we fry a bigger fish." His left hand, his *only* hand, turns another page.

Their mission comes back to Edgar with a jolt. He glances down at the bags by his seat and thinks of the guns inside, his master's weapons. The book he has been reading is still held tightly in his hand, its cover yellow and title blood red, purchased new in London, hot off the press. *The Most Frightening Novel in England!* the advertisement at the W.H. Smith bookstand in Euston Railway Station had said.

He smiles faintly at Lucy. He finds consolation in her face.

"Be there in minutes," says Lear in his deep voice.

———

When the train grinds to a halt at lonely Altnabreac Station, Lucy and Jonathan bounce to their feet: she dressed in a modest brown cotton dress that reaches the floor, her bonnet brown too on her copper-colored hair; he buttoned tightly into a tan corduroy country suit, a cloth hunting cap on his head. Lear is in black from head to foot, as always, his starched white collar barely visible, sliced in two by his black cravat. He stands over Edgar, his massive left hand held out.

"Brim," he says. "It is time."

There had been a day when Edgar feared Professor Lear. But today he fears what they are after even more.

A rough carriage, the transportation for the schoolboys of the College on the Moors, is waiting with the powerful dray horse named William Wilson hitched to it. Up above, the sky is the color of the gruel that Edgar imagines Oliver Twist was served in his workhouse long ago. It always seems that way in this part of the Highlands. Edgar gazes across the barren land, spotting bits of heather here and there, like diamonds in a bog. Where is the demon they seek? Is it out here somewhere, perhaps in the hills killing animals and eating them raw, waiting for this very group to come to it?

The silent driver, whose real name Edgar has never heard, who never speaks a word and apparently cannot speak, snaps the whip in his huge gloved hands and William Wilson begins to amble forward. The driver is hooded but you sometimes see his pronounced scars. His visible features have a patchwork appearance, as if each one belongs to someone else. He is extremely tall and glimpses of his complexion are like pale flashes of the moon.

"We are walking into its trap," says Lear. "But that is what we desire."

They continue in silence. The big wheels turn slowly. The black horse's hooves clap along on the gravel. Lear is deep in contemplation while Jonathan scans the horizon, the knuckles on one hand bone-colored where he grips the seat, the slight bulge in his coat betraying his pistol. Lucy's face is tight and drawn.

Edgar still clutches the book in his hand. He had begun reading it soon after they left London but couldn't take much at once. He had lived it fully each time he turned to it, transported by the author's words to a forest in the Carpathian Mountains in eastern Europe where a dark castle loomed and the hero was being warned not to go. Edgar had *been* that young man when he read. Just a few pages back, he was dropped on a treacherous turn in a road and a freakish, white-faced man offered to deliver him to the castle. The moon was full. Wolves were howling. Edgar had closed the book at that point. The dim light on the moors makes the lurid yellow cover glow, and the scarlet-lettered title, nearly a match for Brim's flame-colored hair, almost vanishes into it.

One can see the college from a long way off, black in this gray and brown world and set upon an elevation against a flat horizon. From a distance, it appears to be a ruin, but as one nears the road that leads to its iron gates, its grandeur is revealed. Its three-and-a-half stories of granite stretch out in long wings and face south toward civilization; its gothic windows, crisscrossed with black lines, are set deep in the stone and seem like eyes. A single black turret towers above.

Lear's leather satchel is beside him on the carriage bench.

Edgar sees a shape protruding in its skin, sharp, as if it wants to slice through. The old man has brought his knife too, as big as a sword.

The mute driver takes them around the curving driveway that winds through the only grass in sight and stops at the wooden doors, like portals for giants.

They open.

Lear has sent word ahead about his two grandchildren. They are expected and are to be employed as his academic assistants, helping him clean up during the last week of school. But that, of course, is not why they are really here, nor has Edgar come back for his graduation.

They are here to kill.

2

Villains in his Bedroom

Sixteen years earlier, little Edgar looked up from his cradle to see a man with dark circles under his eyes approach him in the dimness of the nursery. The man bore a dripping candle in one hand and a fairy tale in the other. He wielded the book like a weapon.

"Ah, the boy and the giant!" said his father, his face becoming clear to the infant.

From somewhere behind Allen Brim, Edgar heard sounds he couldn't identify—sighs and creaks and whispers—sneaking through their barely furnished mansion like the scurrying of ghosts.

Allen began to read and, like magic, the child entered the story. The first part was beautiful—Edgar was a few years older and ascending a fantastic plant into heaven. Everything was green and wonderful, and a shining palace appeared in the distance. But once he went through its doors, there came the thudding of footsteps: the footfalls of a monster. Inside his little mind, the child began to run. He looked behind him as he fled and saw the giant's feet coming around a corner and after him, crushing the stone floor beneath. Terror rose like a volcano inside him.

Fee-fi-fo-fum,
I smell the blood of an Englishman,
Be he live, or be he dead,
I'll grind his bones to make my bread.

The giant reached out and snatched him! He could feel the meaty hands closing around his ribs, squeezing the life from him. The monstrous teeth were thick and blunt and they didn't just slice the boy, they crushed him, tearing him in half and swallowing him in big bleeding bits. Edgar's scream exploded into his father's face and erupted into Raven House, shaking the very walls, it seemed.

The kindly man snapped the book shut and stepped back.

How could this be? he thought. The baby was too small to follow the story. How could it affect him so? Had it been read with too much feeling?

"You . . . you, young sir, must stop that blubbering," said Allen, employing his happy face. The lad began to settle and stared up at his father, who now leaned down to kiss him on his large forehead. Squire Brim's hair was the same color as his son's, their eyes dark blue like a stormy English sky.

"Look, I have ceased reading that tale, my boy," said Allen, holding out his empty hands in their fingerless gloves to his tiny charge. "I shan't do it again."

There hadn't been a fire all day in Raven House, and not a single servant lived or worked anywhere in its many rooms. The squire

9

had so neglected his businesses that he was unable to pay the help, and one after the other, they had left. The Brims came from a long line of industrious country squires and Allen was destroying what they had built. He was a good man, a very good man, but he was a dreamer.

"Shall I offer you something from my own work, my boy?" he asked. He reached for another book, opened it and began to read.

Edgar cried even louder than before.

"A critic!" said Allen. "Well, I do not blame you," he sighed, pulling his woolen greatcoat around his shoulders and his sleeping cap over his ears. He tucked the blanket about his son and they shivered together. "I do not blame you at all."

Squire Brim's latest novel, the one he had just threatened to inflict upon the little one, had sold exactly sixty-six copies. *Pleasant Endings* was an uplifting tale throughout, and tearfully boring. "Should you have troubles sleeping," one reviewer had written, "keep this novel on your bed table and it will solve your problems with admirable alacrity. Simply open it and begin to read. I can assure you that you shall be fast asleep before the first chapter reaches its sunny conclusion."

But wee Edgar Brim disagreed. It was as if the story demanded that he *must* be happy just moments after the life had been scared out of him. He remained wide awake in the old wooden cradle after his father left the room, listening to the footsteps thumping up the stairs and then striking heavily on the bedroom floor above. Edgar had often been up there, carried tenderly in large arms across that big room, and shown the many volumes in the looming bookcase, his eyes drawn to the ones with the brighter covers that were kept way up on the top shelf. His father would sometimes gently set him down on the big bed and simply glow at him.

But now Edgar lay alone as the moonlight streamed in upon him through the bare windows, listening in fear for the sound he knew would come next. And there it was: through the heat pipe that ran between the master bedroom and his room, he heard his father crying, soft, heart-wrenching sobs that filled the air in the nursery.

And in that air, as if on cue, someone began materializing near the ceiling. She floated down toward him, seemingly growing out of the very pain that his father was sending through that pipe. The infant was no longer afraid: she was lovely and smiling at him, like an angel come to soothe him. Edgar reached out his little arms to her, but his hands went right through her. Virginia Brim wasn't really there, for she had died giving birth to him.

Then her face became grotesque and her hands reached for his throat.

3

Fear and Truth

A few years later, in the bleakest part of winter, Allen Brim ascended Raven House's creaking wooden stairs with a smile emerging on his lips. His breath puffed in clouds in front of him and he wrapped his arms close to his frayed coat. Young Edgar was such a sensitive child. Even at age four, it took him forever to settle in his bed. Every night when Allen tiptoed up to his own room, the boy was still fussing. But this evening he seemed to have drifted off!

"It is time," said the squire out loud.

He trembled with excitement. He had been waiting for this for a long time. He wouldn't even think about the empty bed with its two pillows arranged there, just as they always had been when his wife was alive. He would walk past it to the ceiling-high bookcase that ran along every wall. He needed to stand on boxes to reach the top shelf. Books were the only thing he spent his traces of money on these days; that, and a yearly trip to the theater. There was little left for anything else.

Squire Brim was planning to let himself go. Tonight, he would read out loud from one of the stories up there in those lurid covers, exclaiming and gesticulating, wrapped up in its essence. That was the only way to come to grips with a literary work of art. At night in this grim house, these dark tales would arise. He hadn't been able to do this for four years, but tonight, with the boy finally appearing to be deeply asleep, he could unleash them. He knew the words would resonate in the stillness of the room while the blackness glowered through the windows! He tried not to run to the shelves. He wished he had the courage to write such vivid tales, such dark truths.

But which would he choose? He climbed onto his two wooden boxes and moved his shaking fingers along the spines. How about the Russian folktale that told the feats of history's most fearsome witch, Baba Yaga? He imagined that story scaring the life out of him! Or what about John Polidori's *The Vampyre*? Was there ever such a villain as the beast in those pages? Tomorrow, he would go to the village bookshop and purchase *The Strange Case of Doctor Jekyll and Mr. Hyde*, the new novel by Robert Louis Stevenson, just published last week. It was said to be terrifying, the monster so authentic he seemed right next to you. If all went well, Allen could perform it next!

He searched farther along the top shelf. And there it was: the only story for this night. He took it into his hands and descended to the floor. Dare he? He gave it one last thought and reassured himself. His little boy was far away in dreamland, and the floor between them was thick. "*Frankenstein*," said Allen in a cold clear voice, "by Mary Shelley." He opened the novel:

With an anxiety that almost amounted to agony, I collected
the instruments of life around me that I might infuse a spark
of being into the lifeless thing that lay at my feet. . . . His yellow
skin scarcely covered the work of muscles and arteries beneath;
his hair was of a lustrous black, and flowing; his teeth of a
pearly whiteness; but these luxuriances only formed a more
horrid contrast with his watery eyes, that seemed almost of
the same color as the dun white sockets in which they were set,
his shriveled complexion and straight black lips.

The story came down through that heat pipe and found its way to Edgar Brim as he lay in his bed half-asleep. It electrified his brain.

The next day they took their carriage, a little hansom drawn by an old horse, down to London. They shared the threadbare blanket. The child snuggled up to his father, and Allen allowed it. He wasn't one for making a man out of a boy before his time.

"You seem tired, my son. Did you not sleep?"

"I slept well, father."

"What shall we do about those circles under your eyes?"

"Hereditary," said the little voice.

Allen Brim smiled, not just because of Edgar's extraordinary vocabulary, but because the observation was accurate. Allen's own eyes were not exactly sparkling advertisements for a good night's sleep.

"Edgar, you may not have much in life, but you will be smart and caring, you will speak well and be well read. There is no question about it." The boy must learn to grapple with fear too, thought Allen. The day would come, Squire Brim vowed, when he would introduce his son to the dark literature.

They moved along gravel roads through the countryside, south toward the great city. Edgar loved to watch the locomotive trains whistle past at unearthly speeds, and the one that thundered by today was faster than any before, its head hissing steam and its tail like a gigantic snake's. Edgar wondered what it would be like to ride in one. There seemed to be many things to learn in life, many secrets. It made him think of something mysterious the squire often did.

"What do you write in your journal, father?" he said suddenly.

Allen was taken aback. He kept the journal locked.

"Oh, nothing, my good fellow."

"Nothing, sir? It can't be nothing, for there are words in it. I have seen you putting them there."

When Squire Brim wasn't writing novels, he liked to record his thoughts. And one subject dominated his journal's pages. His interest in it began with an idea a wise man had offered him long ago.

"I have a theory about stories," the gentleman had whispered, almost as if his words should not be spread about, "especially in sensation novels and horror tales with demons and dark characters." He surveyed the room from behind his desk and lowered his voice even more. And what he proceeded to say had stayed with Allen Brim to this day. He could remember every word.

"Father?"

Allen had been gazing off into the distance. Now he turned back to his son and smiled.

"Well, perhaps I shouldn't say I write exactly nothing in my journal, Edgar, but it is nothing with which to concern yourself."

These trips into London were monthly journeys. Little Edgar found the city disturbing—horses and carriages, rattling omnibuses, pungent smells and absolute rivers of people moving at top speed. Squire Brim's destination, however, was a quiet place—the world's greatest library at the British Museum where, he told his son, he researched the backgrounds for his novels. But he always dropped Edgar at a tall, narrow home in wealthy Mayfair beforehand. Allen Brim would walk his young son up to the entrance and before he even had time to grasp the bronze knocker, the door would be flung open and a smiling woman would pull Edgar into her arms.

Mrs. Annabel Thorne had been Virginia Brim's dearest friend and had loved her from the moment they met, through the days before the Brims' fortunes had slid, right up until Virginia's death. Allen's unusual American wife—the daughter of actors, of all things, from Baltimore, Maryland—had been shunned by London society, but Annabel would have none of it. "Such spirit!" she told others, who often soured when she said so. Now the childless Mrs. Thorne loved Virginia's son with the same devotion.

These were the only times Edgar ever felt the embrace of a woman. Perhaps his mother had clasped him to her the day he was born, the day she had died, he didn't know. Mrs. Thorne's hugs always made him feel warm inside, and he loved to sit with her at tea in front of the drawing room's big fireplace, tasting raspberry scones and sweets, the sorts of things he never had at home.

But there was a mystery in that house, a deep, dark one. Mr. Thorne never appeared. He inhabited a space upstairs at the top of the house, all the way up on the fifth floor, and never came down when the boy was about, and Annabel said nothing of him. Edgar wondered what he was doing up there.

Allen reappeared late that night, lit up from his researches and the play he had attended. Edgar questioned him closely as they walked down the white stone steps of Thorne House past the black wrought iron fence toward their old carriage.

"What was it like?"

"What, my boy, the British Museum Library or the theater?"

"The former first, father, then the latter."

Allen hesitated. Though he said he sought information for his books at the library, he rarely did. He often searched for something else, something he dared not tell Edgar. But he hated to lie to his son.

"Well," he said, "the library is an enormous, round, dim room, as quiet as a cathedral, with walls of books that ring it from floor to ceiling and sliding ladders that allow you to reach them. You hear only the muffled sounds of people moving dusty chronicles and other echoes as you sit at your wooden desk with your little lamp. It is marvelous!"

Edgar could see it as his father spoke. He imagined the books he would find there. Not one like the story his father read last night, which was inhabited by a monster and had given him a terrible nightmare, but calmer tales like others he was now being allowed to hear, with colorful characters and happy endings. They took him to intriguing worlds.

"You are forbidden to make any noise. You must imagine the things you are reading."

Edgar loved that. He hoped there would always be places like this magical library. Would they still be there when he grew up?

"I am a transgressor, though."

"A what, father?"

"Well, I sometimes make a little noise."

For some reason, they both laughed at that.

"I find particular things in books that make me say, 'Ah!' Today I did so and it brought a rebuke from a gentleman nearby."

Allen laughed again, but Edgar didn't.

"What things, father?"

This appeared to make the elder Brim uncomfortable. The carriage was a good distance down the street, and they walked a few more strides along the footpath before he answered.

"Oh, nothing, really."

"If I were in that library with you," said Edgar, "and I heard you say, 'Ah!' I would whisper something to you."

"And what would that be?"

"What, exactly, are you reading, father?" whispered Edgar.

"Oh, nothing," said Brim. He realized he had said it again. "I am sorry, my boy." He wondered how much he should tell his son. "It was an obscure account of a day in the life of an author named Mary Shelley. In the book, she saw something frightening in the woods in Switzerland near a renowned scientist's laboratory."

"Something frightening?"

"Yes, but it was a long while past, my lad, and Mrs. Shelley has been dead for some time. Her work is most certainly not for children. You won't even know of her."

But of course Edgar did know. His heart started to pound when he heard the name that had traveled down the pipe to his ears the previous night.

They reached the carriage. Allen noticed the anxiety on the boy's face as he reached down to lift him into his seat. "Perhaps we should speak of something else. You asked about the theater?"

"Yes, father, might I attend the play next time?"

"Come now, Edgar, it wouldn't be right. The theater is not for individuals of your age."

"When can I come?"

Allen got into the carriage. "Perhaps in a few years."

"Then tell me the story of the play you saw tonight."

"I traveled east on Piccadilly after I dropped you here, my boy," he said, as he stared out into the fog that had settled over Mayfair, "then down Bow Street into the West End, past the Royal Opera House. Bow became Wellington Street and the Royal Lyceum Theatre appeared, its pillars rising on the pale exterior, gaslights illuminating the entrance so it became some sort of palace, a palace of the imagination. The roadway was teeming with gleaming carriages. There were shimmering dresses and famous faces."

"Was that the theater you attended?"

"No, my boy." He had seen a silly musical at the Gaiety and could barely recall the story.

"Then why are you telling me this?"

"I like to imagine the plays that happen at the Lyceum."

"So, why do you not see them?"

"I am not sure I am up to it. The man who performs on that stage has a talent given to him as much by the devil as God." He paused. "There was a giant drawing of him on a banner above the main doors."

Allen remembered the face as if he were seeing it coming toward them out of the London fog, the skin painted with dark makeup, looming there like a monster.

4

A Fatal Mistake

E dgar woke on a dark morning five years later with the old
woman sitting on his chest again, pressing the life out of
him. She came for him at dawn now, not just a horrid face
growing on his mother's body, but the full hag. She dug her knees
into his rib cage, her filthy hands gripped him and her wrinkled
face was inches from his. He couldn't breathe and felt like he was
dying, but he struggled against her and, slowly, she began to fade.

He sat up, trembling.

"I mustn't tell father," he said out loud. "He will worry. A nine-
year-old boy is far too old for such things. And besides, who would
believe it?"

During the night he had heard his father's voice again, reading
one of those frightening stories, the tale echoing through his room.
Nightmares always came later, and then the hag. She seemed *so* real.

"I shan't tell him that I can hear him. He will stop and he enjoys
it. The old woman won't kill me." But he wasn't sure.

He pulled on his clothes and walked out into the hallway. He
could hear Allen's familiar whistle in the kitchen far away and

moved toward it with a smile, ready for whatever the squire had found for them to eat. It wouldn't be much but they would have it together. It was earlier than Edgar usually rose, so his father would be surprised to see him. He paused as he neared the bare sitting room: two chairs were next to the squire's desk in there, where they often sat while working on Edgar's studies. Much of it was reading. They read everything in their big library, except the books on the top shelf. There wasn't enough money for formal schooling. "Not yet," his father said almost every day. "But sometime . . . soon."

Edgar noticed something on the desk that usually wasn't there. *The journal.* And the lock was undone! His father obviously intended to come back to it.

"What if I opened it and looked inside, just the first page?"

He walked into the sitting room, treading quietly, feeling guilty. His father's whistling had stopped, but he was two rooms away. The squire wouldn't suspect that his son was awake yet.

Just the first page.

Edgar moved to the desk and stood over the journal for a while. He reached for it.

But as he did, he heard the creak of a bad floorboard. He turned and saw his father just outside the room.

"What are you doing?"

"Nothing."

But Edgar's hand was on the journal.

Allen's face grew pale. "I have told you that its contents are not for you to view, my boy."

"Yes, father."

"And you disobeyed me."

"I . . ."

There was a hard hickory cane in the room, the one the boy's grandfather had used for disciplining his father long ago. It leaned against the doorframe gathering cobwebs. Squire Brim didn't believe in its use. His eyes went to it now. So did Edgar's and his heart rate accelerated.

But then Allen smiled at him. He moved to the desk and pressed the lock closed. "I shall share it with you when you are older . . . soon."

They traveled to London the next day to the British Museum Library. The Thornes were away on a trip to Germany, so Edgar had to wait in the cold stone atrium, his thin bottom on a hard marble bench, two pleasant children's novels in hand. When his father finally emerged from the Reading Room, his face was tense.

"Is there something the matter, father?" asked Edgar.

"Not a thing, my boy," he smiled. But his words were forced.

After they left, Edgar learned the reason for his father's nerves. Allen didn't pass by the Royal Lyceum this time. He took the boy in.

"I am preparing to write a different sort of story," he told his son as they rushed through the theater's towering front doors. "I feel I must. It is a frightening tale with a sort of devil in it and it explores human fear. I need to prepare myself, and there is no better way than to see the production that is at the Lyceum now."

They were almost late. Inside, Edgar stared wide-eyed at the red lobby with its giant golden chandelier. The room was beginning to clear. Edgar, of course, couldn't go all the way into the auditorium. He was to wait, again, in the lobby on a bench, a softer one this time, plush and comfortable. His father spoke to a coat-check girl, handing her a coin to keep an eye on his son, and then said a few reassuring words to Edgar before he turned to go. As he did, someone came through the entrance, well behind the crowd. The man neared them, tall and thin, dressed in a long black coat and a black bowler hat that was pulled down over his forehead, his big, aquiline nose sticking out like a parrot's beak. Edgar noticed how the man stopped when he saw his father, and then looked back and forth, examining both of them. Something about him made Edgar shiver.

But Allen didn't notice. He strode across the thick carpet toward the inner doors, dressed in the worn-out evening clothes he had put on in the water closet at the museum, the tall man not far behind him. The theater's burly, red-haired manager was standing in the doorway eyeing the lagging patrons. Allen swept by him and entered the auditorium. Instantly, he was in another world. It belonged to the man whose image had loomed above the theater five years ago, the one and only Henry Irving.

Allen's knees were quaking as an immaculately dressed usher walked him up to his seat at the very back of the last section of the upper balcony, nearly two thousand packed seats below him. He had never seen Irving in the flesh before but he, of course, knew all about the great actor. One had to be living under a rock on the Scottish moors not to be aware of exactly what he looked like, things he had said and the roles he had played. It was said that his face, when seen in person, was like porcelain; his eyes like burning coals; his black hair, long and parted down the center and graying a little now, like the feathers of a strange tall bird. Tonight, he would play Satan in the flesh.

London had never seen a production like this. It was huge and lush, and it mesmerized everyone who saw it. Its special effects were astonishing and Irving was spellbinding. Even his leading lady, the great and gorgeous Ellen Terry, rumored to be his lover offstage, seemed unimportant beside him upon the boards. It was difficult to put a finger on just what Irving did to people. He pronounced words in strange ways, dragged his leg as he performed, didn't simply stand facing the audience and declaim like other actors. He *became* his characters. No one could take their eyes from him.

There was always music during an Irving production, all the way through. The orchestra was playing the overture now, the strings rising in crescendos, building the excitement. A buzz ran through the audience, growing with the music.

And then the curtain rose.

For a while people held their breath, waiting for *him* to appear. Soon, a creature materialized out of a mist, red from head to foot. It slithered as it moved. Then it rose up and began to dominate scene after scene, forcing the hero to sign a pact in blood, giving him everything he craved, summoning witches. Allen was glad that Edgar was safe in the lobby, for the great artist took him places he would not want his child to go. He believed in evil that night. He believed he should live only for himself, that wealth and power were all that were important, that women were playthings for his pleasure, that powerful spirits existed that could help him fight God. He believed in the devil.

The play seemed to go by in a moment.

Afterward, Allen staggered out of the auditorium in a stupor, his face pale. His chest hurt. He had been so entranced during the action that he had felt as though he had been dragged down from the balcony to the stage and thrown upon the boards before Irving, where he watched him in the lurid stage lights, that made-up face lit up, those black eyes penetrating his, all the goodness inside him sucked away.

As he struggled toward Edgar in the lobby, he saw the manager again. Another patron whispered his name: *Bram Stoker*. The stolid Irishman looked dazed and glassy-eyed. Irving, thought Allen, had infected Stoker too. How could *he* still be that way after so many performances?

The truth is unbearable, Allen told himself, I dare not write it. He took his son's arm. The boy was stunned and silent, having sat there in wonder for hours as strange sounds came from inside the auditorium's doors, as though a demon were on the loose. Allen led Edgar out under the street lamps and they moved in silence through the remnants of the crowd. The squire felt absolutely exhausted and could barely walk. He got into his carriage like a dead man. The boy was staring at him, peering right into him. Allen knew something then that terrified him. Edgar could see and feel his agony.

As they drove home through the countryside, the squire tried to tell happy stories. All he could manage were old tales from the boy's earlier years. But he was careful even with them. He took the big bad wolf out of the *Three Little Pigs*, the witch from *Hansel and Gretel* and the three ugly sisters from *Cinderella*. He made Edgar laugh once or twice. But the stories were flat. It took so much effort to sanitize them. And Allen remained tired, very tired. When they arrived home, he was barely able to make it to his bedroom.

When Edgar woke the next morning, he noticed the silence in Raven House. Had his father gone out without waking him? Edgar searched for him in the kitchen. It was empty, with no evidence of breakfast on the table. He went into the sitting room; also empty, the mysterious journal nowhere in sight. Then he climbed the stairs to his parents' bedroom. He rarely saw his father there now, though he knew he always slept on one side of the bed, as if keeping the other free for his wife's return.

"Father?"

Allen Brim was lying absolutely still. Edgar approached the bed. The fear that engulfed him when he saw the rigid white face was unlike any he had ever experienced, though fear often dominated his mind. He sat down beside his father on the big bed and stayed there for hours, shaking, the tears pouring down his face. The hag sat in a chair nearby, smiling at him.

"What shall I do?" he whispered. "What shall I do?"

Finally, he rose and left Raven House and walked many miles through the countryside until he found a doctor who would return with him. It was the strangest thing, thought the physician: a perfectly healthy man, not yet forty, dead in his bed of a heart attack, his eyes wide open.

5

Alfred Thorne

"My child, my dear boy!" cried Mrs. Thorne, gliding down the staircase of her Mayfair home as if her feet under her bustled purple dress weren't touching the steps. All the ladies were showing their ankles these days, but just glimpses. Mrs. Thorne's were on full display. The boy stood silently beside the uniformed footman, head bowed toward the gleaming black-and-white tile floor. As soon as Annabel heard Edgar had nowhere to go, she told her husband she wanted him. Alfred had barely responded.

Edgar Brim was shabby in his only suit. It was tweed and threadbare and done up almost to his chin. He held a soiled cap in front of his chest in both his hands. He raised his head and looked her in the eyes.

"Oh! You are such a brave one!" She reached for him and held him close. Then she stood back and gazed at him. "I shall summon Mr. Thorne. You must finally meet him. Beasley, call the master!"

It took a while. It was as if Thorne didn't want to see his new son. But eventually Edgar could hear footsteps from high up in the tall, narrow house: first accompanied by the creaking of wood, then coming closer on the grand marble staircase that rose from the hallway. When Alfred Thorne finally appeared at the top of the last flight, he came to a halt.

Edgar had never seen a man like him. He was of modest height and as thin as a flagpole. He wore a black suit with a cravat, even now in the middle of the day, and on his lapel were bright smudges of unnatural colors. His skin was pale, his hair and mustache dark brown, his brown eyes clear and his head inordinately large, especially in the upper story, as if stretched to contain his big brain. And the left side of his face, from eye socket to jaw line, was scarred. Perhaps something he had done up there at the top of the building had one day gone awry? As Thorne resumed his descent, he turned that side of his face slightly away from Edgar.

"I shall assume this is Edgar Brim."

"Yes, Mr. Thorne, it is," said his lovely wife, her blond hair and blue eyes and bright dress in marked contrast to her husband's stiff presence. She leaned down toward Edgar and whispered in his ear. "His bark is much worse than his bite. Take courage."

But Edgar began to shake. He hated himself for it but couldn't stop.

"He is quivering, Annabel."

Thorne brought his hand up to the left side of his face, as if in thought. It covered the scar. But the boy saw the wound fully for an instant and it caused him to gasp. Thorne frowned at him and Annabel came to the rescue.

"Say hello, Edgar."

"H . . . hell . . . hell . . ."

"The child cannot speak!"

"He is simply a little frightened, Mr. Thorne. It is reasonable."

"There is no reason about it, none whatsoever!" He began to pace about the boy, circling him. "Let me lay down some rules, Mr. Brim." Mrs. Thorne, from behind her husband's back, put her hand over her mouth to hide a smile.

"First and foremost, there shall be no reading of novels. Do you understand that?"

Edgar shook harder and feared he was about to cry.

"He is sniveling, Annabel!"

"I should do the same, Mr. Thorne." He glared at her but she met his gaze.

Edgar stifled himself. "You will excuse me, sir."

"We shall not raise your son to—"

"Our son," said Annabel firmly.

"Our son, if you will, to read the flighty imaginings of such moral reprobates as Charles Dickens or Wilkie Collins or the despicable Ouida! He shall read science and mathematics and self-instruction, self-improvement!"

"And he shall die of boredom."

"Mrs. Thorne, do not contradict me. It is unseemly in a woman."

"Yes, Mr. Thorne. Or should I say, my lord and master?"

Alfred stopped suddenly, as if unsure of what she meant. Her face was unreadable. He turned back to the boy and cleared his throat. "Your bedtime, young sir, shall be strictly adhered to, as shall the time you arise and your study habits. You are weak. That will not do. A manly boy is what you shall be. Do you have that?"

The boy nodded.

"I believe he is almost mute. We have adopted a nearly speech-less child."

"I doubt that, Mr. Thorne. You may go. It is time for you to return to your labors."

He paused again, as if to protest, but then turned to the stairs. As he did, his wife seized him from behind and kissed him, loudly, right on his scarred cheek. For an instant, a grin flickered across his face. It vanished quickly.

"Mrs. Thorne, we are in the presence of a servant!"

The footman wasn't watching. Annabel let her smile show this time.

Thorne climbed the stairs and disappeared.

That night, long after the house grew quiet, Edgar Brim lay wide awake in his huge bedroom on the third floor. He always tried to stay conscious as long as he could because monsters came to him when he slept: it might be the Frankenstein creature one night, a beast named Grendel that had deeply scared him in one of his father's stories the next, or a new villain entirely from his own imagination.

Hours earlier, Annabel had sneaked one of her books into his room and sat on his bedside reading to him. She had chosen Lewis Carroll's *Alice's Adventures in Wonderland*. He had read it when he was younger and still loved it. There was a Mad Hatter always having tea, a talking March Hare and a rabbit with a watch who was constantly late. But he had always skipped over the part with the Queen of Hearts. She was a horror, constantly threatening to cut off people's heads, even poor Alice's. This time, Edgar pretended to fall asleep when the Queen appeared. His adoptive mother noticed, as she noticed everything about her new son. She kissed him, turned off their fancy electric light and left.

Alone in the strange room, he stared into the darkness. Mrs. Thorne's footsteps faded down the stairs toward the master bedroom.

An hour later, desperately trying to keep his eyes open, seeing vague shapes floating on the walls, fending off images of trolls and the Grim Reaper and a dead little boy, Edgar heard heavier footsteps, this time descending from the mysterious upper floors of the house. Thorne was finally making his way to bed. Or was he? The footsteps paused. Edgar sensed a hand on the doorknob. But then the footfalls began again, and withdrew.

Moments later, Edgar arose. He was wearing silk pajamas from India that Mrs. Thorne had purchased for him. They were a little long in the sleeves and trousers and he stepped awkwardly across the room, opened the door and ventured into the hallway. Anything was better than being in bed with the demons. Other than the tick of a grandfather clock, it was silent and dark. He started to move toward the stairs.

"My husband is an inventor," was all Annabel had told him about Mr. Thorne.

"Of what sort?" the boy had asked.

"Of a military sort," she sighed. "Alfred is very scientific."

He was a mad inventor, the boy was sure, with a laboratory in which he conjured up experiments that blew up in his face.

Edgar decided to go upward. But his first step on the wooden stairs brought a creak that seemed to echo throughout the house.

He paused. There was no response. It was strange how this house seemed to shut out sounds, even London outside its doors.

Up Edgar Brim went. One flight and then another. The stairs creaked more as he went. The hallway on the top floor was tiny. In fact, it was really just a landing. There was a door a few feet away. The entrance to the laboratory!

Edgar tried the knob. Locked. His eyes were focusing a little better in the dark. There was a sign there at the height of an adult's eyes.

NO ENTRY!

He bent to the keyhole, which was rather large. He peered through it and saw a tall window inside and moonlight shining in. In front of it was a table with test tubes and tools and beside it a rack bearing two strange guns and a crossbow in various stages of invention, and just beyond was part of a battered bulls-eye target. He shifted his gaze and tried to look toward the walls and saw the edges of books on a shelf. Thorne needed books for research, he supposed. But when he tried to focus on those that were visible, he could have sworn many were novels—DICKENS read one spine, COLLINS another and LE FANU a third. Before he could consider the meaning of this, he heard a door closing below him, perhaps two floors down. Then footsteps started coming up the stairs. They didn't indicate the delicate walk of Annabel Thorne. They were much heavier.

6

Sent Away

"**B**oy!" Thorne bellowed as he approached Edgar, keeping the scarred side of his face turned away, though he was barely discernable on the stairs near the dark landing. "Y-yes, sir."

"I can see you there, quivering. Retreat to your room and I shall decide what to do with you." Edgar wasn't quivering, at least not visibly. He turned to descend the stairs and slipped past his adoptive father. Three steps down, Thorne's disembodied voice reached Edgar from above. "At the very least you will be removed to a school for part of each year. I cannot have you snooping about. And besides, you need to . . ." Thorne frowned, ". . . *change.*"

Poor Allen Brim's effects were brought, via a nag and cart, to the Thorne home the next day and left for Alfred and Annabel to sort out. Beyond Allen's meager wardrobe and the few paintings, silverware and furniture that had remained in Raven House, there were his many fairy tales, sensation novels and horror stories (at which Thorne snorted) and a sealed strongbox. Inside it was the deed to the house (to be given to Allen's brother, who had distanced himself as the family's mansion and fortune crumbled), unfinished manuscripts for more happy novels, and a journal. The latter was black and leather-bound with a latch on it, though no key was found among the effects.

"I shall force the lock when I have time for such things," said Thorne, tucking the journal under his arm and turning to withdraw to his laboratory.

"Is it our right to even have it, dear?" asked Annabel, sitting on her favorite settee in their lavishly appointed drawing room. She had supervised the decor, and the furnishings were brightly colored. The walls and ceiling were white, the fireplace elaborate with carvings, the mirrors gilt edged. "Perhaps the journal is of a personal nature? Might we not give it to Edgar?" She nodded her head up toward the boy's bedroom where he had remained, silent, since breakfast.

Thorne paused on the bottom step. "I am sure it is full of nonsense. Brim was a dreamer."

"He was a lovely man."

"Man is perhaps too strong a term to be applied to Allen Brim, Mrs. Thorne. There was not a great deal of the masculine about him."

When her husband turned, Annabel rolled her eyes.

Up the stairs Thorne went, past Edgar's room with a slight pause and then beyond. As he fumbled in his pocket for the key to his laboratory, the journal made contact with the doorframe, dislodged from under his arm and landed on the floor with a slam. The lock didn't disengage, but the impact knocked a small card from the book's pages. Thorne picked it up and read what was written on it.

The College on the Moors (for Boys)
The Highlands, Scotland

That was all it said, a simple card, the text written in heavy Gothic script. "The Highlands," said Thorne to himself and smiled. It was a long, long way from London. He had considered sending the boy to Eton College, his own alma mater. "Better, perhaps," he mused, "to send him far away." That very night he authored a note to the school and four days later received by post a reply from the school's headmaster, Reverend Spartan Griswold, detailing the school's heritage, curriculum and disciplined way with boys. The rod and the whip were not spared at the Moors.

"It will make a man out of your child, sir, I can assure you," wrote the headmaster.

"Aha!" thought Alfred Thorne.

Annabel delayed Edgar's departure for as long as possible. She made the excuse that he needed time to settle, that appropriate schoolboy clothing had to be purchased, and that his constitution had to be built up with proper food and out-of-door exercise. But even she could not put off her husband indefinitely and so, one very early morning in September, Edgar was readied in the vestibule of Thorne House, Alfred pulling him from Annabel and handing him over to the footman, who stood waiting with the family hansom and horse. Had the boy left just a few months later, he might have been driven to the station in the motorized steam vehicle Thorne was building. As the weeks of the eccentric child's residency in the house had passed, the inventor had been filled with a strange desire to show it to him. Though Thorne would never admit it, Edgar Brim, this child who sleepwalked through his house at night pursued by monsters, had begun to intrigue him.

The sun had barely risen. Edgar sat silently beside the footman as the carriage rattled through their elegant neighborhood, then along Oxford Street, and up Tottenham Court Road near the British Museum where Allen Brim had investigated the origins of *Frankenstein*. Edgar was then ushered across the hard floor under the arched glass ceiling of the Euston Railway Station and pulled toward the platform and through the door in the first-class car with his luggage. Small for his age, he sat on the cushioned seat with the silent footman, dangling bare legs below the short pantaloons of his sailor suit, desperately missing Annabel but thrilled when the great locomotive lurched forward and steamed out of the station.

He kept near the window as they zoomed through the many miles of his journey through England, past villages and towns and countryside—somewhere out there was Raven House—past poor people and rich, under rain and sun, all the way to Scotland, and onto Inverness Station, where the footman rushed him to a Far North Line train for the Highlands . . . and left him alone. Shaking in his seat, Edgar tried not to make eye contact with the few other passengers as the train began to move. Outside the windows, the green landscape soon disappeared and nothing seemed to thrive.

It grew misty. A foreboding rose in Edgar's heart. At distant Altnabreac Station, he disembarked on his own and was met by a tall, hooded man in a cloak and gloves with a scarred face, on a cart drawn by a thick black horse. The driver didn't say a word. Above them, the sky at mid-afternoon was dim. From there, Edgar was taken out onto the moors.

He would never forget his first view of the college. You could see it for miles, alone in the pelting rain and mist, a dark turret looming above it, the building shimmering as if a massive black heart was making it pulse.

But what Edgar found inside was worse.

Left alone at the front doors, he struggled to open them and then emerged into a huge entrance hall made of stone and lit dimly by a giant chandelier ringed with candles. An ornate staircase faced the entrance. The air was clammy, shadows moved about, and a few dull sounds echoed. A bell rang, loud and shrill, making Edgar start, and students began to appear in a whirlwind of activity: along the stone floor and up and down the stairs. No one noticed Edgar Brim.

But then a large boy, coming down the wide staircase in his black school jacket and followed closely by several friends, fixed his gaze on the little newcomer in the ridiculous sailor suit. Fardle's shining brown hair was luxuriant and his teeth as white as snow. "Look here," he said loudly, "it's a sailor!" Edgar knew at that moment that he had a powerful enemy supported by a regiment of lieutenants: one tall and slender, another with white-blond hair and skin like pock-marked flour and a third with a face so ordinary that Edgar forgot it the moment he glanced away. They all gleamed with anticipation at what they might do to this new boy and shrieked with laughter at their leader's witty comment.

A round, bloodless face appeared in front of Edgar, materializing out of nowhere, looming there. Its head was bald. In a deep voice that seemed to go up its bulbous nose, it introduced itself as Usher, the porter, and without another word, led Edgar up the staircase to his room on the Early Years floor, one above. Wrapped in black robes with vertical red stripes, Usher barely made a sound. Edgar fell on the bed after the porter left, and heard doors creaking and closing and a whistling wind coming up from somewhere far below in the building. He pictured his father's kind face and tried to imagine his mother's, but got through that first evening focused on Annabel Thorne, reassuring himself that she would be there to greet him in London when he returned for Christmas. He even thought, somewhat fondly, of Thorne himself, for despite his cold ways, he seemed a fascinating man.

But in the night, the monsters came again.

The cry brought Fardle right out of his bed and onto his feet. His room was just down the stone hallway. He wasn't a sound sleeper. His father, the Duke of Fardle, often beat him when he came home drunk, so he had learned to be on his guard, even in the middle of the night. There was a sob, then silence. Fardle sat down.

"Frankenstein!"

The big boy stood up again. He stepped silently into the hallway. The fevered exclamations were coming from the new boy's room! Fardle moved to the thick wooden door and peered through the barred window into the darkness within. He couldn't see anything but he could hear Brim begging someone, something, to spare him.

Fardle grinned. He moved to another room farther down the hallway. "Maggett!" he whispered as loudly as he dared. "Rise up, Maggett!" In seconds he had Smith and Jones with him too. They stole back to Brim's door.

"NO!" Edgar cried out. There was absolute terror in his voice this time, so chilling that for an instant the four bigger boys were frozen in their places. But then they broke into giggles.

Inside the room, the hag was upon Edgar Brim.

7

Dear Friend

E dgar tried to avoid Fardle, scurrying quietly through the dim halls and sitting alone at a long wooden table in the cathedral-like Great Dining Hall, where students were required to consume their meals with a minimum of fuss. It had the appearance of the nave of a medieval church, all wood and stained glass windows, though neither Jesus Christ nor even the Queen looked down upon the proceedings from the eight-foot portrait that hung above the stage. The subject was Headmaster Griswold himself, apparently the dictator of this place.

Neither Griswold nor his professors, collectively known as "the dismal dozen," were any help to Edgar at meals or any other time. The towering headmaster and his three closest colleagues, Professors Lovecraft, Numb and Lear, sat together in their robes on the Hall's dais, distant from others and unapproachable.

Edgar heard the other students whispering about them. Lovecraft was the only instructor they liked: he never struck a boy or raised his voice in anger and he taught literature as if it were a never-ending story. Barely over five feet tall, he was an elf of hope in a world of darkness. But he had a strange habit. He became monsters. He liked to dress up as literary villains and walk the hallways at night, supposedly to scare students who might be late getting back to their rooms. His portrayal of the vampyre from the novel of the same name was a particular killer. The boys were thankful that Griswold, or the muscular Numb, or especially the hooded "Driver" (who seemed everywhere) didn't do such things.

But Edgar was most unnerved by the bearded Lear. There was something frightening in his very presence: one-armed and massive and with a full head of dark hair streaked with gray, his silent ways seemed to inspire dread in every boy, even from a distance. And right from the beginning, he appeared to take an interest in Edgar, staring down at him from the dais.

The dark stone hallways, the looming portraits of dead professors on the walls, and the men who now inhabited the college, were unsettling enough during the day, but at night the ancient building seemed possessed. Edgar could swear there was something large moving about in the cellar two floors below, something moaning; he thought he heard sawing, the pounding of a hammer, and little shrieks. Outside his window, the wind howled over the moors and things seemed to be running for their lives. One night, Edgar found himself alone in the entrance hall, having lingered in Lovecraft's classroom finishing an essay. It was pitch black outside and the big dim room and its shadows were silent. As Edgar hurried toward the stairs, he saw something moving at the top of the first flight: a black, red-striped robe swirling and the side of an ancient face like a cadaver's. The figure was floating upward. *A ghost!*

Then the apparition vanished and Headmaster Griswold somehow took its place, his big master key ring jingling from his hand. Or was he in pursuit?

"The creature from the moors is coming to get you tonight," Fardle loved to tell Edgar. "Something is out there, you know."

"At least five boys have seen it!" Maggett added.

"There's a demon in the cellar too!" cried Smith.

"And a madman in the turret!" said Jones.

Only Fardle, it seemed to Edgar, spoke without some fear in his voice.

Edgar Brim put up with villainy and taunts, even as his torments increased. He avoided confrontation and kept to himself.

"Can't you do something to help Brim, Headmaster?" asked Lovecraft one day as they spoke in Griswold's office, a room with one window on the third floor. The big desk was littered with papers, great stacks of lists of rules and documents on conduct. The shelves held just a few books and not one of them was within arm's reach. Griswold leaned over Lovecraft and looked down his huge, aquiline nose from more than a foot above.

"It would run counter to the beliefs of our institution, sir. He must learn to be a man. He has a challenge before him and he must take it up or perish! He has never complained, anyway."

In order to survive, Edgar concentrated on his studies. Within a few months, he was at the top of his classes (which didn't help his popularity), strong in every subject, but best in literature. Lovecraft pronounced Master Brim "a genius" and wrote in his reports that "his empathy for the characters is unparalleled in a student in my recollection." He didn't know that Edgar actually entered the stories he read, or that when he wasn't studying or focused in class, he was disturbingly anxious.

But then, at midterm, a sort of present arrived for Edgar. It took the form of a boy named Tiger Tilley. He wasn't a big lad. In fact, he was about Edgar's height and just as slender, maybe even more so. He was pale and smooth skinned with black curly hair and big dark eyes and a rather full mouth above a fragile-looking chin. But there was nothing fragile about his spirit.

"What of it?" he demanded of Fardle his third day at school, coming out of his room across from Edgar's and encountering the big boy. Fardle pointed toward Brim's door and sneered.

"You heard it, didn't you? He whimpers at nights, talks of monsters."

"Yeah, I heard it . . . fatty."

Fardle almost fell on the floor. If there hadn't been professors near enough to come running, he would have splattered this upstart against a wall.

"I beg your pardon?"

Maggett, Smith and Jones gathered behind Fardle, peeking past him at this skinny little boy who had dared to question their leader.

"He seems like a nice lad to me."

"Nice? He is afraid of his shadow."

"That isn't true. He merely has a nightmare every now and—"

"Join us in taking the piss out of 'im, Tilley, or we'll roast you."

"Roast you, we will," said Maggett.

"That's right."

"That's right."

Jones and Smith often said the same thing.

Edgar emerged from behind his door. He had heard every word. He couldn't believe the new boy was defending him. They were in a few classes together and had barely spoken, but this fellow had seemed to like him right away, had even complimented his unique red hair, staring right into Edgar's blue eyes, holding his gaze. Tiger smiled at Edgar now, then turned back to Fardle, who had stepped closer. Tiger stared up at him.

"Edgar Brim has more intelligence in his left nut than you have in your skull, Fat-tle."

It looked like Fardle was going to faint.

"Say . . . say that out on the rugby pitch at five o'clock behind the tree."

"See you then," said Tiger.

When the other four trotted off, the new boy put a hand gently on Edgar's shoulder. "You can be my second, Edgar."

"Second?"

"You know, like the way it is in a duel."

"A duel? Are you going to be shooting each other?"

Tiger smiled. "I don't think so, my friend. You are such a worrier." With that, he clapped Brim on the back so hard that Edgar nearly fell down himself.

Out behind the tree by the rugby pitch at five o'clock, big Fardle and little Tiger went at it tooth and nail. First, the smaller boy knocked the large one flat on his face by sweeping his feet from under him with a kick. It was a most ungentlemanly maneuver.

Then he leapt on him and popped him hard on his noggin four or five times before Fardle could use his superior strength to shove him off. The big one continued to take blows from the little one, all delivered as if he knew his art quite thoroughly. But Fardle's strength, in the end, was too much for Tiger. It was like the power of Frankenstein's creature. Oh, Fardle looked the worse for wear in the end (a bit like Mary Shelley's famous monster, in fact), his nose red from being soundly pinched, some of his hair pulled out, his cheeks scratched and his shins bruised, but he finally succeeded in sitting on Tiger for an extended period. Not that Tilley surrendered. He refused to say "give" even when it seemed he might die of the pressure on his lungs from the weight of his huge opponent. At last, Fardle staggered to his feet.

"I hope that teaches you," he said. But his tone was unconvincing. He was breathing hard and seemed absolutely done in, as if he wanted no part of Tiger Tilley ever again. Fardle turned away. By the time he reached the school, he was leaning on his followers' shoulders.

Edgar helped Tiger to his feet. The little battler could barely breathe at first but soon regained his composure.

"I don't think he will bother you as much now, Edgar."

But Tiger was wrong.

Fardle, whose wounds convicted him of the crime of fighting, was shamed not just by the brutal whipping he took from Headmaster Griswold but also by the weeping he did because of it. The fact that Tilley bore his lashing without a single tear made it worse. From then on, the big lad was careful to keep clear of Edgar if Tiger was with him (and Tilley tried to stay by Edgar's side as much as possible) but still found moments to torment him. Edgar stuck to his old plan: avoid Fardle and keep silent. He only spoke in class . . . and sometimes, now, to Tiger.

Edgar was called to the headmaster's office right after Griswold thrashed Fardle. The sweat was still dripping from the tall man's brow, the excitement still evident on his face. The knock on the door was strong.

"Ah," said the headmaster under his breath, "there *is* some courage within the boy, but still, he won't fight back." He cleared his throat. "Advance!"

The door creaked open and Edgar's head peeked around it.

"You wanted to see me, sir?" His voice was barely audible.

"Come in and sit."

Griswold eyed him, this curious boy with that unruly red hair and dark brows, brilliant mind and violent nightmares. The headmaster rocked back and forth in his wooden chair, his few books— none of them novels—behind him along the stone wall. A portrait of Griswold's predecessor, a frightening man named Emeritus, who still lived somewhere in the building—some said in the dark turret way up at the top—loomed over them. Edgar looked back at the headmaster without flinching. Griswold stood up and moved to the window, which afforded a view of the moors. The sun was shining today, a rare thing. He didn't speak for a while.

"Brim," he finally said, "do you know where I have just been?" His features extended forward on his face as if they had been sucked outward from his skull, culminating at the tip of his long nose and protruding mouth. He was like a pale-faced praying mantis on a six-foot seven-inch frame, with thin limbs too long for even him, held inside his robe and ready to strike. He spoke as though he were teaching others how to pronounce.

"Yes, sir, all the boys know when you are away, sir. I believe you were in London for a few days."

"And do you know what is going on in London now, my boy?"

"I would imagine many things, sir."

The headmaster actually smiled, still turned toward the window. Many things had gone on for the Reverend Spartan Griswold while in the teeming city. He had, for one, taken part in a meeting of a secret organization called the Hermetic Order of the Golden Dawn. They discussed the occult. They discussed evil. They talked about the invisible powers that ran the world. There he had seen Bram Stoker, Henry Irving's manager at the Royal Lyceum Theatre. They had had a marvelous chat and Stoker had been kind and given him complimentary theater passes. Griswold had loved Irving's performance in *Macbeth*. There was cannonading thunder and blood and a severed head on a pole.

"But there is one particular thing that has been going on for some time there, Brim. Murder. In the East End, a great deal of it. A man, well, one thinks he is a man, has been on a rampage."

"I have read that, sir. It sounds beastly." Edgar often read the *Times of London* in the school's library, though it was always several days behind.

"Do you know exactly what this beast does, my boy?"

"I believe he kills women with a knife."

"Indeed, a good long, sharp one. He appears to know a great deal of anatomy, and though he kills his victims with brutality, he carves them up with careful thought and some knowledge of their interiors. The police think he may be a doctor or a butcher. He is scaring the life out of the women of London, many men too. There is a sort of electricity in the air down there. What do you think should be done?"

"Well . . ." Edgar swallowed, "they should seek him with all they have and arrest him, and if they can prove that he did these terrible things, they should hang him, sir."

"But what of the people, Brim, now? They are in danger. Should they not do something immediately, something preemptive? Should good men not take to the streets with weapons and track this demon and murder him in cold blood? Is that not what he deserves? Is that not almost necessary?"

"It might not be justice, sir."

"But are there not times when we must take an eye for an eye? This sorry excuse for a human being, if that's what he is, is murdering left and right!"

"It is difficult to say, sir."

"And what of this Fardle fellow? How shall you deal with him? You know I beat him, just now." Griswold's smile was again cast through the window.

"I am sorry for that."

"Sorry?"

"One never likes to see anyone beaten."

Griswold turned on him. "You think he didn't deserve it?" His voice was raised.

"He did, sir. It is just that I do not take pleasure in anyone else's pain, even Fardle's."

"How noble of you. I will not suggest how you deal with this boy, but the day may come when you will want to take justice into your own hands. That is all, Brim. You are dismissed."

"Thank you, sir."

Griswold remained at the window. The muffled sounds of students moved through the hallways. "Ah, the Ripper," he said quietly, "and Irving as *Macbeth*. It was like he wasn't acting! I *believed* he knifed the king to death in his bed. All that red dripping from him, his big blade gleaming with it!I swear he looked out at *me!*" The headmaster shivered.

When the students in Edgar's grade were initiated into full-contact rugby the following year, intimidation and physical poundings were not just allowed but encouraged.

"Kick it to him, right to Brim, and then stand back and let him pick it up," Fardle instructed Smith, Maggett and Jones as they lined up together the first time they all played a real game of rugby. They spread the word among their team (and the opposing squad) that everyone was to make Edgar field the ball.

Tiger was on Brim's team. He wasn't told of the plot.

On Fardle's side's first possession, Smith had a clear opening to run with the ball all the way to the other team's goal line, but instead, he searched for Edgar, who was keeping far from the battle and behind his team, hoping the action wouldn't come his way. Smith booted it hard in his opponent's direction, apparently giving up possession to make the other team field the ball deep in their end. Edgar was his own worst enemy that day for he was so far away from the others that no one was near him to handle the ball. It had been kicked right to him, though, so he had to take it up.

But Tiger saw what was happening. "LEAVE IT!" he roared as he raced back toward his friend from the midst of the action. Tiger still hadn't grown much, but he dove upon the ball and turned to run with it aggressively, right back at the other team.

The whistle sounded.

"That was Master Brim's ball," smiled the wide-headed Professor Numb, pronouncing each word carefully in a ridiculously smooth voice, still wearing his black and red-striped robes on the field of play. "Master Tilley, you must allow Brim to play the ball!" he shouted with excitement. Numb had a disturbing tendency to admire wounds when the boys were injured. "Now, both sides line up!" He tossed the ball to Edgar and licked his lips.

Edgar dropped it immediately, of course. Then he looked down at it. A good portion of both squads readied themselves to pummel him the instant he laid a finger on the leather again.

"Now, Brim! Play the ball, please!" cried Numb, barely able to contain himself.

Edgar had to do it. He reached down. The instant he touched it, his classmates flew at him like wildcats. Maggett hit him low and Fardle high, knocking him unconscious. Professor Numb, eyes on fire, made the boys stand back and they all gazed down at Edgar. He lay still for a long time. The color drained from Tiger's face. No one had ever seen him frightened before.

Edgar was absolutely motionless. But finally, deep in his unconsciousness, swimming about with the spectacular characters of his imagination, he saw Baba Yaga, the child-eating witch, and awoke, ready to run from her.

"It was good for the boy!" exclaimed Griswold when Numb told him of the event over dinner that evening. The athletics director could not agree more.

During the ensuing few years, as the boys moved into adolescence, Fardle grew bigger and more muscular and then leveled off, Edgar turned long and lean and approached his enemy's height, and Tiger became taller than both for a while but then seemed to stop growing altogether. And these sorts of rugby-field scenes continued to play out. Edgar learned to get rid of the ball quickly. He never fought back.

But then, it all began to change.

8

The Journal

Edgar was sure that Professor Lear was watching him. Sometimes, he even thought the old man was following him. The boy would sense something, glance over his shoulder, and see Lear moving down the hallways a good distance behind, head above the crowd, looking in his direction. Once or twice, Edgar could have sworn he glimpsed Lear's craggy face through the barred window of his bedroom door at night. And then, one evening late in his fourth year, he woke to find the one-armed man *inside* the room sitting on his bed!

"You were speaking in your sleep," said the esteemed professor of sciences in a voice so deep that it seemed to resonate in his head.

"Y-yes," said Edgar.

"Why?"

"I do not know, sir."

"You mentioned the name Grendel this evening as if he were alive in front of you. You are aware of who that is, the evil monster from the epic poem *Beowulf*?"

"Y-yes."

"Why Grendel?"

"I don't know, sir."

Lear regarded him with a penetrating stare. Edgar wished Annabel Thorne were with him, back in the safety of his bedroom in London.

"I see," said Lear finally, "the cat has your tongue, does it? I want to give you something." He pulled a card from a pocket. Edgar looked down at it.

THE CRYPTO-ANTHROPOLOGY SOCIETY
OF THE QUEEN'S EMPIRE,
LONDON, DRURY LANE

"Keep this with you. There may be a day when it will be of use." Lear turned toward the door, as if worried that someone was spying on them, then turned back to Edgar.

"You may be a remarkable boy," he said, and went out.

Edgar often felt worthless. So when Lear uttered those words, it was almost shocking. He had said it like it meant something. Edgar wasn't sure if that was good or bad. So he didn't speak of it to anyone, not even Tiger.

Edgar sometimes went to his door at night and looked out into the dim hallway, wondering what he might find if he ventured farther: if he ascended to the black turret or descended below the ground floor. One night, he tiptoed to the top of the staircase, and as he stood there, realized someone was looking up at him in the darkness from the bottom step. It was a round, bloodless face. *Usher.*

Edgar stumbled back to his room, found his door ajar, and wondered if he'd left it that way. But no one was inside.

"We can't keep doing this!" Edgar whispered, holding the big wooden door of the Great Dining Hall open on a late night just before the Christmas holidays the following year. Tiger had done the dirty work, but Edgar was his partner in crime.

"We'll stop, but this is a festive treat!"

Tiger had been not just inside the Hall, but in the larder room where the food was kept, and dancing in the dark on the headmaster's table on the dais. His arms, as usual, were filled with goodies.

"Let's go up to your room!"

In the corridor, they encountered the driver, his face, as always, deep in his hood, making no sound when he walked. They had seen him trolling the stone floors before on their late-night missions. For some reason, he never betrayed them. But he seemed unable to speak; the professors communicated with him by sign language. He was a bizarre man, rumored to have been found on the moors many years ago.

Back in Edgar's room, the boys gorged themselves on stolen tarts and slices of pie and delicate sweets. The little thief knew the hidden spot in the larder where Griswold and his allies horded the best treats.

Tiger liked to sit against the wall on the bed with Edgar and chat into the night while stuffing his face. Edgar thought they were a bit old for this—both in their second last year at the school, advancing fast up the forms. But Tiger was in heaven. He had a constant love of danger—in the hallways, on the rugby field and late at night. It was strange for a boy of his breeding to be accomplished at so many criminal arts. Edgar could hardly object, since he loved eating the spoils of their adventures, but one of these days, he was sure his friend would be apprehended, probably expelled, and perhaps bring him down with him.

"How do you get the larder door unlocked, and then locked again?"

"You'll have to learn yourself, Brim. I can't do everything for you."

There was a sudden moaning sound. It came up from the cellar and ran along the halls. Tiger laughed and offered an imitation. But Edgar didn't smile. He had never become accustomed to these strange, late-night sounds.

Tiger could be a bit of mystery. He was usually bold, and yet was shy in the changing room during athletics where he chose to disrobe behind the closed door of the water closet. Edgar understood. The smaller boy hadn't grown the way he and Fardle and the others had. Though his lower body appeared powerful, he didn't have the muscle in his arms and shoulders that he wished. It bothered him. He was that sort of boy. He often commented on how Edgar had grown.

"Coming home with me for Christmas this year, Tilley?"

"Certainly. Just ask Mrs. Thorne."

"I already have. I've asked her three years in a row now and she's always said yes and you've never come."

"I will this year."

But Edgar knew he wouldn't. Tiger was always excited when

Edgar brought up the subject in the fall but refused when Mrs. Thorne's invitation was extended later on. He gave all sorts of reasons, but none were convincing.

"What are you afraid of?"

"Don't say that to me," said Tiger abruptly, "not you, of all people." He climbed out of the bed and walked to the other side of the room and was silent for a while before he spoke again. "I want to tell you about the accident now. I need to get it off my chest."

Edgar knew what that meant. Tiger had mentioned the "awful" accident in which his parents had died many times, but had never given any details. Since Edgar lived out any story he read or was told, even drifted into paintings when he stared at them, he wasn't anxious to hear what promised to be a bloody account. But once they graduated, they might not see each other much, so if his friend was ready to talk about this now, he would listen. Tiger had often followed Edgar down the hallways when his nightmares made him walk in his sleep, quietly returning him to his bed so others wouldn't know, but Edgar hadn't told him of the anxiety that was always inside him, or how real the demons in his dreams seemed. He steeled himself for Tiger's tale.

Edgar knew that the Tilleys did not have old money, nor were they members of the aristocracy like many other families whose boys attended the College on the Moors. Instead, they were recently wealthy barons of the theater world, suppliers of costumes and scenery to the best performance palaces in London's West End. "As a child, I was lucky to meet the biggest stars of the stage, including Irving!" Tiger often said. But tonight he didn't mention any of that. He came to the day of the tragedy instantly. He spoke without sadness, which Edgar found strange. The image of his own father lying motionless in bed still haunted him.

"We had just visited the college for the first time, the three of us, the whole family. We had met the headmaster and I'd been enrolled . . . but Mother and Father didn't make it home." Tiger put his hand over his heart when he said this, but still didn't seem upset. In fact, he appeared to be excited.

"They left Altnabreac Station on the afternoon train. It traveled south on the Far North Line to Inverness and then roared toward Edinburgh at full speed! But . . . at a valley over a river half an hour out of the city, the unthinkable happened! Up ahead, workers were replacing a track on the viaduct. They were to flag down approaching locomotives some thousand feet before the precipice. But the man charged with that task made a grave mistake. He held the flag only five hundred feet away and the locomotive couldn't stop. Its brakes screeched and whined, but it plunged into the abyss! Down into the valley the carriages fell, first class, second and third. Many went to their deaths, among them . . . my parents. It was said limbs and heads were severed and blood was splattered on the walls like paint."

Edgar knew that if he listened closely he would be inside that deadly train, so he fixed his mind on a day long ago, reading a happy story with his father.

"I was fortunate," Tiger added. "When my parents enrolled me here they left enough money for me to stay in the Highlands for the duration of my education with all my meals and accommodations paid."

"I believe you've mentioned that."

Though Edgar read the *Times of London* every day, he could not recall ever coming across a report concerning the crash Tiger spoke of. But it did sound a good deal like another he had read about—at Staplehurst in England some three decades earlier, a much-documented incident in which the author Charles Dickens was nearly killed.

But why would Tiger lie to him?

And so Edgar prepared to go home to Thorne House that snowy Christmas wondering about his only friend, again left behind with the dismal dozen. "Have a marvelous holiday, Brim," said a deep voice as Edgar felt a presence behind him at the front doors. He turned to see Professor Lear. The dark-bearded man dropped his voice. "Sleep well."

As fond as Edgar was of his adoptive mother, he always grew bored at Thorne House during school holidays and that Christmas seemed even worse. "Eddie, would you not like to be out of doors?" Annabel asked, as she had many times before. "The pond in the park is frozen over and there are many others your age using it." She purchased new ice skates for him every year.

But he never wanted that. He wanted to be with Tiger. And he wanted to climb the stairs at night and find a way into Alfred Thorne's laboratory. He had sneaked up there a few times when the inventor was away and seen more strange weapons through the keyhole, and once a well-dressed man whose face he recognized from a newspaper had visited the lab: the Marquis of Lansdowne, the Secretary of State for War. "If Tiger were here," Edgar told himself more than once, "we could break in. He would know how."

But two days before Christmas that year, Alfred Thorne unwittingly brought an end to his adopted son's boredom. And in doing so he changed Edgar's life.

Thorne had just entered the drawing room where his wife and young ward were reading in its two most comfortable chairs. She had a copy of *A Vindication of the Rights of Woman* in hand.

Thorne had only recently allowed her to give Edgar Brim a novel or two. It had galled him to give in, though she argued that Edgar had them at school anyway. As the inventor crossed the room, he saw that the boy had shunned the science books he had left out in favor of a recent H. Rider Haggard adventure story narrating strange and dramatic action in darkest Africa. The boy had even discussed it at dinner the previous evening, speaking of a dashing hero named Quatermain. Thorne hated to admit that it had sounded terribly exciting.

"I think I shall open this tonight," said Thorne. He held something in his hand.

The boy looked up and gasped.

"I shall break the seal and see what is in it. I have been meaning to do this for years but couldn't help but think it was nonsense. We shall throw it in the dustbin after I've had a quick perusal. Pardon me while I retrieve a hammer from the laboratory to break the lock."

Edgar then did something of which he wasn't proud. And when Thorne returned, Allen Brim's journal, the object of the inventor's intended violence, was nowhere to be found.

"I could have sworn I left it here. Did you see it, Annabel?"

His wife said she had not, though there seemed a slight smile on her lips.

"Well," exclaimed the eccentric man, "I shall see if I left it up in the lab." Edgar wasn't sure, but it almost appeared as if there was a very slight smile on his adoptive father's lips too.

When Thorne came back empty-handed, Edgar made a shocking announcement.

"If you don't mind, mother and Mr. Thorne, I am going to take some air. I feel the need for a turn in the park. Perhaps I shall indeed try out those ice skates."

In the park Edgar sat on a cold iron bench, slipped the journal from under his coat and tried to pull it open with his trembling hands. But the lock was secure. Finally, in utter frustration, he stood up and threw it on the frozen ground, jumped into the air and came down as hard as he could on the lock with both feet.

It sprang open!

He retrieved it, his breathing quickening, and opened it.

THE PRIVATE THOUGHTS OF ALLEN BRIM
With love to Virginia and Edgar

Edgar fought back tears and began turning the pages. They were full of notes about the fairy tales, sensation novels and horror stories Allen had read, each page headed with the title of a famous fiction. One entry was for *Frankenstein*, another *The Vampyre*, and then *The Pit and the Pendulum*, *Beowulf* and *Beauty and the Beast*.

"The characters seem to be coming to life," the squire had written on one page.

As Edgar read on, oblivious to the cold, he realized that in every entry his father dwelt upon the possibility that the monsters and supernatural villains in these novels were *real!* There were notes about the lives of the writers. Mary Shelley, it seemed, had lived in a haunted house in Switzerland in 1816 during a legendary summer when the sun rarely shone, and one stormy night, she and two poets, her husband Percy Shelley and Lord Byron, made up ghost stories. John Polidori was with them. His tale became *The Vampyre*. Hers was *Frankenstein*.

Mary apparently knew of scientists who believed they could animate dead matter. Allen wondered if one had created a human being, and if she knew about it. Did she see the creature? He quoted a passage Mary had written somewhere, perhaps in her own private journal, and it shook Edgar:

> *I saw the pale student of unhallowed arts kneeling beside the thing he had put together. I saw the hideous phantasm of a man stretched out, and then, on the working of some powerful engine, show signs of life, and stir with an uneasy, half vital motion. Frightful must it be!*

Edgar flipped through more pages. There were notes about the great American writer named Poe too. The horror master was uniquely sensitive, had "spectral visions" in his dreams and when wide awake. His death had been eerie. "Why can't they discover what killed him on the Baltimore streets?" Allen had written. "Why was his corpse found in someone else's clothes?" Then he added: "Did a demon take his life?"

But of all the spine-tingling thoughts Edgar found in the journal, nothing compared to what he encountered at the end. The final paragraph was in darker ink:

I am worried that I have done a terrible thing to my beloved little boy. He cannot sleep; he seems frightened of so many things. Did I somehow cause this? I have made him learned and sensitive to his surroundings. He will be a fine boy in those important ways. But have I made him frightened of life? If I have done that, I have done the devil's work. The Bible says, "Fear not!" and those words and "Love" are our Lord's greatest. I have not yet had the courage to write the truth in my novels, but if I live long enough (and I have premonitions I may not), I will, at least, instill in Edgar one last and meaningful truth . . . whatever you do in this world, my son, fight your fears. I am with you.

DO NOT BE AFRAID

Edgar Brim could actually hear his father's voice saying those words as if he were sitting beside him on the cold park bench. It gave him great strength. He stood. As he did, the wind fluttered the pages and his thumb happened to find the last one. Edgar looked down. There were two words there, set off on their own and very small:

Lear knew.

9

New Edgar, New Tiger

When Edgar Brim returned to the College on the Moors after the Christmas break, he was almost a new boy. Or at least, he was trying to be.

It was in the very way he moved. Lovecraft noticed it, of course, but so did Griswold and Numb. The lad looked people in the eye, walked with his head up and shoulders back, and spoke to others in a clear voice. It didn't matter that it was obvious he was forcing himself; it was enough that he was doing it. He was only unnerved near the one-armed professor of science. *Lear* must refer to someone else, he thought. It must be a coincidence.

Do not be afraid, he kept reminding himself.

He appeared in the gymnasium on the first day back ready to develop his muscles and endurance. He wasn't even sure what he should do with the dumbbells and barbells. He was "greeted" by an astonished Fardle and his minions. Edgar Brim was still the slimmest student his age in the school—the only other who came close was Tiger Tilley. But Edgar ignored Fardle's needling comments about his weight lifting, stuck to his efforts and made sure he took seconds of everything in the Great Dining Hall. By early February, he began to thicken noticeably. "Excellent," said Tiger, feeling his mate's bicep, "you are becoming a man, Master Brim!" The expression on Tilley's face betrayed admiration. It didn't hurt that Edgar's efforts coincided with a major growth spurt. Before long, he reached Fardle's height.

But it was at night that Edgar faced his biggest challenge. He kept dreaming of monsters, though now he forced himself to fight them. He wielded an ax at Grendel and confronted the witches and made them back down. He no longer cried out in the night or walked the halls in his sleep, but the nightmares didn't disappear. And he couldn't stop wondering about Lear.

He didn't shun the more frightening passages in books anymore. Lovecraft was delighted to see him stand up and offer to read the page in Wilkie Collins's recent novel *The Woman in White* that detailed the appearance of the ghostly female who haunted that story. Edgar read it with such feeling that he actually scared his classmates. Fardle, for one, fought with a desire to get under his desk.

On the rugby field, Edgar took the tackles now and often carried the ball. He even caught it once when Fardle threw it at his crotch after a score, then delivered a bullet-like projection right back at the bigger boy's own groin area. The hard inflated leather ball found its mark and the bully was instantly on the ground, hands upon the precious little engine of the Fardle family's hopes for the future. The big boy lay there for a while, face as red as the blood he had once or twice drawn from Edgar, Tiger looking on with pride.

Fear, Edgar began to realize, was everyone's biggest hurdle to success. Easing it even somewhat changed everything dramatically. Who would have known that such a thing, not even a real thing, just a feeling, could mean so much in someone's life?

Eventually, he grew a few inches beyond Fardle and much taller than Tiger, who almost unaccountably didn't add an inch in their last year and a half.

But then everything changed again, this time, in an instant.

It happened on the field during their last semester of school. Edgar and Tiger, born in the same month and set to graduate a year early, were approaching seventeen. They were on opposing teams: Edgar on Fardle's side, Tiger with the Fardle Followers. The two friends liked to tackle each other now and sometimes had spectacular collisions. Edgar still didn't truly enjoy violent contact but Tiger seemed to thrive on it. But on that day Edgar was the aggressor, soon aided and abetted by none other than Fardle himself.

Tiger was playing wing, as usual, always one of the fastest boys on the pitch, almost impossible to catch. He took possession of the ball after a series of quick passes and swung outside and made for the goal line as if he were riding the howling wind that was blowing across the moors that day.

"Got you!" cried Edgar, coming for him.

"Not in your dreams!" shouted Tiger.

Edgar wasn't going to let him get away. He would show them all. And so, in an action he would later deeply regret, he found speed that even he didn't know he possessed. He powered across the field after Tiger, urging himself to new heights, competitiveness surging through him. "I will catch him! I will catch him!" he cried inside his head.

And he did. But all he could grasp was his friend's thick shirt, or more accurately, shirts. For some reason, and for some time, Tiger had been wearing two layers of the College's rugby shirts, even when it was warm. Edgar grabbed a fistful of cloth in his hand. It seemed for an instant that Tiger had slowed, as if he wanted to be caught.

Edgar violently pulled and ripped the shirts clean off Master Tilley's back.

Beneath them, Tiger was wearing something that none of the boys had ever seen before. It was a piece of material almost like a bandage, wrapped tightly around his chest. When it was revealed, Tiger actually screamed, his voice rather high, certainly higher than usual. Still running, he dropped the ball and thrust his hands across his chest, as if to hide something.

Then Fardle arrived, panting, only catching up because Edgar had slowed Tiger. He saw his chance. He reached out to seize his opponent and spear-tackle him to the ground like an American cowboy pulling down a calf. With his left hand, he caught that strange piece of bandaging that ran across Tiger's back and around his chest from halfway up the rib cage to just below the collarbones. In a vicious yank, he tore it, ripping it from Tiger's body.

This time the fleeing boy was knocked down and landed hard on his back. He screamed again, just as high-pitched but very loudly, and sprang to his feet. They all saw Tiger Tilley's chest for an instant. That is . . . they saw *her* chest. It didn't look anything like theirs.

10

Two Deaths

Tiger Tilley was expelled the same day. She was allowed just one request. She had ten minutes with Edgar Brim to say good-bye.

The knock on his door was gentler than in the past. Edgar knew it was him . . . or her, but he didn't want to answer. She knocked again.

"Please, Eddie, let me in."

Her voice was higher than usual, more like the way she had sounded when they first met. It was obvious to Edgar now that she had been speaking in lower tones for a while, on purpose. He thought of all the time they had spent alone together in his room.

He got up and opened the door. He hadn't intended to even look at her, but it was impossible not to. Standing in front of him was a young woman: black curly hair now washed and combed out, black eyes sad and downcast, her skin soft and without a trace of fuzz. (He had wondered about that.) Even the little bump on her twice-broken nose, the lean muscle in her neck, seemed different now. But most shocking was her dress. Tiger stood there in women's clothing, an old frock that must have belonged to the cook. Long ago, Mrs. Shakewell must have been much slimmer, for this dress fit Tiger perfectly. Her figure, now apparent, was having an effect on Edgar that he tried to ignore. It was the strangest of emotions.

"I owe you an explanation."

"I should think so," he said bitterly.

"May I sit?"

Edgar turned and sat on his chair at his desk, so he only saw her peripherally. He wasn't about to get on the bed with her again.

"I suppose."

She dropped onto the bed. She did it with an athletic little dart, quick as lightning, just like the old Tiger. Edgar stifled a smile.

"I am not who I said I was."

"Oh, really?"

"I deserve that."

"Yes, you do."

"I wish my parents were here." She sounded like she was ready to cry.

That softened Edgar. "I'm sorry," he said.

She smiled at him for a moment, but then her face tightened again.

"It's all right. They've been dead for a long time, so I really shouldn't feel that way."

"Not that long. At least they got to bring you to the school."

"That wasn't them, and they didn't die in a train crash."

"So you lied about that too."

"They weren't my parents. They just came here and went home."

"What are you talking about?"

"Edgar, I was born in a workhouse in London. My real name is Edith Hoffman. Or at least, that was what I was told."

"Edith?"

"Yes."

"Good change."

Tiger couldn't stop another little smile, but then her face darkened again. "They said my mother was a prostitute who died the minute I entered the world and my father, well, he was who-knows-what. I'm guessing, though, given that he was my father, that he was probably a rather special person, maybe a duke or a prince?"

She was trying to be humorous, but Edgar didn't react. Her tone dropped again.

"I was on my own from the time I was born. But I always had spirit. I left the workhouse when I was small and lived on the streets with other pickpockets and purse snatchers. I was a clever one, so maybe my father really was someone important, who knows? I never went without food in London. I could steal better than others; I could pretend I was anything or anyone. Some of the thieves even took to dressing me up and using me to fool folks. But what I really wanted was to *be* like the people we stole from. To do that, I knew I needed an education. I knew that was the key to everything. And I suppose I wanted to be a man, because that is how you get places in this world." She stood up and marched a few strides away from him.

"I lived for a while with about a dozen other street urchins in one room on the third floor of a rookery house in the East End. There wasn't a toilet, not even a hole in the floor. You got to the house down a filthy alleyway and then up a rickety wooden staircase. But I wasn't like them. They spent everything they stole. I saved and waited for my big chance. And it came one day when I was used in a robbery at the Bank of England. I was small enough to crawl up a pipe from the sewer into the cellar to a vault that the gang knew how to open. But I didn't come back with the money. I went up into the ground floor of the bank and escaped out a window. Then I climbed a drainpipe and took off across the roofs until I was miles away. I took all the loot with me."

Edgar remembered how Tiger could steal the tarts from the larder, almost out from under the giant nose of Griswold himself.

"I wasn't proud of my actions but I did what I had to do. I moved to Brixton south of the Thames after that and lived in disguise. But it wasn't long before I could be myself again—the gang that had helped me get into the bank must have been desperate after what I did and within weeks they were caught doing their next job. You can't be sloppy. They've been put away for decades."

"You were fortunate."

"Fortunate and devious, and I was never afraid. The things you are afraid of usually turn out not to be so frightening at all. We've talked about that."

Edgar knew he had learned a great deal from his friend.

"What I did wasn't right. I know that. But I had to survive. I dreamed of being someone, of making something of myself. There was only one way to do it."

"You are wrong there," said Edgar. But he knew he sounded full of himself. What would he have done in her situation?

"I knew actors. Folks in my business are acquainted with all kinds of them, not Henry Irving or anyone like that, like I said, but

I knew a few who acted in lower parts. I paid a couple of them a bag full of money to play the roles of my parents—"

"You did?" He turned toward her.

"I'd heard things about the College on the Moors, an exclusive school in the far northern Highlands that made men out of boys. It had a winning reputation. Graduation from here meant you could do nearly anything you wanted. I decided I'd come here disguised, toughen myself even more and be a man. With the bank job money, I had enough funds to finance my whole education. I made up the story about my parents dying on their way home. They were effectively out of the way, no questions asked. The school only cared that they had my money."

"What did you intend to do after you left here?"

"I don't know for certain." She paused. "I had dreams about starting a business, maybe working in a bank in a high position, I don't know."

"As a man?"

"Maybe. They don't give such jobs to women." She paused again. "But then I met you."

"I think you should go."

"I met you and I never had such a friend. I knew many awful boys and men. I never thought one could be like you. You really care about things. I started thinking that maybe I could become a woman anyway and go back to London . . . with you."

There was a knock on the door. It was the grim porter, Usher.

"Master . . . Miss Tilley, it is time. Driver has brought William Wilson around to the doors. You cannot miss the train."

"Go away, Tilley," said Edgar. "You deceived me."

As she turned to leave, he noticed that Tiger was almost crying. But then color rose in her face. "Is that all you have to say?" she muttered and slipped out the door.

After that, Edgar moved about the halls a truly different and dangerous boy, sometimes downright nasty. One day he even dropped his books to fight Fardle when the other purposely squeezed him into a doorframe as they entered a classroom. Edgar Brim would not be ridiculed anymore—he wasn't in the mood.

He wished that meant that his nightmares would go away too. But they kept coming, defying him as he confronted them. And so did the hag. The hideous old woman did not appear as often, but she didn't vanish. And she was still terribly real.

As he struggled through his final months at the college, there were, thankfully, other things to distract him. The first and most important was a little boy named G. Lancelot Newman, who had arrived at the school just before Tiger left and had been ill almost every day since. The child nearly lived in the school's infirmary. He was said to be of a "nervous disposition." He had nightmares and couldn't sleep, and he intrigued Edgar Brim.

One day, Edgar knocked on Lovecraft's door.

"Ah, Brim, how are you this fine morning?" asked the ever-cheerful little teacher.

"Might it be possible, sir, for me to keep poor Newman company some evenings? I could read to him. It might help him fall asleep."

Lovecraft smiled that electric smile of his. Sometimes, it was almost mesmerizing. "What a lovely idea, Brim. How kind." He kept grinning at Edgar from under his long mop of wildly curling salt-and-pepper hair. "Now, don't you worry about Griswold," he said under his breath. "I shall work my magic on him and procure permission!"

The infirmary was a strange place: on the ground floor at the far eastern end of the building, it was three times the height of the dormitory rooms and classrooms and an extra floor taller than the Great Dining Hall. It was a damp stone place with tiny high windows and not a spot of decoration. Few boys spent time there because it was essentially not allowed. Being sick was considered a disorder of the brain more than the body and one owed it to their family, school and country to get better as quickly as possible. A "nervous disposition" was thought of with great disdain. But G. Lancelot Newman, tiny for his age, cried out even louder in his sleep than Edgar had ever done. He disturbed the other boys, even from the distant infirmary. Thus, when Lovecraft asked Griswold to allow Brim to help Newman fall asleep, the old man did not hesitate to give permission.

The door to the big room, itself about ten feet high and five feet across, creaked as Edgar opened it and echoed when he closed it behind him. His footsteps sounded like heavy slaps to the face, each offering its own reverberation. There was no one in there but the little boy, lying in one of about a hundred cots, alone in the middle of a sea of white. There was no nurse at the College on the Moors. Most of the aid administered to the boys was simply in the form of pep talks delivered by various members of the dismal dozen.

G. Lancelot Newman's little eyes widened as he saw Edgar Brim approach.

"May I sit down, my friend?"

"Y-yes. What do you want?"

"Want? Nothing."

"I will try to be well."

"You shall do nothing of the kind. You shall simply relax."

The boy almost smiled. His hair was like straw, his skin pale and his frame skeletal. Edgar had heard that he never smiled. He was six years old and appeared about three.

"Thank you, sir."

"Not at all. I was once like you, you know."

"You were? There is no one like me, sir. I am worthless."

The word alarmed Edgar, but he collected himself. "Nonsense, no one is worthless, especially not you. You are unique, Lancelot Newman."

"I am named for the great knight."

"Excellent, but you do not have to be him, you know."

"I don't?"

"You are G. Lancelot Newman and no one else, and you shall be a fine knight of your own sort."

"I will?"

"Of course. Do you have nightmares?"

A cloud gathered over the boy's face.

"I am sorry, sir, very sorry, but I do."

"No cause for sorrow. Are you unable to move sometimes when you wake up?"

There was terror in the boy's eyes but he found his voice. "Are you?"

"Yes," said Edgar.

75

"YES?" It was the first time Newman had ever raised his voice at the College on the Moors, at least while awake. The sound echoed in the huge room and frightened him. "I am sorry, sir."

"Do not be. Let your big voice be heard."

The little boy giggled. That startled him too, for he had rarely heard that sound either.

"My father is an important man in India in the Empire government and my mother is a beauty."

"I am sure she is."

"Father has no time for weaklings."

"Then he is a fool."

The child shot up to a sitting position on his cot and looked around. "Quiet!"

"He can't hear us, Master Newman, not from India, and we shan't worry about him anyway. We shall tap him on the nose if he disturbs us."

"We shall?" The little boy paused, then smiled and lay back in the bed. Then he rose onto one arm. "What is that you have in your hand, sir?"

"I am Master Brim, not sir, and it is a thin book with a fiction inside."

"Oh! I don't like those. Are there monsters in this one? I can't abide them. I shall die if you read it!"

"There are no monsters, and what if there were?"

"They are real!"

It was Edgar's turn to be startled. He wanted to say "nonsense" but couldn't.

"Perhaps they are," he said.

"There is no perhaps about it."

"And what if they are, Master Newman? You know, there are frightening things in life. There always will be. All of us have fears. Our response to them is what matters. Even Headmaster Griswold is afraid of something."

"Oh, I'm sure he isn't."

"He is likely afraid of himself. And that fact, like many other things about Spartan Griswold, is kept hidden from the world. That is why he is so mean to others. You must fight your fears. *Do not be afraid.*"

He had never said it out loud. But when he did, it sounded marvelous. It sounded like the truth. It made G. Lancelot Newman beam.

"I think I should like you to read the book."

"It is just something by a man named Poe. He wrote the most frightening stories the world has ever read. They are marvelous."

Lancelot Newman pulled the covers up over his head. "Then I've changed my mind. We shan't read this."

"But this one is not so frightening. It is a poem. He wrote many of those too. And he wrote happy and adventurous stories, as well. He always told the truth, sometimes very difficult truths. Human beings need that. This is a love story and rather sad, extremely sad, actually, but awfully beautiful too."

This little boy lowered the covers from his face. And so Edgar began:

It was many and many a year ago
In a kingdom by the sea . . .

He read with such feeling that it calmed the boy. Yes, it was sad, but it told of real and abiding love, and the boy so reveled in hearing it that he fell asleep. Edgar sat there watching him, observing the little fragile face with the darkness around the eyes. He was so still that Edgar imagined him dead, a porcelain corpse like in a Poe story. He stopped those thoughts and turned away. And when he turned back, the boy's eyes were moving under his lids! He began to toss and turn.

Edgar fled.

But he came back every night for weeks. Each time, he brought another book. He read the boy things that challenged him: Lewis Carroll's second Alice story, *Through the Looking-Glass*, keeping in some frightening parts but leaving out the scariest; Jules Verne's *Twenty Thousand Leagues Under the Sea*, with its fantastic underwater scenes featuring Captain Nemo; and one by the master, Robert Louis Stevenson, called *Treasure Island*, remembering not to say too much about the one-legged pirate Long John Silver. Edgar was building toward the monsters. He wondered not only if Master Newman could stand them, but if he too would be able to remain within the room.

Edgar hated to admit it to himself, but he missed Tiger. In fact, he missed her dearly. It got worse as the weeks passed. He sat alone in his room night after night, remembering the things they had done together and thinking about the fact that he had no idea where she had gone. He might *never* see her again. He had pushed his dear friend away, for the crime of trying to get somewhere in the world. He began to wonder if there was any way he might find her. A solution came to him. But in order to do it, he had to attempt a "Tiger thing."

He remembered hearing Usher speaking to her as they moved away from his door, down the hallway to meet the waiting driver and his black horse on her last day. The porter was a man of few words. "We are making up your records. Once you are settled in the city, they shall be sent to you."

Edgar knew that students' personal records were kept locked in the headmaster's office and the only way to find her address was to get into Griswold's files. He tried to imagine how Tiger would go about it. It occurred to him that much of her technique was simple boldness. She bravely went right to the thing she wanted and pounced at the perfect moment.

Then he thought about the headmaster. Everyone in the school feared him so much that no one in their right mind would enter his room when he was not there. Not even Lear. That meant Griswold would never expect such a thing and likely kept his door unlocked.

Since Edgar was a final-year student, many of his classes were on the third floor, the same level from which Griswold ruled his empire. The day after he'd made his decision, Edgar took a slightly different route between classes than usual so that he passed directly by the headmaster's office. He saw the old man come out, slam his door and head off down the hallway with his whip at his side. There were just a few students in the corridor. Edgar kept walking, then did an abrupt turn and headed back toward the office. This time, the hallway was clear. He opened the door quickly and darted inside, closing it behind him.

The room smelled of old man, stinky with the body odor and secret farts of the headmaster of the College on the Moors. The Reverend Spartan Griswold was a connoisseur of cheese, and Edgar could tell. He held his nose. There was a large wooden desk directly in front of him and on it were what appeared to be a series of upright knives and needles on little stands, and skewered upon them were Griswold's memos to himself. He liked to impale things. The stone room was dim and filled with stacks of papers, wooden filing cabinets and a bookshelf along the wall with just a few volumes in it. Edgar ignored the portrait of old Emeritus staring down on him and moved to the cabinets and examined the labels on the outside. STUDENTS, read one. He slid a drawer open. It creaked as if it hadn't been oiled since the 1600s.

Edgar froze. Would that sound be heard out in the hall? What would Griswold do to him if he found him here? The headmaster had never whipped him. He was certain the beating would be vicious. But all was quiet outside.

The file was alphabetical and, unfortunately, he had opened *A*, the wrong drawer. He pushed it back in a half inch at a time. He examined the others. How many drawers down would he have to go to find *T*? He chose the bottom one. Because it bore the weight of the whole ancient cabinet, he knew it would squeak like a rat. He pulled it back, slowly. It squealed as if it were alive and he was killing it, still no sound from the hallway. He made up his mind. He couldn't stay here forever, pulling out the drawer inch by inch. Griswold could return at any minute.

He yanked hard and pulled it right out. It screamed. But there were the *T* files. He flew through the students' names until he came to Tiger's and seized her pages. There was her new address on Mordaunt Street in Brixton, in London! But written across it was a slash of handwriting: *Moving to America.*

It was like a dart to his heart. He gasped and slammed the drawer shut.

As the sound settled, he heard footsteps in the hallway. They were coming his way and moving fast. They thundered on the floor.

Edgar turned and made for the door. But the footsteps were picking up speed. In a second, they were right at the entrance. Edgar saw the knob turn and the door open. Big-nosed Spartan Griswold, giant in height and strength, and a vicious practitioner of the whip, stood before him.

11

Mission

With a terrifying smile, the headmaster began to slowly close the door behind him. But suddenly a hand stopped it from sealing shut.

"Yes, Lear, may I help you?" asked Griswold impatiently. "I am about to deal with this *trespassing* child." The excitement in his face betrayed his intention: to exact brutal blows to the flesh of another student, *this* particular one.

Edgar couldn't move a muscle. *Do not be afraid*, he ordered himself. He didn't know which of these two enemies was worse. He dreaded the thought of the whip, but Lear, who was glowering down upon him, made him tremble. "Where is the ink!" thundered the one-armed man at Edgar.

"Ink?" asked Brim, barely able to get the word out.

"Don't be smart with me. You know why I asked you to come to the headmaster's office! Do you have your head in the clouds again?"

"Ink?" asked Griswold, beginning to appear disappointed.

"I told him you would have a good supply here," said Lear, motioning to the bottom shelf where the headmaster indeed kept big bottles. Among Griswold's eccentricities was his desire to control all the supplies at the school. "Do you not recall that, Brim?" He seemed to nod slightly as he said it.

Edgar paused. "Yes, yes, I recall that, sir. I am very sorry."

"No need for that. Pick up a bottle and come with me."

"But—" sputtered Griswold.

"Yes, Headmaster?"

"He came in here when I was out. He must be punished."

"My fault. I told him to go in if you were not here. I know you leave your door unlocked. It is an admirable choice and a great lesson to the boys about honor and trust."

"But—"

"Brim, shall we be on our way? We must not keep the headmaster."

Edgar swept up an ink bottle, rushed past the open-mouthed Griswold and was out in the hallway with Lear in an instant. They moved silently down the stone floor for a while. The professor took the bottle from him.

"I didn't know we needed ink, sir."

"We don't. What were you searching for in there? And don't say nothing."

"Miss Tilley's address."

"She is in London. Did you find it?"

"Yes, sir. But there was a note on it saying she was going abroad."

"Would you like to investigate this further?"

"Yes, sir, though I'm not sure how to proceed. I'm not sure I should pursue this at all. I would need permission to go to the city, and money, and I don't know how to get either."

"Come with me."

Lear led Edgar to his classroom. The thick wooden tables were littered with test tubes, mortars and pestles, and Bunsen burners. Rubber tubes led from vats into flasks. There were floor-to-ceiling glass cabinets filled with containers of liquid and powdered chemicals. Skeletons hung on stands. It was the sort of place where you could make a monster, like Victor Frankenstein had.

Lear looked up and down the hallway and then locked them in. Edgar kept his distance. If he was going to find Tiger, he had to do so immediately. She could be gone forever any day now. It was Wednesday. There were no classes on Saturday and Sunday, and a train left Altnabreac Station each Friday evening for London. He could take it and be back to the moors by Sunday night. Graduation was next week. But even if he could muster the courage to go, how in the world would he do it? Alfred Thorne had made it clear that he was not allowed, under any circumstances, to leave school, except for the Christmas holidays.

Lear moved closer to him. Edgar stepped back. The bearded man halted just inches from him.

"You indeed need consent to leave the college, Brim."

"My stepfather, Alfred Thorne, will not give it."

"Then you are in an intriguing situation."

Edgar thought of the strange card Lear had given him that night in his room years ago. It was still in his bedside table. "Were I to decide to go, would you help me?" Edgar asked, though he couldn't believe the words coming out of his mouth.

"You could consider it done," said Lear and turned back to his desk and began rummaging in a drawer.

At first, Edgar didn't know how to respond. Then he found his tongue. "May I ask how you would accomplish it, sir?"

"The Royal Mail is delivered here Mondays and Wednesdays, as you know. I shall forge a note from your adoptive father now, giving you permission to go to London on Friday and return by the Sunday evening train. I shall make up a reason for your absence, something about a family gathering. I will deposit said letter in the bag tonight before Usher distributes its contents tomorrow. I know his habits. It shan't be a difficult thing. Griswold is a lazy man, my boy. He will not recall Alfred Thorne's handwriting nor will he investigate any of this further. I can assure you there will be no inquiries made to Thorne House, London. He will simply call you to the office, likely by Friday noon, to give his official permission and let you go, as long as you return at the required time. If you decide not to leave, you can tell him you are ill, or some such thing."

Lear closed his desk drawer. "Take this." He handed the boy several pound notes. "Return them should you resolve to stay."

"Th-thank you," Edgar sputtered. *Why was Lear helping him?*

"You are dismissed, Brim."

Edgar wanted to ask the old man much more, but he had gotten what he needed and didn't want to push his luck. It might be a mistake to ask Lear why his name was in the journal. It might not even be him anyway. Edgar turned to leave, but as he unlocked the door, he heard the professor's voice.

"Oh, Brim?"

When he turned, he saw that Lear had put his spectacles on and opened a thick novel.

"Should you go to London, I would impose one condition in exchange for my assistance." He lifted his eyes up above the spectacles. "You must visit the society named on the card I gave you some time ago."

Edgar gulped. "All right, sir."

"And Brim."

"Yes, sir?"

"You could give my regards to Miss Tilley."

As Edgar stepped out into the hallway, he thought he caught a glimpse of the edge of a hooded cloak disappearing around a corner.

Edgar spent the rest of the day moiling about what he should do. It would be a daring move, perhaps not worth it if Thorne found out. But Tiger could be lost forever.

That night, he went to the infirmary for another visit with G. Lancelot Newman, and because he knew he might not see the boy for a while, brought a special book to read aloud: *The Personal History of David Copperfield* by Charles Dickens. It began: "Whether I shall turn out to be the hero of my own life, or whether that station will be held by anybody else, these pages must show."

Master Newman was delighted with that beginning. He sat up and looked as bright as a shilling, brighter than he had ever appeared before. He listened intently. There were no monsters, but a good deal of truth and a few nervous moments. When Edgar finished, the child smiled.

"I should like to be the hero of my life. Do you think that possible?"

"Absolutely. You will be, Master Newman, trust me."

"I know the monsters are real, sir, but I think I shall challenge them. I think I shall choose not to be afraid."

"Good for you, my friend."

G. Lancelot Newman went to sleep immediately after that, drifting off with a smile on his face as Edgar watched over him. His eyes did not move under his lids and his rest was undisturbed. A magic moment had come.

Edgar thought of the little boy's last words and repeated them. *"I know the monsters are real, but I think I shall challenge them. I think I shall choose not to be afraid."* But he didn't smile when he said them, for as he spoke a cold sensation came over him, as if a breeze had entered the room and gone through his heart. He couldn't explain it, but it seemed as if there was a presence nearby. He suddenly felt that the child was in danger. He pulled the covers up over Lancelot's little chest and tucked them under his chin. He got up and surveyed the room, sure they were not alone.

"Is someone there?" he asked, his voice trembling. All he could make out were shadows in the corners. Then, for an instant, he thought he saw something move on a distant bed, but when he trained his eye there was nothing. Of course there was nothing, he told himself. He had much to do the next day, so he left, closing the door slowly behind him, with one last glance back at the middle cot in that sea of white.

The next morning he awoke to the news of Lancelot Newman's death.

———

They held the funeral on Friday morning. The entire school—one hundred and ninety-nine students, twelve professors, one driver and groundskeeper, one cook and one headmaster—were gathered about in the rain in the graveyard at the rear near the rugby field, dressed in black. Lancelot's parents were not in attendance, although the rumor was that they were home in England and had simply instructed the school to bury their only son "without fuss." The black horse brought the body on the rugged carriage, a bible passage was read, the small coffin was lowered into the hole that Usher and the driver had dug, and G. Lancelot Newman was put to rest in an unmarked grave at the back of the cemetery.

Most of the students and school officials seemed put out by the inconvenience of having to attend the funeral for this weakling in the rain. Only three people appeared even the least disturbed: Edgar Brim had to fight with every ounce of willpower he had not to break down and cry; Professor Lovecraft wept uncontrollably and didn't seem to care that others noticed; and Lear looked ghastly that day, suit in disarray, cravat poorly knotted, hair more than usually disheveled, as pale as the ghosts that it was said walked upon the moors. Lear's black eyes never once left Brim throughout the service. Edgar felt as if the old man were trying to tell him something—something he couldn't say aloud.

Edgar Brim was not only crushed by Master Newman's death, he was terrified by it. Had he, in fact, felt a presence in the infirmary the night the child died? And why was Lear now giving him that unblinking stare? GO, it seemed to say.

There was only one person he could talk to about this, and she lived in London, he hoped. He lay on his bed after the funeral, his heart pounding, staring at the ceiling. There was a knock on the door.

"Master Brim," called out Usher. "The Headmaster wishes to see you."

Griswold had the letter in hand, tapping it against his desk, but regarding Edgar.

"Your presence is required in London," he said, "at a family gathering. Your stepfather says it is important."

Edgar thought of the night in the infirmary, of the pitiable little coffin, of Lear's warning look. What was happening at the College on the Moors?

"Well, sir," he said, "then I suppose I must go."

12

The Crypto-Anthropology Society of the Queen's Empire

Edgar arrived in London in the early hours of Saturday morning, his black school jacket rumpled from his restless sleep on the hard third-class train seat. He was rumpled too—his flaming red hair unkempt and the dark circles under his blue eyes re-appearing for the first time in months. He was sad and frightened and excited.

He strode from the station on Drummond Street into a crush of pedestrians just beginning their day. He had come here on a mission and there was no time to waste. His first job was to find his friend. But he didn't just want to be near her anymore, simply seek her friendship again; he needed to share with her what had happened the night Lancelot Newman died. She knew about his nightmares and how they affected his life and had always been sympathetic. But he had never mentioned the idea that the monsters might be real, nor had he shared with her Lear's late-night visit long ago, or shown her the card he now carried in his pocket.

Finding directions to Brixton from the map he had copied out at the college, he took the underground railway southeast to Aldgate, near Whitechapel where the Ripper had ruled, and then got out and walked briskly to Monument Station and rode in one of the little electric cars on the new City and South Railway "tube" under the River Thames to its last station in North Brixton. From there, he walked along wide, crowded Stockwell Road, past shops and shouting hawkers and the smells of horse droppings and mongers' wares—pungent fish, aromatic flowers and vegetables a little past their prime—keeping his hand on his wallet to protect it from the street urchins and pickpockets. Five minutes later, he turned and followed a narrower residential road until he came to Mordaunt Street. It was filled with row housing. He approached Tiger's address.

But when Edgar stepped through the little brown-iron gate and walked up two short steps to the door, everything appeared quiet inside. He hesitated, lifted the brass knocker, and tapped lightly. No response. He tapped again, this time harder, and still no one came. He could slam it down with a bang, make sure she wasn't there, but he was reluctant. Though part of him was terrified she was gone forever, another part was almost relieved. It might be best to forget her and Master Newman and the monsters and his past, just graduate from the College on the Moors and return to the Thornes and the future their money could provide for him. It might be easier to never see Tiger again.

But as he turned to retreat down the steps, he heard the door open behind him and then that voice, her real voice. "Edgar?" She sounded sleepy. "Is it you?" He turned back to see her rub her eyes. Then her face hardened. "What do you want?"

He stepped forward and hugged her. He hadn't intended to do that.

For a moment she was stiff in his arms but then went up on her tiptoes and hugged him back, and they remained there embracing for a moment on her front step. He could sense now what he had never really known about his dear friend—she was strong, yes, but a bit vulnerable too. It felt amazing to hold her.

She was wearing her white cotton school shirt and gray flannel trousers, but not the way they were intended to be worn. The shirt had no tie and was undone a few buttons at the collar and hung loose over the trousers, and her feet were bare. Her shape gave the clothes a look they weren't intended to have. Her face was a little puffy, her shining black curly hair, now grown longer, was disheveled. But she was marvelous to him.

She invited him in, made tea, and they sat at the table in her little parlor. By then she had buttoned up her shirt, done up the trousers, put on shoes and fixed her hair a little, but not too much. Her brief joyful expression had been replaced by the tough face she had maintained throughout her years at the college.

"So you're not going to America?"

"I probably will, soon. I can't secure a good position here."

"What sort are you seeking?"

"That is part of the problem."

"What do you mean?"

"I cannot decide if I am a man or a woman. No, that's not it. I mean, I know what I am." She smiled and started to slide her hand over to his and then pulled it back. "But I don't know what I should be in order to get what I want in life."

"You should be yourself."

She smiled again but then narrowed her eyes. "Why have you come?" she asked. "Not just to see me, I'm sure."

"Well, I did come to see you. But there's something else too." He took the card from his pocket and put it on the table. She picked it up and looked at it.

"Lear visited my room one night, years ago, and gave me this."

Tiger glanced up at him. The mysterious one-armed professor had the same frightening effect on her as he did on all the students at the College on the Moors.

Edgar told her about trying to help Lancelot Newman, how their friendship had grown and what had happened a few days ago. He couldn't bring himself to say that he believed in demons and monsters, and really, he didn't think he did. But he told her how the little boy had felt about them, and how at the last moment, just after he had spoken of them, a presence had come over the room, as if someone were in there, watching.

Tiger was listening but also concentrating on the card.

"I know about these people," she said, tapping it with a finger.

"You do?"

"From a long time ago. I remember when I was on the streets as a child, I used to see these cards, usually on Oxford Street or The Strand; street boys used to hand them out. They all asked the same question when they did. If you answered "yes," they inquired if you would come with them to a certain address for a little experiment, for which you would be paid. It was sort of sinister, but there were always children who were desperate, and I suppose whoever employed these messengers knew it."

"Did you ever go?"

"No. It wasn't enough money, just pennies. I had bigger plans. *Lear* gave this to you?"

"What was the question they asked?"

"Let me see." She thought for a moment. "Oh, yes. They asked if you ever had the sensation, just as you wakened, that something or someone was sitting on your chest and pressing the air from your lungs, trying to kill you. Your arms and legs were paralyzed; you were conscious but couldn't move. They called it the hag phenomenon."

Edgar's heart started pounding hard.

"Edgar? Are you all right? You are very white! Do you want to lie down?"

He had never mentioned the hag to a soul.

"They asked that very question? They called it that?"

"What is it? Why does this matter to you?"

He told her. And he admitted that the old woman was still with him.

"You should have told me this before."

"Why?"

"I don't know. You just should have. You shouldn't keep things like that from me. Maybe I could have helped you. Maybe I still can."

Though Edgar certainly appreciated her desire to help him, he doubted she could, not with this. The hag represented something that remained alive in him that he needed to kill—he wondered if someday terror might seize him so thoroughly that he might want to end his life. It was good to have his friend near him and reaching out, but he knew that solutions lay elsewhere. It intrigued him beyond description that the "society" noted on the card that Professor Lear had given him was interested in the very thing that had plagued him since infancy. They even had a name for it. Now, *that* could mean something.

"Will you come with me?"

"Where?"

"To find these people."

Half an hour later they were heading north toward Drury Lane. They walked this time, a long way up to the river and then over Waterloo Bridge with stately Somerset House on one side and the golden Parliament Buildings in the distance on the other. They passed ladies in bustled dresses and fancy hats, other women in torn skirts and blouses that barely stayed on them, men in bowler hats and high cravats, or soiled caps with greasy rags around their throats. On the busy streets there were tram cars and omnibuses and even a few motor cars, new in England and the world, daring the speed limit of twelve miles an hour. It was a fine day for London, no fog or rain, as if the great city, often in a dark dream, was momentarily wide awake. But the couple barely noticed either the weather or their surroundings. They were locked in conversation, Edgar telling Tiger in more detail what happened the night Master Newman died, and about the ominous Lear insisting on a visit to the address on the card. She wore a hat, a pleated shirtwaist and modest skirt, but she had that old intense expression on her face, prepared for a fight.

As they reached The Strand, a wide street just north of the river, Edgar spotted the Gaiety Theatre to his right, its billboards announcing *The Circus Girl*, one of its popular musical comedies. But just ahead on Wellington Street was *the* theater. And the tale to be told inside its walls this week was vaguely familiar to Edgar. "FAUST!" read the marquee. "**Returning after 7 Years!**" He stared at it. Memories of the sounds within the theater's auditorium came back to him, and so did his father's strange state that night, the night before he died. A chill ran down Edgar's spine.

A moment later, they came to the intersection of Wellington Street and Exeter. Down a short block to their left, two men hurried from the side door of the Lyceum. One was tall and burly with well-groomed red hair and beard, dressed in a nondescript Irish tweed suit and brown tie, a brown felt Homburg hat on his head, his hands in his waistcoat as he anxiously followed a surly fellow in front of him. That man was almost as tall but nearly skeletal, his suit black and immaculate, enclosed in a billowing cape, his top hat towering on his fine head, his black and gray-streaked hair hanging down past his collar. The burly man scurried past and seized the door of a hansom cab, opening it and almost bowing to the other man as he did.

"Henry Irving!" said Edgar, and he and Tiger froze.

They were only a few carriage lengths away, the cab pointed straight at them. Irving settled into it looking severe, his face cold and white, his eyes dead like a killer's. For a fleeting second, it occurred to Edgar that the great Irving's features bore a distant resemblance to the hooded driver's at the College on the Moors.

The other man closed the hansom door and waved as the driver snapped his whip and the horse moved forward, hooves clapping on the cobblestones. Irving didn't deign to turn back to his helper but stared at the two young people as the cab passed them. The expression in his black eyes seemed to penetrate Edgar's soul and make it shiver. The devil was staring at him.

When the great man was gone, they regarded the one left behind. The big fellow, too, was watching them, as if he were guarding Irving from all who dared to observe him.

"Come, Edgar, we must be on our way."

They came to Drury Lane. It was a curious street. Narrow and almost closed off from the sky with tall, ancient buildings three to five stories high, it wound its way from its start just north of The Strand to fashionable Oxford Street at its top. In between were many worlds: theaters and shops and offices as well as slums. When you stood at its bottom, it seemed that you could move about in time: back to the bowed shop windows of Dickens, remain in the modern times of steam, or move ahead to the approaching machine world.

They dodged people on the footpaths, noting the plates on the buildings in search of the Crypto-Anthropology Society. They passed J. Sainsbury's grocery shop, the back of the huge Drury Lane theater and several boarded-up buildings. Children ran by, a maid in her uniform, a swell in a top hat whistling and a man with a wide basket of muffins balanced on his head, ringing a bell and crying out his wares. The street smelled both enticing and repulsive.

"Where is it?" said Edgar, frustrated. Why had Lear sent him here? Maybe it was all a ruse. This wasn't the safest street. Were they about to be set upon?

But their destination appeared no more than a minute later, a tall old building of an ochre color, made of brick and wood and likely here when knights and their ladies walked up these footpaths. It seemed to loom out over the street, no lights emanating from the low square windows and the upper ones shuttered. The society's title, so long that it barely fit its plaque, sat below three plates referring to other businesses. There were bells beside each name and Tiger rang the appropriate one. Edgar could have sworn that her hand was shaking just a little.

Edgar's imagination began working on him. Lear, he thought, had set this up. What if they went inside and never came out? He readied himself. He wondered how quick and agile Tiger would be in her women's clothes. Anyone encountering her now wouldn't believe she could do what he knew she could. Perhaps that was an advantage.

The inner door opened. They saw a figure through the smoky glass. Then the outer door moved, but didn't swing wide. Both Tiger and Edgar stepped back.

"Yes?"

Before them, or below them, stood a very short man with an enormous head. It seemed to be nearly the size of his entire torso. The door opened a little wider. He was dressed in black billowing pants and a frilly white shirt undone nearly halfway down his chest. He appeared to be ancient, the folds in the skin on his face like those of a hound dog, his bottom lip hanging down too. He was perspiring, his spectacles up on his forehead. The two young people were speechless.

"Might I, William Shakespeare, chairman of the Crypto-Anthropology Society of the Queen's Empire, be of use on this prepossessing day, filled as it is with azure skies?" He glanced up toward the heavens which were, actually, growing cloudy.

"I beg your pardon?" asked Edgar Brim. Was this a joke Professor Lear was playing on him? Edgar wondered to himself. Was Lear capable of humor?

"In short, what do you want?"

"To . . . to meet the Society?"

"The Society of which you speak is not available to any Tom, Dick or Harriet. It is peopled by gentlemen of the highest standing, and their time is of great value, that is to say, one must have an appointment to meet with them and that appointment must portend of singular moment and significance. Do you understand me?"

"No," said Tiger.

"In short, get out of here."

"But I have come a long way," said Edgar.

The man chuckled. "I thought as much. This is London, my boy, the greatest city upon the earth, this orb, this stately sphere, and our Society has society of this noble metropolis's highest standing. I do not care that you have come from—"

"He experiences the hag phenomenon," said Tiger.

Shakespeare stopped speaking and gaped. He pulled his spectacles down over his eyes and stared up at Edgar. "This specimen here?" He looked as if he wanted to lie Edgar down upon an operating table and start carving him with a scalpel.

"Yes, sir," said Edgar, making sure his voice didn't crack.

"Well, well, well, well, well, well, well, well, well, well, well, well," said the little man.

"I—"

"You must come in!" He opened the door fully, stepped aside, and motioned with an elegant sweep of his hand for his guests to enter and start down the stairs. Once Edgar had passed and taken the lead, Tiger made sure that she brought up the rear, so they were on either side of the strange man as they descended.

The room below was extraordinary. It was round with a very high ceiling. Nearly every inch of its curving wall, from top to bottom, was crammed with books. Edgar scanned them. It seemed like every last one was a work of fiction. Peeking out between the volumes were more animal heads than one might see in a row of cages at the London Zoo. All sorts of exotic creatures gazed vacantly down upon them—lions, tigers, wildebeests, gazelles and even an elephant. And in among the beasts, as if one of them, hung a mammoth portrait of Her Majesty, Queen Victoria, painted at least fifty years earlier. A half dozen leather chairs sat around a wooden table in the center of the room. Each had a stack of papers and books in front of it. There were lit cigars at the settings and smoke filled the space like one of the city's fogs. But no one was present except this man who called himself Shakespeare.

"They are conducting discussions of utmost secrecy and importance," he said in a near whisper.

"Who are?" asked Tiger.

But the little man hushed her with a wave of his hand. "GENTLEMEN!" he shrieked and then paused. "Thank you, kind sirs." He seemed to be internally bubbling with excitement. "I give you . . ." he said to the empty room, then apparently realized that he had not asked his visitors their names. He turned to them. "Uh, whom am I giving to my esteemed associates?"

"My name is Edgar Brim."

"And I am Miss Tiger Tilley."

"Tiger?" asked Shakespeare. "Why, I'll be a camelopard; I'll eat my head if I've ever heard of such a name for a woman." He rolled his R's liberally and caressed each word as if it were a pearl of enormous wisdom cast out toward the swine of the world. He regarded an empty chair. "What is that you say, Mr. Sprinkle? That I may have to consume it, since that is what she said? And, though large, it would be a rather light meal?" He was not pleased. "Thou art a boil, a plague sore!" he shouted.

But then he turned back to Tiger and Edgar and smiled. "And I give you, my distinguished visitors, three gentlemen of unsurpassed renown in the city of London, indeed in the entire Empire, perhaps the world: Messrs. Sprinkle, Winker and Tightman." He indicated three empty chairs.

"Though Mr. Sprinkle Esquire's standing is not of an elevation more mountainous than his colleagues," continued the little fellow, "I shall introduce him first." He paused. "Now, don't grumble, you two. You rampallian! You fustilarian! I will get to you!" He cleared his throat. "Sprinkle is a magnate in the world of hat feathers and an author of extreme distinction. You may sit down, sir." Shakespeare turned to the next chair. "Mr. Winker Esquire, whom you see here, is not to be sneezed at either. He has made an enviable fortune in the world of nose bags. His family, indeed, are the nose bag kings. He is also a sportsman of some standing, having shot and killed great piles of animals." Then Shakespeare turned to another chair. "And, of course, here is the inimitable Mr. Tightman Esquire, a giant in the toilet tissue world and a man now working upon the ultimate refutation of the works of Charles Darwin, following close upon his study of the history of the world in ninety-seven volumes." He uttered a sigh. "And I, kind sir and lady, am the gentle William Shakespeare, as aforementioned, retired now from the beastly world of daily concerns, a direct descendant of, well, need I say his name?"

"Shakespeare has no direct descendants," whispered Tiger.

"Uh, no, sir," said Edgar. He glanced around the table. "It is a pleasure to meet every one of you." He wondered what in the world Lear was up to.

"Mine too," added Tiger.

"Excuse me, guests, but my colleagues are all speaking at once. SILENCE, you long-tongued babbling gossips!" he shrieked and then waited for a good ten seconds. "Now, kind sirs," he said to the table again, "please listen carefully to what I have to say." His excitement was coming to the surface. "This gentleman here, this Sir Edgar Broom—"

"Brim."

"Oh yes, Sir Edgar Brim." He turned to the boy. "Do I have that right now?"

"Yes, sir, except I have not yet been knighted."

"This Brim chap has experienced the HAG PHENOMENON!!!" Shakespeare shouted the last words across the room as if he had been trying to hold them back since he entered. His face had gone beet red. He then waited a few moments as if gauging his audience's reaction. He seemed to receive the response he wanted, for he began to beam. "Well, sirs, do not just sit there, get him THE drink! Or, a drink, I should say." He stood there for a while, tapping his foot impatiently. "The potion? Now, why would you call it that, Mr. Sprinkle, just fetch him a beverage, sir. Just a drink, Mr. Winker, if you please? A mere liquid refreshment, Mr. Tightman?" He paused again, "Well, RETRIEVE IT! You lumps of foul deformity! Must I do it myself?"

Shakespeare turned and stalked toward one of the dark little hallways that led off from the room. But almost immediately he was retreating, backing up.

"I had forgotten you were here," he said, sounding a little frightened.

The person who had unnerved him emerged out of the darkness of the room. He was large and wide shouldered and his head almost touched the low ceiling. His unkempt longish hair and beard were black with gray streaks, his head like a dark lion's. He had just one arm.

13

Lear's Secret

"I have been expecting both of you," said Professor Lear.

"You . . . you have?" Edgar stepped back. Tiger's fists were balled, legs planted wide.

"Indeed."

Edgar clenched his fists too. "Why did you draw me here?" he demanded. He looked around and wondered if there were other people hiding in the passageways that ran from this room.

"I wanted you to meet Mr. Shakespeare. I wanted you to hear the insane things that occupy his mind. I have known him a long while. He wasn't always like this, you know. He was very learned and quite wealthy, as he still is, though now you can't tell." Lear took a step toward them. "And I needed a place to speak with you. It couldn't be at the Moors."

"Why not?" asked Tiger, moving slightly in front of her friend, sticking out her chin.

"Shakespeare!" exclaimed Lear.

"Yes, professor, sir?" He lifted his big head.

"His real name is Nathaniel Nitwick," whispered Lear. Then he raised his voice again. "I do not think it advisable to give these people your potion."

"Potion, sir? I am not sure I follow you. What would that be?"

"Perhaps the one that puts them to sleep so that you may study them and see if the hag appears in the flesh?"

"Oh, I doubt we would ever do such a thing."

"So do I. Not while I am on the premises anyway. I can assure you that the hag indeed visits this boy. Sit down and tell our guests what it is you do."

"Tell them, Lear? You must be joking!"

"As you know, I am not given to humor, my good man. I have something in mind. In order to execute it, you must tell them what it is this society does."

The little man hesitated. "But it is the most secret and sensitive of matters. It is of the utmost importance and cannot be—"

"Tell them or I shall explain everything myself and then resign my position." He surveyed the empty chairs. "And advise the others to do the same."

"Very well," said Shakespeare, not pleased, "if you insist." He turned and spoke under his breath, "You poisonous hunch-backed toad." Then he pivoted toward his two visitors. "Might you sit down, youths?" He glanced around the table. "You may take your seats as well, gentlemen."

Edgar and Tiger sat, careful not to take the invisible men's chairs.

"We, this most distinguished organization," said Shakespeare, "believe—" He turned to Lear. "Must I really tell—"

"Continue!" bellowed the professor.

"Beetle-headed flap-ear'd knave," said Shakespeare into his collar. Then he lifted his head again. "We investigate, that is to say, we analyze, theorize and speculate into the possibility that . . . the chance that there may be . . . the—"

"Tell them."

"In short, there are monsters." He shut his mouth like a peeved little boy.

"What did you say?" asked Edgar.

Lear turned to him. "These gentlemen gathered here fund research into the possibility that there are aberrations on this earth some might call monsters or demons, some of which have been described in famous stories. There will be a meeting tomorrow at noon to which you are both invited."

"Oh no," said Shakespeare, "they are not." He checked the table. "The others seem to agree, so you are overruled, Lear."

"And I overrule them."

"You do?" He seemed wary of the professor and Edgar wondered why. But Shakespeare found his voice again. "You neglected to mention that the center of our work is the presentation of learned papers upon the aforementioned subject. For our discussion upon the morrow, I shall be holding forth on the subject of Mary Shelley's Frankenstein creature and the night both it and the Vampyre were unleashed."

"Yes," said Lear, sighing, "you will, won't you."

"Or would you prefer that I speak about the monster from the epic *Beowulf*? What do you think of that, of the accursed Grendel? Should I speak of who truly killed him?"

For a moment, Edgar thought Lear might strike the little man.

"I am sorry," whispered Shakespeare.

Moments later the professor steered Tiger and Edgar out of the society's quarters and onto Drury Lane.

"He is beyond mad," said Tiger.

"But perhaps on to something," replied Lear.

"Surely you don't believe what he believes."

Edgar again remembered those words: *Lear knew.*

"I do not think, generally speaking," said the old man, "that demons written into frightening stories are real. That strikes me as nonsense."

"So why did you bring us here?"

"Because there may be some sort of truth to it."

He then offered Edgar a room at his hotel, the Langham, off Oxford Street, well known for its wealthy patrons. Lear's only income, as far as Edgar knew, came from teaching, and he doubted the professors of the College on the Moors were growing rich from their occupations. Edgar tried not to look suspicious.

Lear flagged down a cab for Tiger, but she was reluctant to get in. "He may want to be rid of me," she said quietly to Edgar as he stepped toward the carriage with her. "Are you sure you want to go with him?" She motioned back at Lear with a slight turn of her head. "He hasn't even mentioned Lancelot's death. We don't know what he's up to." She leaned closer. "I could come with you."

"I'll be careful."

Edgar stepped back and said good-bye to her until the morning, then walked up Drury Lane with Lear toward their destination. He kept some distance between them.

"Sir, can you afford a stay at the Langham? And a room for me, as well?"

"No, my boy, I cannot, but the society can. Shakespeare puts me up there when I come to London. There was a day when I could have sprung for lodgings at such a place. But I chose the investigation of literature for my profession and gave up the conduct of our family's business to my brother. You can see where it has gotten me."

Edgar thought he glanced at his right shoulder where his jacket sleeve hung empty.

They reached wider Oxford Street and turned west. The crowds were much thicker here.

"There will be others there tomorrow," said Lear, eventually.

"Real ones?"

The professor smiled. "Yes, real people."

"Tomorrow is Sunday, sir. The society meets on the Sabbath?"

"Shakespeare feels it is a sacred task."

Edgar chuckled.

"This, Master Brim, is far from a laughing matter."

The Langham was a magnificent stone building of a beautiful light-yellow color and seven stories high, a sort of castle north of Oxford Street on Regent Street. Edgar was in awe of the regal lobby, the big chandeliers and the polished staircase.

"I have another appointment, my boy," said Lear as they entered. "Just give them your name at the front desk." But Edgar stopped him before he could leave.

"Sir, do you really believe there are such things as these aberrations you speak of, even just a few?"

"I cannot say for certain, but I have some reason to believe it. And as you know, something recently happened at the college that disturbs me. I knew when it occurred that you *had* to come here, and not just to see your dear friend. And I knew I had to follow you and speak with you frankly."

"Master Newman," said Edgar. His heart began to pound. They were finally getting to it. "What killed him, sir?"

"I wish I knew. Perhaps it was really just his nerves."

But the boy could tell from the old man's tone that he didn't think that was so. "Can there *actually* be monsters among us?"

"This matters a great deal to you, doesn't it, Brim? Why?" The big man with the dark brows stood close.

"Because I was afraid. Because I *am* afraid."

"Afraid of what? Tell me."

"I see the hag."

"But there is more, is there not?" Lear put his hand on Edgar's shoulder and leaned toward him. Edgar couldn't look at him.

"I have seen monsters in my dreams since I was an infant. They are terribly vivid. I . . . I used to be so afraid that I thought I would be better off dead. It affects my whole life. My heart used to pound for no reason." Edgar can feel Lear's grip on his shoulder intensifying. "I think I gained this fear from my father. He kept a private journal and in it he wondered about the very things that frightened me—about demons in stories . . . and if they might be real. He wouldn't let me see it when I was a child, but I read it recently." He swallowed. "There was one passage where he said how important it was to *not* be afraid. He wanted me to know that. He said it like it was the key to life."

"He was a wise man."

"Your name was in that journal."

"That isn't a good thing."

"Why?"

"I . . . I will tell you before long."

"Sir," said Edgar, summoning all his courage. He didn't know why he asked this question at this moment, but something compelled him. "How did you lose your arm?"

Lear paused for a moment.

"I lost it, my young friend, to Grendel."

Edgar stood stock still in the lobby of the Langham Hotel staring at the professor. His father had read the famous epic *Beowulf* aloud in that room with the heat pipe that ran downward, sending the chilling story to his ears when he was a child. Its huge monster Grendel attacked in the dark, ripping human beings apart, eating them.

"You should sit down, my boy. It is time I told you this part."

They found two seats in an alcove in the lobby, out of the way. Lear dropped into his with a sigh and began.

"I loved literature as a boy and chose its study. One must do what one loves. Great stories not only entertained me but I felt they dared to tell great truths. That thrilled me. What is of more value than truth? I excelled at university and found a position teaching English literature at an esteemed school in Denmark, which was where I met my lovely wife, Gretchen." He paused for a moment and gathered himself. "As a student, and later as a teacher, I was particularly interested in how fiction and fact related. I was intrigued by where and how great authors found their characters. Sometimes, I even wondered if the well-drawn ones were, in some way, real." He drummed his fingers on his leg. "Then it began." He didn't say anything for a long while.

"It?" asked Edgar.

"There were reports in the papers from time to time about children disappearing in the vast forests in Sweden to the north. They speculated that this was due to the little ones getting lost or being attacked by wild animals, but there were whispers spread about by peasants in the area that the children were being eaten by a monster. Some even said it was the great Scandinavian demon from literature, the creature Grendel. It was an outrageous idea and I scoffed at it at first. But I investigated the disappearances and was surprised to discover that as far into history as I could find, journals and newspapers had been reporting similar incidences. I had taught the epic *Beowulf* and had always been struck by the way it, in particular, blended fact and fiction. The hall where King Hrothgar of the Danes was attacked by Grendel was real and in a real place. I had visited the location near Lejre. Some academics believe that Beowulf was based on a real person, a hero of the Geat people in Sweden, who may have indeed come to Denmark to help the king destroy a creature or whatever it was that threatened him and his people. Whether there ever was a Grendel, of course, is unknown and is certainly a strange idea to contemplate as fact. In the great story, Beowulf kills Grendel and then Grendel's mother and severs both of their heads to make sure they cannot return from the dead." Lear paused. "Beowulf himself is later killed by a dragon." He sighed. "Why are there so many dragons in stories, my boy? Did we simply make them up or was there once something like them?"

Edgar thought of the many dragon adventures he had read. He thought of dinosaurs, those great lizards science was uncovering. Sometimes it almost made him laugh to think that these gigantic creatures were once real.

"I traveled north to Sweden," continued Lear, "taking my wife." For a moment, he seemed about to dissolve into tears. Edgar felt uncomfortable. But the old man went on. "I went to the forests and began talking to the peasants. I went year after year. A child had been born to us during my first semester at the college in Copenhagen—Abraham was perhaps seven the year it happened. I—" He seemed to not want to go on.

"Sir?"

"Give me a moment." Lear sighed again and stiffened his shoulders. "I had begun to be intrigued, though certainly not convinced, by this far-fetched idea that Grendel might be alive in the Swedish forests. It was like the Loch Ness monster in Scotland or the Sasquatch in Canada, but it was better: this was from literature! A colleague had told me with a laugh that there was a scholar in London who actually believed this sort of thing. I contacted him. A man named Nathaniel Nitwick."

"William Shakespeare?"

"The same. I went to see him. In those days, he was simply an eccentric man with strange ideas. He was teaching at the university in London though he was wealthy and didn't need to work. He had gathered a group around him who liked to speculate about life on other planets, ghosts and monsters, and loved the idea that some of the famous demons in literature might have anchors in reality. They jokingly called their group the Crypto-Anthropology Society of the Queen's Empire and met in a room—the same room as today—in Drury Lane. When I spoke to him about the Grendel stories, he was fascinated. In fact, it was a bit disturbing, since as we talked he grew very excited, his big face became quite red, and the veins stood out on his forehead. In his eyes, I could see the madness that later consumed him. He offered me a good deal of money to further my research, and I wasn't wealthy, so I took it. But he also warned me that he had some evidence, however scanty, that there were people who actually had these ideas at various times in history, and that a creature or two had been pursued. But those hunters, as he called them, had not lived long. Something had either killed them or they had died prematurely. 'What if there was more than one aberration in the world and they knew of each other?' he would say. 'What if they killed anyone who got close to their secret?' I found that amusing. I also felt guilty about taking his money because I knew these were just peasants' tales, but I thought I might find some way to connect their legends to *Beowulf*. Perhaps there was some way in which fact met fiction and I could write a groundbreaking paper? I believe it was my twelfth research trip when—" He stopped talking again, gasped, and said, "Gretchen," under his breath. He dropped his face into his hand. Edgar looked away. But the old man gathered himself in a moment, muttering something about being brave, especially now, and went on.

"We camped that night, far into the forests. Gretchen always woke first, that was her way." He smiled. "We had left our boy in Copenhagen, safe with friends, so she felt free. She was excited about what we were doing. She was like that—intrigued by my work. I loved her dearly for it. So, that morning, she wandered off into the forest alone. And she never came back." Lear's eyes were glistening. "I searched for months. But she had vanished just like the children. I found evidence that she had been killed: dried blood on leaves, bits of her clothing. Something horrific had attacked her. But there had been no bears or wolves spotted in that area for more than a decade and none appeared there in the month or so that followed. I grew obsessed by the idea that something else had killed her, perhaps something supernatural."

"Grendel."

"I couldn't bring myself to believe that, but I was big and strong and angry, and I took to the woods and hunted for the thing that had killed her, whatever it was. I spread my search throughout the forests and interviewed every peasant I could find. Then, I found footprints."

"But there must have been many—"

"Huge ones—and I found a cave where something like an enormous bear was living. I shouted into the forests that I would find it and kill it. Before long it seemed that this creature, this beast, whatever it was, was on the run. I tracked it west through Norway and all the way to the North Sea. It seemed to vanish there, leading me to believe that it had taken to the freezing waters, either swimming or stealing away by boat. I stood on the shoreline and imagined what was on the other side of the sea."

A sinking feeling came over Edgar. "Scotland," he said.

"Indeed! And where would it go in Scotland if it felt it had to get away from me and stay hidden from the world? To the Highlands, the moors, the most godforsaken parts! I tracked it north and west in Scotland from Cruden Bay way up into the moors. It settled there. And so did I, to be near it, hunt it and destroy it!"

At the College on the Moors, thought Edgar.

"I started teaching in the Highlands in 1858 when Abraham was nine. I left him in London with my brother's family. And that is where he grew up. I went down to see him often, poor boy." Lear was sad about this too and Edgar wondered why. He imagined that Lear still saw his son. It was something deeper.

"I would go out onto the land at night and search for this thing. I still don't know what it was. But I know that I killed it."

"Y-you did?"

"I am six feet two inches tall and in those days I weighed over 15 stone and most of it was muscle. I was prepared to die to kill the thing that took my wife. Losing the person you love most in the world makes you capable of anything, my boy. It took me more than a year to find it. It was staying away from people but inhabiting the land near the college so it could steal the things it needed to survive—food, clean water, even clothing. I wondered, at times, if it was somehow living somewhere in the college, but clearly it was out on the wasteland, eating the wildcats and hares and moles, raw or cooked over fire. Each time I would locate a blaze, it slipped away. God, I remember the night I came upon it!" He paused again and looked across the lobby of the Langham Hotel. People were passing back and forth, eyes and minds intent on their daily lives. "I had gone out to an area where I thought it might be and simply lay down on the moors, staring up at the black sky. I heard it approach. I could hear it grunting as it moved. I stood up.

"But I quaked with fear when I saw it. It was on two feet, of human shape, but huge and hideous in appearance. It stood a full foot taller than me. Naked but for a loin cloth, its skin like an alligator's, its arms huge and hanging low like an ape's, its giant face so repulsive it was hard to look upon. This was some sort of aberration, some mistake of nature, a living monster! It still seemed incredible that it could be the creature from the book, but in the epic, it hated loud sounds, so I began to shriek, perhaps as a strategy or in fear or desperation, I don't know. I guessed that it preferred to strike by surprise and would have escaped if I had simply attacked it or even if I'd cowered or tried to get away. But enraged by this noise, it attacked me, just as I had hoped."

Edgar could see the scene on the moors long ago! He could feel the hag entering the room.

"It came at me with superhuman speed and was on me in a flash. It seized me and, in anger, chose to torture me before it killed: it sank its massive canine teeth into my right arm at the shoulder and ripped it from its socket. The bone crunched and the ligaments tore away. The blood flew. I shrieked even louder. And yet, in the midst of this horror, it seemed my plan might be working: Grendel was incensed and irrational. It pulled back from me, knocking me to the ground, and began to eat my arm."

Edgar is in agony as he listens. His right arm aches.

"I gaped up at it in terror, the pain almost rendering me unconscious. But I had spent years readying for this moment. Whatever this creature was, I knew that only a warrior of as stout a heart as Beowulf could defeat it. I had to be that way that night. Grendel loomed above me, devouring my limb and yet a perfect target. Still crying out in agony, I pulled my pistol from my cloak. My left hand would have to do the work. I started shrieking louder. It dropped my limb for an instant and put its hands over its ears. It was directly above me, just a few feet away, its wide chest open: an easy target. I extended the gun toward the monster, still crying out. Then I stopped shrieking. It took its hands from its ears and bent over, groggy from the effects of the noise, its chest actually pressed up against the gun. I knew that in the epic Grendel's skin was as strong as armor and bold warriors had been unable to penetrate it with swords, and others in ensuing centuries who may have glimpsed it would have merely shot at such a beast from a distance. But now, with this modern-day gun pressed directly to the creature's chest, the barrel within an inch of its huge heart, I believed I could kill it. I fired. Not once, not twice, not three times, but six, unloading every one of the bullets in the newly invented six-shooter I had purchased from America with the society's funds, emptying the chamber directly into the fiend's vital organ. It staggered and then fell like a giant, thundering down onto the earth. It seemed as if the landscape shook. I took my big knife and severed its head and left it for the ravens out on the moors."

Edgar can feel the hag receding from the room, but can sense her, still standing near the lobby door, watching.

"I reeled back to the college, pressing my coat to my gaping wound, nearly bleeding to death. The cause of my injury, I told Headmaster Emeritus, and Spartan Griswold and Numb, was a wolf. They had never heard of wolves being on that part of the moors, but they accepted it, assuming it was a freak encounter. What else could they do?

"But I feared the consequences of what I had done. I couldn't stop thinking of what William Shakespeare had said about "hunters" being killed by other monsters. I left the college for a year to recover and live with Abraham here in London. But I couldn't stop wondering if there were other aberrations out there, maybe worse than Grendel? It seemed a mad idea, as mad as believing the creature that I had killed was a demon from a story. But what if something even more terrifying and powerful knew what I had done? Would it come after me? All my anger drained from me and I lived in fear from that day until now."

"But nothing has pursued you, sir."

"Hasn't it?" He got up. "I must go. We will speak more of these things tomorrow."

14

You Have No Choice

Tiger joined Edgar at the society's meeting the next day. There was a surprise waiting for them when they gathered in the big room. In fact, there were two. One was beautiful to Edgar and he took note; the other was handsome to Tiger but she tried not to notice.

Lucy and Jonathan Lear were sitting near their grandfather at one end of the big wooden table, with Tiger and Edgar at the other, and William Shakespeare presiding in the middle, with three empty chairs apparently containing the other curious gentlemen of the society facing him. Lucy had a china-white face and pale blue eyes, hair a unique copper color and wavy and worn a little longer than fashionable. She seemed anxious. Jonathan, fit and bronzed by the sun, acted as though this meeting was nothing but a lark. Everyone was introduced, Lucy quickly glancing down from Edgar's flame-colored hair to the table as she nodded to him, and Jonathan smiling broadly as he stood and shook Tiger's strong slim hand.

Edgar peeked across at Shakespeare while everyone was exchanging greetings. The little man was staring at him with a dark face, but then quickly glanced away and the mad expression came over him again.

He started the meeting off by singing "God Save the Queen" . . . solo. Everyone present used all the willpower they had not to stick their fingers in their ears. Then he called the meeting to order. He held his right arm in the air above his shoulders, palm out in an oath, nodding to the others (including the men in the empty chairs) to do the same. He barked out the goals of the society and swore to "initiate investigation of these demons, and ultimately, their elimination, for the betterment of man." Then he threw back his head and uttered a hideous cry, the trademark monster call of the society. None of the others did the same, though one imagined that in Shakespeare's mind, his good friends were complying. Edgar and Lucy each noticed the other stifling a laugh.

Shakespeare then held forth, orating for close to three hours.

". . . These aberrations are mistakes made by God or nature, of crypto-human origin, likely given birth from the loins of human beings. They are part of our real world, but nearly immortal, living for centuries unless someone finds a way to destroy them. Great adventurers guided by scientists such as ourselves . . ."

Jonathan yawned loudly.

". . . may have killed a number of these creatures, their activities kept from the world. It would not be good for the average person to know such things." The little man looked condescendingly at the four young people, one after the other. "We tip our hats to these brave men. None have lived long afterward! Their courage is unparalleled."

"And well beyond your own, Shakes," murmured Jonathan.

Shakespeare stopped for a moment, glared around the table, cleared his throat and went on, entering upon (what he felt was) the meat of his subject for the day: Mary Shelley's character, the Frankenstein monster, and how she created him. He spoke at length of a night long ago in Switzerland.

"A mixture of fact and fiction," mused Lear under his breath to Edgar.

Shakespeare then discussed interviewing Robert Louis Stevenson about Mr. Hyde, then amended that to say he had known someone who had interviewed Stevenson on the subject, then amended that to say that he knew someone who knew someone who had read said interview. He briefly referred to Grendel and paused. But the professor, stationed at the far end of the table, was by that time snoring loudly.

After saying on at least five occasions, "And so, in conclusion," Shakespeare finally came to an end. "If there are aberrations left, they are the worst, for they must be almost unkillable, the ones from whom to stay away. But they must be destroyed!"

The little man stopped suddenly. He was sweating profusely.

"I must ask the chairman for permission to speak," said Lear, rousing.

"I shall consult the others," replied Shakespeare. He nodded at each of the three empty chairs and turned back to the professor. "Proceed." He sat down.

Lear looked like he wanted to beat him with a stick, but he went on. "I should like funding for the purchase of numerous weapons."

"Weapons?" asked Shakespeare, starting onto his feet again.

"We shall need, first and foremost, a powerful pistol, a hand-gun that can be concealed on someone's person, the most deadly rifle we can locate and perhaps something with a much larger bullet. This is why I am in London at this time."

"Really?" asked Shakespeare. "You are going to strike again after all these years? There shall be action? We shall attend! Sprinkle, you bolting hutch of beastliness, you must wear your hunting outfit and bear your musket!"

"No need, gentleman—though I'm sure your brave actions would be invaluable—just funds for guns, some useful clothing and train fare for a number of people are required."

"A number?"

"I do not know how many yet. I may need a few other things as well."

"What exactly are you after?" cried Shakespeare. "Tell us!" He sounded like a child. Edgar's eyes were widening too.

"It is a matter, as you often say, sir, of utmost importance and secrecy. There shall be a full report."

"A report!" cried the little man. "Why, yes, a report!"

A short while later, Lear, his grandchildren, and Tiger and Edgar were on Drury Lane. Edgar was shaking a little and trying to hide it. *Weapons and monsters!* He could see the excitement on the others' faces. Lucy's freckled skin now had a good deal of color in it, going well, he thought, with her copper hair. Both young Lears were restless, as if anxious to tell Edgar and Tiger something. Tilley was flushed too, apparently thrilled by what she had just heard. Only the professor appeared composed.

"I should like you all to come with me to the Langham for a moment. Perhaps we shall have some tea?" said Lear.

Up Drury Lane they went, Lear in the lead followed by Edgar and Lucy side by side and then Jonathan and Tiger.

"Would you take my arm, Miss Tilley?" asked Jon after a while. Edgar wondered if Tiger might slap him, and the athletic, dark-blond young man seemed like the sort who might actually like that, take it as a challenge or an opening salvo.

"That isn't necessary," said Tiger. "I believe I can keep myself upright on my own."

Edgar considered offering his own arm to Lucy. Not everyone might think her attractive, but she exuded something that was perfect to him. He couldn't put his finger on it. Tiger had a bold gait, but this slender girl walked in sways beside him, eyes sparkling with some idea. Then she stumbled. As she did, she reached out for him and slipped her arm into his, apologizing, but keeping it there.

"May I speak frankly, Master Brim?"

"Of course, Miss Lear."

She looked up at him as if she had known him forever. "My grandfather has something he must accomplish before he dies. It is a matter of life and death." Her intensity took him aback; her thin lips were held in a straight line. "You know what it is."

"I'm not sure I exactly—"

"I think that is why you are here with us. I will help him with my very life, and so will my brother. We have ample reason."

She turned her face forward and said nothing for a while. After another block or two, she gathered herself and spoke of other things. She asked him about school, about his past. He was alarmed at how much he told her. He even spoke a little of his fears, and this to a person who was a stranger but a few hours ago. It was as if she had some sort of power to draw things out of others, or at least, from him.

Time seemed to fly. Behind him, Jonathan appeared powerless not to unload his whole life to Tiger too, though she said almost nothing. Edgar heard him mention that he was about to enter a respected military school, was already training for it, and that he and Lucy lived alone. Edgar wondered where their parents were.

At the hotel, Lear asked for tea to be sent up to his suite and gathered them around at a table. He stood with his hands on the back of a chair, so no one else sat either.

"I have something of importance to ask of you."

He sounded solemn. Edgar waited for one of the others to respond. But the professor was gazing directly at him.

"Yes, sir?"

"I want you to be my ally on a sacred mission."

It had sounded almost thrilling when Lucy had suggested something similar, but now, in the professor's deep voice, it was ominous.

"I beg your pardon, sir?"

"I want you to return with me and my grandchildren to the College on the Moors tomorrow, leaving in the early hours of morning."

"That is a slight change of plans, but yes, sir, of course, I need to go back anyway and—"

"Not just to finish the last week of school, not just for your graduation."

"Sir?"

"That child whom you befriended. I believe he was murdered."

Edgar swallowed. "Who murdered him?" He tried not to imagine a creature from his nightmares coming to life.

"I do not know for certain."

"Then how can you—?"

"A force that may have murdered many times before."

Edgar wanted to leave. He turned to Tiger, but she was fascinated. Lucy was still eyeing him, hope in her face. Jonathan sat back, trying to seem unimpressed.

"Master Brim, there is something on the moors right now, an aberration, whom I would like you to help us pursue and kill." Edgar felt dizzy. He pulled a chair back from the table and sat down. The others gathered around him, Tiger included. It almost seemed as if she were in league with them, though she was only just learning about all of this too.

"Yes," said Jonathan, "a monster." He walked away and took a position at a window, as if he were concerned that they had been followed. "A lovely fellow."

"Will you help us?" asked Lucy.

"Why?" Edgar asked. "Why do you need me?"

"You have no choice, sunshine," said Jonathan.

"What does he mean?" asked Edgar, still addressing Lucy.

"Don't worry about that," she said, shooting her brother a cross look.

"Yet," snapped Jonathan.

Lucy knelt in front of Edgar and took his hand. Her red dress was spread out around her on the floor. She stared directly into his eyes.

"Look, Edgar," she began, "we know grandfather encountered some sort of aberration on the moors long ago. If one existed, is it not possible that there is another, or even more? What if they *do* know of each other's existence, watch out for each other?"

"You are talking like Shakespeare. This is madness."

"What if that is why this thing is on the moors, right now?"

"This thing? Listen to yourself. Lancelot was ill. He was frail." Edgar squirmed in his chair but didn't pull back from Lucy's hand. Her grip was strong. "This so-called Grendel could have been just some strange ape lost in the wrong part of the world."

"But haven't you always feared such things were true?" said Lear. "What did your father believe?"

"That was just a theory." Edgar wondered if they would seize him if he bolted for the door. He looked at Lear. "How did you know my father? Where did you meet him?" But the professor didn't respond. Edgar turned to Lucy. "Why me?" he asked again.

But she still won't answer his question. "What if they kill anyone who destroys a fellow demon and always have, with one hundred percent efficiency? And that's why they are unknown? Maybe it's true that no one who has killed an aberration has ever lived to kill another?" She paused. "Except my grandfather."

"Yep," said Jonathan, "the old codger is still on the loose!"

"Well, that's proof, isn't it?" said Edgar. "If it were real, sir, you would be long dead."

Lear shook his head. "After I went to London that year to recover from my wound, something else happened on the moors." He held up his hand as if to wave off any questions. "It made me think that another creature was near the college. I was terrified. I wondered if it would be up there when I went back, waiting for the right moment to pounce. I had to protect myself. So after I returned, I stayed off the moors and made sure I was never alone. But I also prayed out loud every night, assuring God or nature that I was done with monsters, real or imagined. I told the air that I would not pursue them and I even apologized to the Grendel creature. I felt a fool, but I hoped something would hear me, sense me. I also let it be known that I had written a paper with a groundbreaking theory, and if I were to die in a mysterious way, that paper would be published, but were I to die in old age of natural causes, it would be burned. If this demon was somehow aware, somehow watching through the windows, listening through the walls, following my conduct, somehow understanding out there on the moors, we would be in a stalemate: kill me and the existence of Grendel and another would be exposed; leave me and the secret was safe. . . . And I have lived!"

"But—"

"But I have been watched for nearly forty years. I haven't seen anything, but I have felt it." His head fell. "And my plan has had fatal flaws."

Jonathan left the window, stomped across the room and slammed the door on his way out. They heard his footsteps marching up and down the hallway.

Edgar saw pain in Lucy's eyes. He sensed she was about to cry and squeezed her hand tightly. She seemed surprised.

"My mother died in childbirth," she murmured.

"Just like mine," he said, not letting go.

"I know."

How did she know that? he wondered.

"I don't have a father anymore either." She wiped her tears. "He died last year."

"I killed him," said Lear.

"No, grandfather, don't!" She turned back to Edgar. "They said it was his heart, but there is no history of such problems in our family." Edgar thought of his own father's death, but dismissed it. "Grandfather viewed the body. He won't tell us what he saw."

"I know why he died," said Lear. "That's all you need to know."

"And a few days ago," said Lucy, "that dear little boy died too, the one who believed in monsters! That was when grandfather told us everything."

"It is warning me. Will it come for my grandchildren next?!"

The door opened and Jonathan re-entered the room. "Fat chance of that!" he said and headed toward the window again. "Are we done with this and had our tears? Told our sad little stories?" Tiger noticed his strong strides.

"Not yet," said Lucy, wiping her face. "Sit, Jon-Jon, and keep your mouth shut."

"Those deaths may be just coincidences," said Edgar.

"You know as well as I do, Brim," said Lear, "that there have been reports from boys at the college of something on the moors at night, a human-like being out on the wasteland." He paused. "Those stories began just after I killed that creature."

"But they're nonsense, children's fears. We imagined all that." Edgar tried to look like he believed it.

"Or perhaps you didn't. Will you help us?"

"We have an idea of how to kill that sucker," snapped Jonathan.

"Yes," said Lear and there was a strange gleam in his eye. Edgar wondered if the professor, like Shakespeare, was going mad. "We plan to concentrate on the head."

"But we need a weapon of extraordinary power," added Jonathan. "Blades are only useful in close. A cannon would be best, or at least something with its capability."

"Tonight," said Lear, "I will finish a deal to procure the most lethal guns possible, and if we find this thing and use them correctly, pray they are enough. We have no choice. We must kill or be killed. I will not wait for it to do more evil."

You, thought Edgar, *you* three have no choice, not me.

"But there is another reason we have to act," said Jonathan, leaving the window and approaching Brim. He walked right up to him, apparently holding back a rage. "You see, there is a certain boy in his last year at the College on the Moors who dreams of monsters to the point where he worries they are real, says it out loud in the night. He told someone else too, doing it while this *thing* may have been on the moors, watching and listening! He was in the room just before our enemy appears to have taken the life of that poor child. He made the child state his belief out loud! This boy is suspicious of what happened. And he has spoken to others of his suspicions."

"Me," said Edgar, terrified.

"Give the man a prize!"

"Oh, don't be beastly, Jon!" said Lucy. "He is frightened."

"We are all frightened, my earnest little Lu. We all know the consequences if this thing exists and has made up its mind to act."

"This is incredible," said Edgar quietly, shaking his head.

Lear walked slowly toward him. He held his one hand down to Lucy and helped her to her feet. "Perhaps it has noticed my interest in you, Brim, though I tried to be discreet. Perhaps it thinks I am, finally, about to reveal what I know. Perhaps there are other reasons."

"What about Shakespeare?"

Lear smiled. "It doesn't care about him. Shakespeare is barking mad, or so it seems. He only speaks to his invisible friends and me. It cares about me because of what I did in the past and what I can do now, and it may care about my grandchildren if it discovers that I told them what I suspect. But it may now have a deep and abiding interest in someone else. It likely knows of the young man who did all the things that Jonathan just said. It has probably been aware of him since he came to the Moors with his nightmares. It knows that young man is from a new generation, from outside my family, young and vigorous, growing in mind and body, anxious to kill his fears."

Edgar shuffled in his chair.

"My dear Master Brim, I am not really asking you to help me. I am imploring you to take refuge among us and save yourself. You have no choice. *You* are the next accident. If this monster is about to act, then I believe it will be coming after you!"

"But I don't—"

"You may be the key to destroying it. We may need you to draw him to us."

Tiger moved to Edgar's side and put a hand on his shoulder. "If he goes," she said, "if he's in danger, I'm coming too."

"Couldn't do it without you," said Jonathan, smiling for the first time in a while.

They all turned to Edgar. His heart was thudding. He sat there thinking about his childhood, about everything he had been through. It seemed to him that it had all led up to now. He had to fight what he feared or be killed. He had found a mission.

"All right," he said. "I'll do it."

Jonathan clapped him on the back. Lucy leaped to her feet and hugged him, almost ripping him from Tiger's hands. But he gently pushed her back.

"And I will do something else. You said you need extraordinary weapons to destroy this thing."

"Yes," said Jonathan.

"I know where to find some."

15

Armed

Edgar needed Tiger for this job. Not that she was going to stay behind anyway. The instant he suggested that he might lay his hands upon weapons with monstrous capabilities, she insisted that she accompany him. In fact, she told him that she would pin him down and make him let her go. He didn't think she could pin him anymore, though he thought that activity might be fun.

They arrived in Mayfair that night both excited and nervous, Tiger wearing her trousers and a man's shirt, Edgar carrying a bag with two blankets and a small lantern inside. It was one o'clock in the morning. Tall Thorne House was the only five-story building on the block. Edgar pointed out the top floor, which contained the laboratory. It sat up there as if lowered from above and attached to the rest of the house, its windows with wrought iron bars and a flat area on the roof for Thorne's outdoor experiments.

All the lights were out.

They checked up and down the street, slid up the few stone steps, and Tiger produced a tool from somewhere in her trousers.

It had a handle like a screwdriver but was narrower at the other end and slightly hooked.

She had the wide black entrance open within seconds, then put her finger to her lips and nudged the door gently, testing it for sound as it swung open a few inches. It didn't offer any noise at all.

"The rich make it so much easier," she smiled.

Inside, all they could hear was the dull and distant ticking of Thorne's grandfather clock. It was strange for Edgar to be in the house at this time of the year and stranger still to be sneaking about in what was supposed to be his home. He wished he could slip up the stairs to the second floor and wake Annabel and draw her into the hall for the same warm welcome he always received, wrapped in her arms. But he couldn't do that to her. If she knew what he was attempting, she'd be deceiving her husband. He was about to steal from the man who was supposed to be his father.

The servants were all asleep too. Up the stairs the two intruders went.

"Nice place, rich boy," whispered Tiger.

It was funny. The Thornes did have money, most of it acquired from the sale of armaments that Alfred had made to the military, but they weren't the sort to show off their wealth and they (or at least, Alfred) didn't lavish it on their "son." He was to be brought up with "an appreciation for money." In other words, he was given almost none. Edgar wondered what Alfred's plan was for him once he graduated. The mysterious man had said nothing about it.

On the next floor, they passed Edgar's bedroom. He nodded toward it and pointed to himself.

"I want to see it," said Tiger quietly and moved in its direction. He grabbed her by the hand to stop her but she pulled away. When he entered the room, she was lying on his bed, giving him a come-hither look. He rolled his eyes and sat beside her. She instantly jumped to her feet and headed past him up the stairs. Edgar had warned her that those last flights, wooden, creaky and creepy, especially near the top, would be a problem.

The steps winced the instant they put their feet upon them. The two friends paused and listened. There was no response in the house. They tried several more steps, but those groaned too. With every noise, they paused, and with every pause, they listened.

There was only a landing and the entrance to the laboratory up there, a door at the top of the stairs like a portal into the heavens, or maybe hell. When they reached the last step, they heard a creak that wasn't of their own making, sounding like it came from inside the laboratory!

They stood stock still for a long time. Their eyes were locked on the door with its ominous sign: NO ENTRY!

Finally, Edgar nodded at Tiger. She took out her lock tool again.

But she couldn't make it work. Edgar stood beside her for a full five minutes holding the bag with the blankets and lantern, watching Tiger grow more and more frustrated.

"I've never seen anything like this," she muttered. "He must have invented a new kind of lock." But at last, she sprang it. The door was thick and turning the big, tightly fastened steel knob was almost a feat of strength. Edgar accomplished it with a pounding heart. He was finally about to enter Alfred Thorne's laboratory!

He took his time pushing the door open, nudging it just an

inch at a time, making sure it made no noise. It didn't, as if designed to perfection: it was jammed tightly into the frame to make the laboratory soundproof.

When he was younger, he would have shoved Tiger in first, but now he stepped inside without waiting, into the forbidden realm.

They let the door close gently and stood still for a moment. Edgar lit his small lantern, keeping his hand over it so the glow remained dim. Bobbies often patrolled the Mayfair streets. He didn't want one inquiring about a suspicious light on the fifth floor of Thorne House.

They could see only a small area at a time and had to move slowly, carefully illuminating their path so they wouldn't trip or knock anything over. It was a surprisingly large room, much larger than seemed possible when viewed from outside or through the keyhole. There before Edgar were the things he had glimpsed when he spied on this room: countertops like operating tables littered with test tubes, vices, saws, scalpels and chemicals. It smelled acrid and burnt. There were strange weapons on some surfaces, others on racks—crossbows, pistols, cannons, rifles—unlike any they had ever seen, some equipped with cogs and containers filled with liquids. There were targets everywhere, a few with holes in them, others nearly blown apart. An imposing wooden desk with a black lamp sat at one end of the room. And all around, evident as Edgar shone his lantern on the walls, were books, some he'd glimpsed before. Few dealt with science. He saw names on the spines that thrilled him: Beowulf, Dickens, Le Fanu, Mary Shelley, Robert Louis Stevenson, and volumes by the American, Poe. Really, what good would *those* books be for *Thorne's* research?

Edgar shone his light toward the ceiling and his mouth fell open. There was a window about the size of several shop fronts up there. He hadn't been able to see it from the keyhole. Then he realized that the horizontal blind that was drawn partially over it extended the full length of the room. Alfred Thorne's entire ceiling was made of glass, crisscrossed with black iron bars. Imagine, thought Edgar, being here on a starlit night, your imagination soaring with the twinkling black heavens above you.

"Eddie!" hissed Tiger. He had lost his concentration. She hadn't. She was standing in the center of the room where two tables had been pulled together, away from the others, and on them were two extraordinary weapons.

"Bring your light. I think it says something here."

Edgar tiptoed forward and turned the lantern on the weapons. Up close, they were amazing. Edgar wasn't a violent young man, but something inside him made him want to pick them up and use them on something, anything.

"I want to fire them," he said.

"Yeah," said Tiger.

They had hit a gold mine.

The first instrument was a rifle. It was so unusual that it appeared to have come from the pages of a supernatural story, one set far in the future. It was a sort of revolver rifle, with a round cylinder and chambers where the butt met the main part of the gun and a sleek barrel that was slim near the trigger but grew slightly wider toward the muzzle. It was black from one end to the other. There was a bag of six bullets with it and a sheet of paper beside them with handwriting on it, as if put there for them to read.

NOT FOR MILITARY USE.

Rapid-fire revolving rifle with six new-fashioned expanding bullets that explode on contact with their target. Sighted. Can kill anything within a fifty-foot range.

Edgar reached out and ran his hand along the shaft. But the other weapon was even better. Its barrel was several times the width of the first's and a little longer. It was like a miniature cannon, complete with small wheels. It was telescopic, with the barrel receding in size in sections from the muzzle, and a cylinder with six chambers, near the pull-cord that fired it. A translucent container was attached below the cylinder, with two liquids evident inside, one green, the other black. The weapon was shiny red, as befit its devilish capabilities. There were big round bullets as big as fists sitting in the chambers.

NOT FOR MILITARY USE.

Short-range, rapid-fire cannon with new-fashioned projecting mechanism. When cord is pulled, chemicals mix and explode in massive concussion, firing five-inch diameter cannonballs with extraordinary force and accuracy. Bullets expand on contact. Next bullet then moves into firing position. Can smash a foot-wide hole in a concrete wall. Can be folded smaller and moved on wheels.

Could this thing destroy a monster? Edgar gave a low whistle. At that moment, as if in answer, they heard another creak, like a single footstep. It seemed to come from inside the room.

They stood still for a long time. Then Edgar broke the silence.

"We have to leave now. We're taking these two."

In seconds, they had both weapons and their ammunition down from the tables and wrapped up in the blankets and shoved partly into the bag, and were tiptoeing toward the door. But Tiger turned back. She had spotted another rifle bullet on the table. "For good luck," she said, and swept it into her pocket. They were down the stairs in a flash, the steps groaning as they went. They flew along the marble stairs, through the vestibule and then out the main door, which Tiger had left open just a crack. She closed it behind them and they ran up the street, heading north toward the Langham. Edgar was so excited he couldn't speak. He had done it! He had not only been in the laboratory but had seen the guns and actually stolen two. He, Edgar Brim, was growing reckless. At this moment, he didn't care about the consequences.

When the two thieves got to the Langham, they could barely contain their excitement. They showed off the weapons and Jonathan, who was grinning, eagerly took each one in hand and aimed them at objects in the room. Lucy thought that ridiculous; she didn't want to touch them. But the others took time to understand how to use them, and then Lear made sure they were wrapped tightly in the blankets and placed, with their bullets, into their big traveling bags. He packed a long knife too.

A few hours later they were at the Euston Railway Station to take the five o'clock morning train north to Edinburgh, change up there at Inverness and then on to the moors. Tiger, who was not allowed in the college, would be on a later train and join them that night. They couldn't risk someone from the college seeing her with them. There was an abandoned farmhouse a fifteen-minute walk from the school where she told them she'd stay. Lear had telegraphed Griswold and Usher, saying that he was not only bringing Brim with him, but also his grandchildren, to help him during the last week of school. Lucy's presence in the all boys' institution was going to be a challenge.

They scurried through the station, the stars still twinkling in the black sky above the bowed glass ceiling. As they passed the W.H. Smith bookstand, Edgar noticed a tall man in a black bowler hat and cape standing next to it with his back to them, his nose a beak peeking out. When they neared, the man knocked a book from the stand. Edgar picked it up. He looked at the cover, yellow with a blood-red title, and then up at the sign in front of him: *The Most Frightening Novel in England!* It was like a challenge, dropped into his hands at precisely the right moment. He had to take it on. He paid the shilling and caught up to the others. The tall man had vanished.

Edgar read the story sporadically as they moved north, enjoying the first few pages, written in the form of a young English solicitor's journal about a trip into the Carpathian Mountains in eastern Europe. Then it became more and more frightening. Edgar was the hero, in a carriage on a winding road leading to a dark castle. He had to stop reading several times.

The four of them were in a compartment facing each other. That way, they could speak quietly and without fear of eavesdroppers. But mostly there was silence. It was only as they neared Scotland that they really talked. Edgar began by asking Lear more questions.

"What if it isn't up there anymore? What if it has gone somewhere else? We aren't even sure what we are after."

"You raise excellent concerns," said Lear. "But we have the beginnings of a plan."

They hadn't given Edgar many details, which worried him.

"The key will be the little boy," said Lucy, finally.

"First, we try to prove that it killed him, so we will know it was there last week," added Jonathan, "and perhaps how it operates."

"How do we do that?" asked Edgar.

No one answered him.

"How do we prove it killed Newman?" he repeated.

It was Jonathan who finally spoke. Edgar couldn't believe what he said.

II

First Pursuit

As soon as you trust yourself, you will know how to live.

∞

Faust, Johann Wolfgang von Goethe (1808)

16

Grave Concerns

The doors of the College on the Moors creak open as if moved by invisible hands as the four friends enter. Outside, the hooded driver sits on the carriage, with his black horse hitched to it, watching. Inside, Usher floats toward them, emerging out of the shadows, dressed in his black school robe with vertical red stripes. His round face is especially white in the dimly lit entrance hall. Voices echo off the stone walls as if their owners were speaking down a well.

"Good evening, gentlemen, my lady," says Usher, bowing to Lucy, who starts.

"Good . . . good evening, sir."

"I might observe that I am not 'sir,' my lady. I am a mere servant, the porter."

"Usher," says Lear, "I trust you received my telegram. These two are my grandchildren, Lucy and Jonathan. They will be accommodated in the empty rooms on Master Brim's floor. We shall handle our own bags. Our young friends are tired from the long journey. Could you arrange for their meals to be sent up to them? That is all."

"It is as you wish, sir."

He glides back several steps, stops directly under the chandelier in the cavernous room, and his bald head glows as he lowers it and bows to them.

"I shall meet you all later," says Lear quietly, "as discussed." He lumbers toward his quarters on the ground floor.

The others climb the big staircase with the ornate balustrade, their boots making sweeping sounds on the stone steps. The staircase opens wide at the first floor, where they turn left under the dim gaslights toward Edgar's room. Classes are still in session and the halls are deserted. Each room's wooden door is closed and only the muffled sounds of professors barking instructions and the students' responses are heard.

"This is nice," says Jonathan, "such a sunny, welcoming place."

"Lovely. How do you stand it, Edgar? It is nine months of the year, isn't it?"

"Thirteen, I believe, Lucy. Wait until you see your room."

"Fit for a lady, I'm sure."

"*The* lady, sister dear. Do you not feel honored?"

Mrs. Shakewell, the cook at the College on the Moors, is round with hairy arms and a stained uniform. That is it for females.

"Tiger should be here by dusk," Lucy says.

"Yes," says Edgar and smiles. It's the only thing about this evening that doesn't make him tremble inside. He thinks of Tiger the Brave finding her way to the abandoned farmhouse out on the moors. Only she would volunteer for such a thing.

Edgar shows them their rooms. Lucy is directly across from him, where Tiger used to be. Jonathan is next to her.

"Remember," says Edgar, "we stay in our rooms until midnight."

Perfect silence usually reigns in the college once darkness has descended. It is a hard and fast rule, and rules here are not meant to be broken (thus, loud nightmares and sleepwalking are particularly frowned upon). But there are whispers this night in the corridors. Three figures are sneaking down the stone steps, meeting another one near the entrance. They slip out the door, almost through it, like ghosts. Usher stands in the shadows in an alcove near his counter, observing.

They keep their voices low as they walk toward the graveyard. Sounds carry remarkably far on the treeless moors. The wind is cold tonight, though it is early summer. They wrap their coats close as they move across the back grounds, the college rising behind. Lear has distributed the tools they need: Jonathan is carrying the shovel, Edgar two coils of thick rope. The professor keeps looking up to the moon, which is far too big and bright for their purpose. A vigilant eye could spot them from an upper window.

Do we really have to do this? wonders Edgar.

When they reach the grave, Jonathan raises his hand, although no one has spoken. He has seen something, far out past the boundary of the school grounds. They all cast their eyes through the moonlight toward the horizon. A figure is on the move out there. It seems human but it is hard to be sure. It stops, appears to spot them and then runs. It is coming right at them.

Edgar left Thorne's guns in his room. He wishes now he hadn't. But Lear had said they needed their hands for other things—the weapons were for later. Edgar tosses the ropes to the ground with a thump, ready to confront the approaching figure.

"It's Tiger," says Lucy, relief spreading across her face.

They wait for her to arrive. She is wearing a thick coat and cap, gray trousers and black boots. Edgar has often thought that he has never met a more practical person.

The grave is a small one, befitting its inhabitant, at the back and freshly filled in. It has been less than a week since the funeral.

"Let us begin," says Lear. "Jonathan?"

His grandson sighs and drives the spade deep into the soil. It cuts through the gravel and clangs against stones like a sword encountering bone. He pauses. "And so, our happy task commences." Jon's dark-blond hair and sideburns are almost black in the dim light. He puts his back and his big arms into it and doesn't stop digging for a long time. The others stand motionless near each other to block the wind. Lear keeps alert, scanning the horizon, examining the few trees on the grounds for a figure in hiding.

"Shall you give it a go?" asks a perspiring Jonathan, turning to Edgar when he is three or four feet down. "It's quite fun, it is."

Edgar doesn't want to do any digging. In fact, he doesn't want to be in the graveyard or at the College on the Moors or even in Scotland. But he knows he must face this. His father had told him so. But he hesitates to answer Jonathan. Though he can do many difficult things these days, can he do this?

"I'll finish the job," says Tiger, stepping forward and reaching out for the shovel.

"No!"

Edgar seizes the spade, leaps down into the grave and begins to dig. It smelled damp and earthy up above. Down here he finds the stinking odor of death. It almost makes him gag. Jonathan had pulled his scarf over his mouth as he worked, but Edgar is determined to face the stench. Life, to him, can be like a series of stories connected by vivid scenes, and the one he is in now deeply worries him. But he keeps digging.

His shovel strikes wood. He steps back and drops the spade as if an electric shock has hit him. Tiger leans down and offers a hand. He takes it and scrambles out.

They all stand staring into the grave for a moment. Then old Lear struggles down into it, his movements heavy but purposeful. He takes the shovel in his only hand and scrapes another few inches of soil away before dropping to his knees and sweeping back what remains, revealing the outline of the coffin beneath. It is tiny, just four feet by a little more than one.

Lear looks up toward his partners in crime. Lucy turns her face away, but inserts her arm into Edgar's. He is thinking of the dead child in the box below.

"Get the rope," says Lear, his face like granite in the night. "Let's pull the coffin out and open it."

Edgar bends down and gets one of the ropes and soon Jon has the other. They drop into the grave and get the ropes under the coffin. Tiger and Edgar take the ends of one and Jonathan and Lucy and Lear the other and together they hoist it up. But as they do they realize that one of them could have lifted it alone because it is shockingly light. They set the little oblong box down on the wet grass under the moonlight. It is a simple wooden container. The child's parents could have afforded much more; Driver had made this meager final resting place.

The smell is stronger now. Lucy pulls the collar of her coat up around her mouth and long-ish nose. She can't look, but she keeps holding on to Edgar, to comfort him, he thinks, as well as to seek solace. Tiger frowns. Jonathan is staring at his grandfather as Lear takes up the shovel and jams it into the crack between the lid and the main body of the coffin, beginning to pry it open. It creaks and squeaks as he leans on the shovel. One side pops up. Lucy utters a little cry but stifles it. The other side pops up. All the nails have been released.

"We must do this," says Lear. "You all know that."

"God forgive us," says Lucy.

"He will."

Lear pulls back the lid and the smell is overpowering. Lucy turns and walks several strides away and Jonathan steps back too. Tiger and Lear peer down into the coffin. Edgar stands still, pushed forward by his willpower, pulled back by his nature.

"My God!" whispers Tiger.

Lear's face is transfixed on what is beneath him. He takes out his knife, his huge sharp one. For an instant, Edgar sees it gleam in the moonlight and catches Lear's face reflected in the blade. His expression is deadly serious but it contains something else, almost a smile, unlike any Edgar has ever seen.

Edgar steps forward and peers down too, Lucy coming forward with him. Then she buries a scream into his chest. He wishes he could cry out too. But he can't. He can't do anything. They are looking down upon a corpse that is as pink as life. The cheeks are rosy. The lips are red. The eyes are wide open . . . and moving.

The child is alive.

17

A Grim Decision

Tiger finds her voice first. "Can it speak?"

The little corpse is staring right at them.

"My friend, can you . . . ?" asks Edgar into the coffin, not sure if he wants a response.

The child's eyes start darting back and forth, but they don't focus. His chest is pulsing up and down, but he remains silent.

"He is paralyzed." Lear leans forward, bringing his big knife toward the little boy's chest. Lucy can't stand it. She grips her grandfather's arm.

"No!"

The professor gently removes her hand. "I am not going to harm him, not yet."

None of them like the sound of that. But they stand back and watch as Lear brings his blade nearer the child. He inserts the tip into the shirt near the stomach and in one quick motion slices the material right up to the boy's throat. Lucy starts.

Lear reaches down and pulls back the shirt like a science student peeling back the skin of a frog. There is the pitiful little chest, the ribs evident, the beating of the heart almost visible in the rising and falling of the torso. Edgar wonders if it is just him, but the child's eyes look terrified now.

"Look!" says Tiger.

There is a wound on the boy directly over his heart. It is small and circular, about the size of a shilling coin. It is indented as if it were once a little hole.

"What does that mean?" asks Edgar.

"Perhaps it is an old wound," says Lear. He takes the child's jaw in his hand and turns his head from side to side, examining his neck.

"Why are you doing that?" asks Edgar sharply.

"The neck is clean, not a single mark on it."

"What do we do next?" asks Lucy. "We can't leave him like this."

"No, we can't, my dear."

"*It* was here," says Tiger, clinical and calm.

Children die mysteriously, thinks Edgar. It happens. But they don't look like this in their coffins beneath the ground almost a week later. He glances around the graveyard and out over the moors.

"I am guessing the child is in agony," says Lear. "He is not alive nor is he dead."

"We need to kill him," says Tiger.

"No," whispers Lucy.

But Lear had nodded at Tiger. "And when we do it we need to make sure that he is dead."

"What sort of creature could do this?" demands Edgar out loud. "What are we searching for?"

"I am sure it will introduce itself soon," says Lear.

Jonathan is standing near his sister. "Lucy, you should go."

"I'll walk her to the door," says Tiger.

They turn and head back toward the building.

Lear looks at the two remaining boys.

"There is one sure way of driving evil from a corpse, for rendering it dead beyond a doubt. It is done in all ancient cultures." He picks up his sword-like knife. "We must sever the head."

18

An Offer

As they enter the Great Dining Hall for breakfast the next morning, they say nothing about what was done to the child's corpse. Lucy doesn't ask. No one who walks upon the back grounds of the college today will notice that the grave has been disturbed.

"What do we do next?" asks Jonathan.

Lear brings a finger up to his lips. Griswold is approaching.

"May I be the first to welcome your grandchildren to the College on the Moors," he says, attempting a smile. He curls his thin red lips and his gums show. His teeth are unusually long and a little yellow.

"Thank you, sir. This is Lucy."

The giant headmaster extends a long skeletal arm down toward her, raises her hand to his lips and kisses it wetly.

"It is a pleasure to meet you, sir."

Edgar admires her ability to show not an ounce of revulsion.

"The pleasure is most certainly mine."

"And this is Jonathan."

"Good day, sir. Welcome to our institution." He attempts another smile and pumps Jon's hand, which despite its substantial size disappears into Griswold's.

"It is good to be back, Headmaster," says Lear.

"Of course it is. How was London? Did you see Irving?"

"I didn't have time."

"He is a genius!" Griswold's face lights up, but then he remembers himself. "Brim," he says, nodding at Edgar. The boy nods back. "It was a shame to not see these young ones at dinner last night." He pauses, an expert employer of silence. "What did you do with them?"

"They were tired, sir."

"Yes, quite exhausted," says Lucy.

Griswold turns to her again. "Of course, my dear."

"They stayed in their rooms."

"No moonlit strolls?" asks Griswold. He regards Edgar when he says this.

"Of course not, sir," says Jonathan. "Slept like a corpse the whole night. I look forward to a hearty breakfast."

Griswold pauses again. "I am forgetting myself. I must let you eat. I shall watch over you all whilst you are here, make sure you have no needs that are not fulfilled. Good day." He is about to walk away but turns back to Lear.

"You are dining with the children?" He pronounces the last word particularly clearly. Jonathan looks like he wants to strike him.

"Yes, sir, for today. I thought I might."

"I suppose we can make an exception."

The headmaster pivots and departs, taking his usual long strides toward the table up on the dais where he dines. He still has his favorite companions at mealtimes, though they have changed from year to year. Lear is no longer a regular honored guest; his time appears to have passed.

Edgar watches the back of the headmaster's bulbous skull move away, its bone color showing through wisps of white hair and shining under the candled chandeliers that line the center of the ceiling. Griswold ignores the nearly two hundred students filling the wooden chairs at the thick tables, not deigning to say hello to even one of them.

Edgar looks at the two professors at the table of honor, awaiting their headmaster's return. Numb is looking the boy's way with a hard expression, but the other is smiling and waving. Edgar waves back.

"Lovecraft looks so out of place up there," he says as he and his friends take their seats.

"Looks can be deceiving," says Lear. "Now, we may not have much time. We must examine what we learned last night and decide on a course of action."

They keep their voices down, especially since talk, in general, is subdued here. The mere movement of a chair echoes in the room.

"Well, no marks on the corpse's neck," says Jonathan, "which rules out one of our more famous monsters. I bet you are disappointed with that, Lu."

"But what about the one on his chest?" asks Edgar.

"Little boys have many scars," says Lucy. "It could have come from anything."

He wasn't very active, thinks Edgar.

"But it was indented, like a hole," says Jonathan. "It seemed recent."

"The open eyes," says Lucy. "And they were moving!" She shudders.

"A lovely look, I thought," says Jonathan.

"I was told," said Lear, "that Newman's eyes had to be closed when he was found dead in the infirmary."

"And they opened again in his coffin!" says Lucy.

"How is that possible?" asks Edgar. "Some reaction of the nerves? Some return to his expression at death? Was he seeing something terrifying the moment he died?"

"An interesting way of putting it, Brim," says Lear. "Some . . . thing."

"Yes," says Edgar, ". . . not a presence or a spirit—"

"Not a fog or a floating poison in the air," Lucy nods. "The child saw something that reached out and put a hole in his chest!"

"Scintillating debate," says Jon, "but as I said, methinks some time ago, what's next?" His leg is pumping up and down under the table. Some might call it a nervous twitch, but he wouldn't. He is ready for action. "I suggest we do something that you tall foreheads are dancing around. Whether it is a body or a phantom or the big bad wolf, we need to hunt this thing and murder it, now."

"I agree," says Edgar.

"But even if we're sure it can be seen," says Lucy, "we have no idea where it is." She glances around the room and up at the table on the stage where Griswold is staring back at her.

"Maybe we can find out," says Lear.

"Yes, I'll get some cat food and we'll go out onto the moors and call it," says Jonathan. "What do you think it would respond to? Here, kitty, kitty?"

"No," says Lear, "but you are close."

His response makes Jonathan swallow. The old man is deadly serious.

"We must offer it something."

"What do you mean?" asks Lucy.

"I should think that predators, whether they be human, animal or monster, prefer to attack their victims one at a time, when they can catch them alone. The odds are better that way. Not that this thing likely needs much in the way of odds." He turns to Edgar. "Do you have any thoughts on the subject, Brim?"

"Well . . . Tiger is alone."

"She is indeed," nods Lear.

"You can't!" says Lucy.

He regards his granddaughter. "Tilley agreed to be part of this." Edgar knows that only too well. It was because of him. "Someone alone in that little farmhouse would be an enticing target. That is why I took Thorne's biggest weapon out there this morning at dawn."

It is some consolation for Edgar, but not enough. He looks through a stained glass window toward the murky outdoors. They have no idea what it will take to bring their enemy down. Would Thorne's weapons, as remarkable as they are, do anything? Would a bullet or even a cannonball simply pass through it? Need the bullets be silver? But that's for vampires and the boy had no marks on his neck. Edgar wishes that they knew, at least, what form their pursuer takes. Will they *really* be able to see it? At least, he reassures himself, Tiger is as tough as nails.

"Brim," says Lear.

"Yes, sir?" He doesn't like the tone of the professor's voice. It makes him think of the old days at the college when he feared this menacing man.

"You need not worry so much about Tilley. You have enough to be concerned about."

It sounds like a threat. Edgar thinks of the sound of Lear's sword-like knife cutting through the muscle and bone of the boy's neck last night, the little one's eyes still wide open. He had felt vomit coming up from his stomach and had turned his head. Jonathan had pretended to look, but Edgar is sure he too looked away. He had told himself, again and again, that the ritual destruction of the corpse was necessary.

"What do you mean, grandfather?" Lucy moves a little closer to Edgar.

"It is a good plan to involve Tilley as an enticement, but we need to do more than that."

"More?" asks Jonathan, leaning forward.

"Master Brim, you agree it is wise to offer the demon something, do you not?"

"Yes, sir." Edgar's hands are shaking under the table.

"Tilley is just the tease. There is something else I believe it truly wants. I've told you so."

Edgar asks anyway. "And what is that?"

"You."

19

Bait

Edgar has his book with him, the one with the blood-red title. He sits reading it in the lantern light, the hag peering over his shoulder, as he waits on a hill on the moors for the monster to attack him. Inside its pages, he becomes the hero again, deep in the forbidding forests in the Carpathian Mountains in eastern Europe. But now, he is inside the terrifying castle. Only one man lives there, the same one who picked him up on the road, pretending to be the driver. He is old and ashen and unearthly, as if he were dead; he only appears after the sun sets and doesn't seem to eat or drink. Edgar sneaks from bed in the darkness of his room in the castle to shave. But the old man is suddenly behind him, causing him to slice himself with the razor. The freakish man reaches for his throat when blood appears, then quickly excuses himself. Edgar is filled with dread. He thinks about escaping, but knows the castle has been locked shut and is on a steep precipice. He is a prisoner.

Edgar closes the book. He listens and hears a distant wildcat growl. He swings around. He is a prisoner out here on the moors too, for real. Can he escape what is coming? He wishes again that he knew what was going to attack him. And what will it do to him? Kill him instantly or take its time? But he keeps his wits about him, his body still, his heart thudding. He must face this.

"Can you see Edgar?" asks Lucy. She is lying on the ground in trousers next to her grandfather and brother, who has pocket binoculars trained on Edgar's little light in the distance.

"Oh, my God!"

"What? Tell me?"

"He is being attacked by something! It's eight feet tall."

"What?"

"It's got him down. It's bending over him. It's tearing at his head!"

Lucy swipes the glasses from him. She scans the horizon. There's the light. There's Edgar, sitting beside it, his head turning as if it were on a swivel, but securely attached to his neck. He is still alone.

"You're an idiot!" she tells her brother.

"Well, why would you ask me a question like that? Of course I can see him. What do you think I'm looking at?"

"Be quiet, you two. Give me the glasses."

Lear swings them west toward the old farmhouse where Tiger is living. There is a light in its window. All seems well.

They have positioned themselves on a small mound about a quarter of a mile from the college. They are another quarter mile from where Edgar sits on a hill in an undulation in the moors, and about the same distance from Tiger's stone house to their left. The three observers could run to either human bait in a short burst and pick off whatever attacked either friend. They have the weapons with them to do it: Jonathan with the smaller of Thorne's two remarkable guns, the rifle-like item with the chambered cylinder and deadly accuracy, and Lear with his grandson's pistol. Jon will enter the Royal Military Academy in Sandhurst in the autumn and has been training himself with unbending dedication. He is already a crack shot. Lear has always known his way around a gun, but the old man has his big knife holstered to his leg too and has made sure that Lucy and Jonathan have one each, though theirs are not quite as prodigious.

"If we have to confront it," he told them before they left the college, "you both must be armed."

Lucy doesn't want a gun. She has something more valuable—her senses and her intuition.

"I would wager that you will feel the villain's arrival before either of us sees it, Lucy," Lear had said as they walked out to their location. "One uses everything at hand in this game and females have powers males do not. Their wariness in the darkness is an antenna of great strength."

"Oh, really," said Jonathan.

"I would rather have a woman than a man with me in a tight spot," Lear added, "especially at night."

"Thank you, grandfather," said Jonathan. "One is always seeking a vote of confidence."

A few hours before sunrise, Lucy sits up.

"Something's coming," she says.

"Where?" asks Lear.

"Over there, near the college grounds."

They squirm around and lie flat, Jonathan training his gun in the direction she pointed.

"I can't see it!" he gasps. "Tell me where it is."

"Wait," says Lucy.

Then they all see it. Something large, upright on two legs, moving without a lantern west of the grounds and out toward the moors, black on black.

"I don't know if I can hit it!" exclaims Jonathan. He sounds a little nervous.

"Don't shoot yet," says Lear. "See where it goes first."

They hold their breath and watch. Lucy runs her hand down to her knife, strapped as if in a garter to her leg. The creature moves well for something without light, floating over the moors, up and down through its undulations.

"Does a human being move like that?" asks Jonathan. His hand is twitching on the rifle's trigger.

"Quiet. Watch."

It glides silently, coming to within a dozen carriage lengths of the three bodies on the ground on the hill. It stops when it nears. It turns toward them. Lucy hears Jonathan quietly cock the gun.

It grunts and then moves on. In minutes it is halfway between Edgar and Tiger. It seems to spot Edgar. It stops.

"We must do something," says Lucy. She tries to get up, but Lear holds her down.

"Wait."

Off in the distance, the creature takes a few strides toward Edgar.

"We can't wait. Edgar only has a knife! It will kill—"

"Wait."

"The whites of its eyes," says Jonathan and grins.

The being stops. It stands still for a moment and then turns toward the farmhouse. It is almost instantly moving at top speed.

"It's going for Tilley!" says Lear. "Jonathan, after it!"

He leaps to his feet. "Alone?"

"We have to stay here and watch Edgar. This could be a tactic. There could be more than one of them."

"Now you tell us," says Jon, and in a moment he's vanished into the darkness over the moors.

The creature stops when it nears the farmhouse and Jonathan stops too. He can see now that it seems to be wearing a cloak or a robe of some sort that is billowing in the wind—human clothing? He knows then that he can't just shoot it. He needs to get closer, see what it is about to do. He thinks it is fitting that he has this task, saving the remarkable Tiger Tilley.

He sees the light go out in the house. The creature approaches the door.

Half a mile away Edgar is startled by a cry upon the moors. It comes from very close to him. He stands: an ill-advised move. He has made himself visible.

"Show yourself!" he cries. He hopes his friends will hear him.

"He's being attacked!" shrieks Lucy. She gets to her feet and runs, Lear stumbling after her, Jonathan's pistol in hand. They can barely see in the moonlight. This is the worst possible situation: all they have is the little gun and just two of them coming to the rescue—a slender girl and an old, one-armed man.

Edgar isn't going to wait for reinforcements, for a shot to come whizzing through the night. And anyway, he must make their prey visible, so Jonathan can train Thorne's great rifle on it and destroy it. What will this thing do if the bullet can't stop it? Edgar stifles his vivid imagination, stopping his visions of ripped flesh and blood. He walks toward the sound, the lantern held out to illuminate whatever may appear.

"I am here!" he cries.

Lucy and Lear hear him clearly now. But they can't say anything. They can't betray that they are nearing. Lucy sees Edgar moving down the other side of the little hill where he had been ensconced. He stops, his head still visible, holding the lantern out.

"Hurry!" she says to herself.

Thud!

The intruder has its back to Jonathan as it strikes the farmhouse door. Jon takes a chance. He gets down and crawls past it in the dark, keeping well away, moving around to the side of the house. From there, he can observe through a back window, train his gun through the glass, and if this being so much as approaches his friend, he can destroy it: a frontal shot to the head.

Standing on the far side of the hill, Edgar sees the thing that screamed. In fact, he sees *them*. They are glaring at him, their eyes glowing red in the night.

"Wildcats," says Lear, out of breath as he approaches Edgar. It is two males and they have just stopped fighting. The sounds they make in battle are almost unearthly, especially when heard this close.

Lucy puts her hand on Edgar's shoulder. The big cats, ring-tailed and evil-looking in the night, run off.

Lucy lets out a deep sigh. Edgar stifles his. But then they hear another sound, a thudding, coming from the direction of the farmhouse. Without a word, they start to run again.

Jonathan can see the back of Tiger's head through the window. He also notices that the cannon is ingeniously hidden from the view of anyone who might enter the building, behind Tiger and against a wall by the big wood stove but still pointed at the door. She can move back a few steps and fire it. He trains his gun.

"Let me in!" croaks the intruder at the door.

"Stay calm," Tiger tells herself. She undoes the latch with a kick and then stands back, legs wide, one slightly forward, hands not quite balled but ready. The door is instantly driven open from the outside, smacking against the wall.

Professor Numb stands in the entrance, muscular and hairy. His face is almost purple. He doesn't seem like himself. It is as if a transformation is happening.

Jonathan takes aim.

Despite Lucy's diminutive size, she is strong. She keeps up with Edgar, who is lean and powerful. The professor is huffing and puffing, struggling to stay with them.

"Go on!" he gasps, slowly. He tosses the pistol to Edgar.

The farmhouse door is open and something large is standing in it.

———

"I thought so!" shrieks Numb, not sounding like himself. He reaches a beefy hand toward Tiger's neck. She slashes his arm down and takes three strides back toward the cannon behind her. She pulls the cloth off her lantern, lighting up the room.

Jonathan keeps dead aim. He sees Tiger strike Sebastian Numb and step back. As far as he can tell, the weird professor has no weapon. As far as he knows, he is *just* a professor. But he isn't certain. "Do not intervene unless necessary," he says out loud. Tiger will understand. But his finger begins to press on the trigger.

Lear sees Lucy and Edgar come up close to the little stone house twenty or more strides in front of him. Then he hears something approaching from behind.

When Numb receives the blow from Tiger, he seems dumbfounded. He stares at his former student and the dark color fades from his face.

"I suppose I should expect nothing less from you," he says, assuming his smooth voice again. "I was instructed by Headmaster Griswold to come out to this location, Tilley, to investigate whether some person might be inhabiting it. Evidently, it is you—you who were once expelled from our great institution and who are forbidden to come back. You must leave. That is what I was asked to convey to anyone I should find here."

Tiger is directly in front of the little cannon and Numb can't see it. She shoves it with her foot, rolling it behind the big stove.

"You have no right to evict me. This isn't the college so I can be here if I like."

"No, you may NOT!" thunders a voice from behind Numb. Griswold has entered, out of breath. He has to bend down to get in the door. Lear is beside him and so are Edgar (pistol hidden under his jacket) and Lucy. Jonathan moves from the side of the farmhouse and fades into the night. Lovecraft approaches the house from behind his leader.

"Oh, my dear Tilley!" exclaims the little man. "Welcome back!"

"Shut up, Reginald!" says Griswold. He turns back to Tiger. "The college expropriated this house when the peasants vacated it. You are thus upon our property. You shall leave, and you shall do so *now!*"

Tiger simply stares at the headmaster.

"And Professor Lear," says Griswold, "I suppose you knew nothing of this?"

Lear pauses. "No, sir," he says.

"Just what I thought you'd say. Your grandson appears to have vanished, by the way."

"Perhaps he is out taking the air, sir. He has a great interest in astronomy."

"Perhaps Tilley will encounter him, then, for she is just about to leave the premises. Such a person cannot stay within a mile of the college. Such a person can make its home out on the moors with the wildcats, as far as I'm concerned."

"I shall, old man," says Tiger. "Just give me tonight and I will be gone. I promise you."

Griswold hesitates. "I am not sure what a promise from the likes of you counts for, but all right. Make no mistake, however, if we see you here or anywhere upon the property of the College on the Moors after tonight, Usher and Driver shall clap you into William Wilson's chains and put you onto the train on a short trip to Inverness prison, do you hear me?"

Tiger says nothing.

"DO YOU HEAR ME?"

Lear nods to his former student from behind Griswold's back.

"Yes, I do," says Tiger.

"Fine decision, Tilley!" exclaims Lovecraft. "Lovely seeing you!"

"Shut up, Reginald." The headmaster glares at the happy little man, who barely notices. "Everyone else, leave! Now!"

Edgar tries to linger but Griswold pushes him from the room, nearly knocking him into Lucy. He steps into the night. All he hears is the sound of their footsteps trudging over the barren landscape. His thoughts spin: Is their enemy watching them? Observing from a distance? Or is it in the air?

He imagines Tiger alone, cast out on the moors.

Griswold, Lovecraft and Numb are barely visible, well ahead of them as they lead the way back to the college, the low murmur of their conversation inaudible.

Something leaps from the heather and seizes Lucy . . . her brother, whom she slaps. Edgar isn't amused. He's thinking about Tiger, wondering if he should return to the farmhouse and convince her to go home to London, now. But he knows she won't.

"Jon, you are on first watch in your hallway tonight," says Lear. "Keep the rifle loaded near the door in one of the rooms." Edgar wonders what he would do if he was on guard when something broke into the college and came into that dim passageway, in that enclosed space, attacking without warning.

"Aim for the head," Lear reminds them. "Keep shooting until it is blown completely off."

They reach the grounds and pass by Driver's stable. His dim light is on, as usual. The three professors are entering the college.

"Ah, we didn't get to see it attack Brim," says Jonathan, clapping Edgar on the back. "Rather disappointing, that."

"Great fun postponed," remarks Edgar.

"We learned nothing," says Lucy, "and now we've lost Tiger."

They trudge up to the main doors.

"I was out there alone, perfect bait, and it didn't come after me."

As Edgar says this, Lucy comes to a sudden halt, her eyes wide.

"What if it isn't out there?" she says. "What if it's *inside*?"

20

Hiding Place

The next morning, Professor Lear climbs the staircase that leads to the top floor and beyond. There, in the black turret that sticks up high above the rest of the College, lives an ancient man he wants to interview. Edward Emeritus had been the headmaster at the College on the Moors for sixty years. Griswold is eighty himself, though one wouldn't know it when he is whipping a boy, his few wisps of white hair flying up, spit coming from his mouth below his hooked red nose as he whacks children with blood-drawing roundhouse strikes accomplished with more flare than the best blows of the boys' bats on the cricket field. He had spent nearly all of his six decades at the college waiting to succeed the old man. But in a sense he never did, for the legend of Headmaster Emeritus lives on, so much so that he is allowed to stay in the college, kept there in that room above everyone else's, his counsel sought on every issue until just the last few years.

Lear is breathing heavily by the time he reaches the great man's room. There is no answer to his knock. For an instant Lear wonders if Emeritus has expired. The old man's one hundredth birthday was toasted the previous year, though he had been too frail to come downstairs. In fact, no student currently at the college can be certain to have ever seen him, and most professors, Lear included, haven't spoken to him in years. Lear gently pushes open the door.

And there the old headmaster is—sitting at his desk with his back to the door, staring out over the moors, mumbling to himself, still wearing his robes. Lear needs him to be sane, not perfectly sane, not bright with awareness and suspicion, but somewhere in that unguarded state that very elderly people reach, almost as if they were between sleeping and life, in their own sort of dream.

"Headmaster Emeritus?"

The old man keeps staring out the window, muttering.

Lear walks around so he can be seen. His presence doesn't startle the ancient man in the least.

"Yes, my child, have you come to be whipped?" Emeritus speaks in explosive bursts in a thin, hoarse pitch.

This man had been the king of whippings. He made Griswold look like an amateur. Though his body is withered and shrunken today, his face fallen as if it is beginning to melt, his hands, resting on his lap, are as big and powerful as ever. He is said to have left scars on some students that will last lifetimes.

"Sir, it is Professor Hamish Lear."

"Oh. Oh, Lear. Yes, I recall you, young man. Are you settling in nicely?"

"Sir, I have been here for forty years now."

"I see."

"I have a few questions for you."

"Questions!" The old man tries to get up, but he can't and falls

170

back into the chair. "Questions about discipline? Do you have a problem I must straighten out? Send me the boy!"

"No, sir, there is no boy involved."

"No boy! But how can this be?"

"I want to ask you a few questions about the history of the College on the Moors."

"Yes, well, I was the headmaster there, my boy."

"Smooth sailing?"

"For the most part, yes, thank you for inquiring."

"No problems? Nothing suspicious happened during your tenure that you still think about?"

"Well, there was the case of the murdered boy."

Lear feels the blood drain from his face. He is glad that the old man can't see well. He doesn't want to talk about this and there is no reason to now. The boy Emeritus has just spoken of was precious to Lear, though he hasn't mentioned him (or what happened) to his grandchildren and certainly not to Edgar Brim.

"He wasn't murdered. There was nothing suspicious about it."

"Well, killed, at least. Erasmus Scrivener was his name, a lovely boy, had a deformed foot, if I recall correctly. I never had the pleasure of whipping him, not once. He didn't need it." The old man is sad for an instant, but goes on. "He was a genius in literature. A man named Lear, who taught him, told me that."

"That would be me."

"You! No, no, can't be; he is a young man."

"Scrivener committed suicide, sir, nothing more."

"Ah, yes, that was what they said. The prints of his boots led to the lake."

Scrivener had been Lear's prize student in the days when he taught literature. He had often secretly veered from the curriculum and taught modern works to his classes. He remembers even instructing them on the writings of Poe. They loved those stories— the tale about the man who pulled his wife's teeth while she died, another about a boy who killed an old man because he didn't like one of his eyes, and of course, the poem about the ghastly raven.

"You are Lear, for certain?"

"Yes, sir."

"Has your arm healed? That was one nasty business. A wolf, was it not? Wolves are rarely seen here."

"Yes . . . a wolf, sir."

"The boy died while you were on sabbatical getting well, did he not?"

Scrivener had indeed died when Lear was away. It had pained him even more than the loss of his limb. He had done nothing about it, and there had been something to do. He had been afraid.

"It was suicide, sir, the police were sure."

Though there are few lakes on this part of the moors, the one in question, Loch Blue, is about a mile to the north. It seemed obvious that the boy had walked out there alone and perished in the freezing waters. A few prints were clear the next day, leading up to the edge; no remains were ever found. He had been a happy boy from a loving family and with excellent prospects; he had no reason to despair. Lear still sees Scrivener sometimes these days, in his nightmares.

He needs to change the direction of the conversation, get

directly to the point he has come to investigate. The old man is nodding off.

"Sir, were you to want to hide somewhere in the college, where would you do it? Are there any old, secret places that no one else knows about?"

"Hide? Why would I do that, young fellow? That sounds like an impertinent question. Are you an impertinent boy? Are you here to be whipped?"

"Could you hide anywhere in the walls?"

"No, my boy, they are solid throughout the building, no exceptions. But there is another place, one that is a different story indeed, one with potential! Were I that Brontë woman who wrote those dreadful novels—"

"There were three Brontës, sir."

"The one who wrote that modern nonsense for moral reprobates about that lunatic woman, insane as a rabid dog, kept in that hidden apartment in that dreadful gothic mansion—"

"*Jane Eyre*?"

"That's the one! If I had a lunatic, whom I wanted to hide, I'd—" He pauses. "Not that I do, young man."

"I am sure you don't, Headmaster."

"I do *not*, you scoundrel, you can be sure of it! I am hiding *no* lunatic woman on these grounds! Do I make myself clear?" He made a motion to get up again, but fell back.

"Headmaster, I am—"

"Do you doubt me, young man? I HAVE NO LUNATIC WOMAN HIDDEN AWAY!"

"Yes, sir."

"Are you here for a whipping?"

"Where would you hide her?"

"Why, in the cellar, you fool."

The cellar. It's really only Usher who ever goes there, braving it to fetch bottles from its wine racks. The moans that seem to come from it at night are just the winds blowing low across the moors. If something were there, would Usher not see it?

"There's a hidden room down there," says Emeritus. Lear has never heard this. He leans forward. "A catacomb! Come even closer, Griswold, for I can only tell *you* this. It is an old secret passed down from the previous headmasters. I thought I wouldn't tell you. There is no need for you to know. It would just scare the boys. But since you are here—" He notices the moors through the window and completely nods off, snoring like he has a bass trumpet in his mouth.

"Sir!"

He comes awake with a start.

"Are you here to be whipped? Take down your trousers, under-clothing and all!"

"The room in the cellar, sir?"

"Oh, no one knows about that, boy. Why would I tell *you*! You *are* impertinent. Down with your trousers!"

"You would hide your lunatic woman where, sir?"

"*If* I had a lunatic woman! I am not saying that I have! Are you accusing me?"

"Yes, sir, I am. Tell me about the room or I shall expose you."

The old man pauses and examines him. "I do *not* have such a woman, but *if* I did I would put her at the far eastern end of the cellar where they built an ice room when the college was constructed in the 1590s. A fine school for boys, mind you!"

"They made an ice room? Because it was cool down there?" Lear thinks this strange because the college has an ice room deep in the ground just outside the gates.

"But it wasn't cool, lad, no."

"It wasn't?"

"It was as *hot* as hell, sir, as the devil's own home, so they filled in the doorway to it! And that is why no one knows it is there! You can see it if you search, though no one would dare to do that these days even if they knew it existed. It is filled in with modern cement and stones. Though I hear there are holes."

A room in the cellar, thinks Lear. He has what he needs.

21

The Cellar

They are moving quietly and quickly in the utter blackness of the ground floor of the college toward the cellar staircase, unlit lanterns in hand. They have Thorne's smaller gun, the rifle, and Jonathan has his pistol. Tiger is with them. She has taken up residence out on the moors and made it through the day, hiding the little cannon in a lonely shrub, too stubborn to take the train back to London. Jonathan had volunteered to go out there with some food and tell her their plan for investigating the cellar that evening. As the stroke of one o'clock on the school's big clock echoed throughout the building, they creaked open the front door for Tiger and closed it in the reverberation.

The professor leads the way in the darkness and Brim takes Lucy's hand. Tiger and Jonathan keep to themselves. The cellar door is at the back of the entrance hall, past the grand staircase and the doors to an office where Usher rules his porter's counter. Once you go by the stairs, two hallways run off on either side. It is there, close to the doors, so as to intercept anyone who might be trying to get in or out of the building, that the professors, every one of the dismal dozen, have their quarters.

Their snores are sawing back and forth, as if they are competing.

"I give you the Nose Orchestra of the College on the Moors," whispers Jonathan.

"Ssshh!"

Most of Lear's aging colleagues probably sleep so soundly that he and his young friends could fire their cannon down one of these hallways and none of them would awake. But Lear isn't sure. One loud sound could end everything.

The professors may or may not be listening as the five intruders move toward the rear of the main room, but someone else is most certainly aware of their presence. Henry Usher sits in his alcove with the lights out.

"It's here," says Tiger in the dark.

They are at the top of the cellar stairs. Lear gives the order.

"Lights."

Edgar, Jonathan and Lucy light the lanterns they carry. The bolt is large and thunders when Tiger pulls it back.

"Proceed," says Lear.

"Yes!" exclaims Jonathan under his breath. "Let the bad boy make his entrance!"

Lucy's grip on Edgar's hand tightens and it fills him with courage. He hopes she knows that.

They close the door behind them.

What would happen, thinks Edgar, if someone were to come along and lock it from the other side? The terrifying sensation of being confined reminds him not only of the little boy alive in his coffin but of Poe's story about premature burial, where the narrator calls out in the darkness of his grave, awaiting starvation and decomposition.

"Come on," he whispers, "let's get this done."

Tiger smiles at him.

The stairs go on forever. There are cracks in every step, causing the intruders to walk carefully, worried that the whole thing might collapse. When they reach the bottom, the scene before them is daunting. The massive cellar is dark and damp, and they hear water dripping into unseen pools. The strange howling that is heard distantly up above is louder here, moaning through this huge space. Shadows lurk on the only wall they can see: beside them on the staircase. The other walls are out there somewhere in the black distance. Edgar wonders if anyone could hear them scream down here. They are deep in the bowels of the moors.

They gaze around with open mouths. The monster could be near them now. Edgar begins to try to picture it, a faceless foe attacking them from behind and ripping them apart, eating them alive. Just my imagination, he tells himself.

"All right," says Lear, "Emeritus says the room is at the eastern end of the cellar." He points straight ahead. "That would be this way."

"Where is the wine cellar?" asks Tiger.

"Need a drink?" says Jonathan.

She ignores him. "It must be close to the staircase." They would all like to see some sort of guidepost. The wine cellar *should* be near. It is unbelievable that even Usher would come down here if he had to walk too far in this ghastly darkness.

Seconds later, they find the racks and wooden barrels, cobwebbed and mostly undisturbed in a little area built into the wall no more than twenty steps from the bottom of the stairs.

But then Lucy screams and kicks at something on her boot. She folds herself into Edgar, shaking. He can't believe how good this feels, so good that, to his surprise, *he* doesn't cry out. He just lowers the lantern. As he does, he catches Tiger's face in the light, looking their way, on the verge of a scream too, and then frowning. It surprises Edgar. He sometimes thinks Lucy has the right approach: she doesn't pretend she isn't afraid. Something is scurrying below, several things. They squeak.

"It's all right, Lucy. It's only rats," says Edgar.

"I hear they're tasty, sis," says Jonathan, though in the lantern light, Edgar can see that he is a little paler than usual too.

"Keep your eyes wide," says Lear. "Watch below you and in front. We can't afford another sound like that. Who knows how noises travel from here. Maybe it goes right up into the bedrooms. We may have warned whatever lurks down here too."

"I'm sorry," says Lucy.

"Not at all," says her grandfather. "These clowns would have screamed too. At least your voice doesn't carry as far. Females are stealthier too. I've told you before: I would rather have women with me in a pinch."

"Thanks again, sir," says Jonathan.

They move forward for another few minutes. It is difficult to believe that the cellar can be this large. It is as if they walk the full length of the college and then on past it and over the athletics field and out into the moors.

Cobwebs catch on their faces. Lucy doesn't make another sound, even when a rat runs up her leg. Edgar can swear that he hears Tiger and even Jonathan let out little noises of alarm, though they both stifle them quickly. He would be happy to be told at any minute that there is no secret room down here and they must turn around. But they can't.

They move on in silence. Edgar thinks again of the novel he is reading, and of the imprisoned hero in the grim castle, descending into its cellar too, seeking to escape his frightening captor. Earlier in its pages, Edgar had seen the terrifying old man through his window at night, crawling down the sheer drop of the side of the building, *face downward* with his cape billowing, glued to the wall like a spider! And there were witches in another room, strangely beautiful, with wet, red mouths, ready to fall upon him. When Edgar got to the castle's cellar, he found it was filled with vaults, and in them, coffins. He opened the biggest one and saw the old man inside, his eyes wide open.

They reach the eastern wall. But when they shine their lanterns on it, the surface is uniform everywhere. There is no sign of another room, sealed up or otherwise. They turn right and walk along the wall together, casting their lights up and down its rocks and crevices.

"We should try going the other way," says Tiger after a while.

"No," says Lucy. "I smell something. It smells different here."

Edgar isn't sure she is right. It still seems like the same damp, rat-infested atmosphere that has been invading their nostrils since the moment they entered the cellar. But he has read that women have a better sense of smell than men. Annabel Thorne can scent everything he has done: the professor's cigar smoke on his clothes when he comes home from college or even an extra sweet he has stolen from the kitchen. It is maddening. "You know, my son," she once told him with a smile, "young ladies will be able to smell others' perfume on you in a few years, so you had better be a loyal young fellow!"

They keep moving forward. Edgar begins to sense a different odor too. Tiger sniffs the air and nods at Lucy. "I think you're right."

Moments later they detect changes in the wall. It is discolored as if the rocks have been plastered in the last few decades rather than three centuries ago like everywhere else.

Lucy holds her lantern high.

"Up there!" she says.

There's a hole in the wall nearly eight feet up. It's not very large, less than two feet in diameter.

Edgar thinks he hears a sound behind them. "Quiet," says Lear and they all hold their breath for a moment and listen, but there is silence. "Let me examine the hole," whispers Lear. He takes Edgar's lantern and gazes up at the wall for a while. "Too small," he finally says.

"I can bust it up," says Jonathan, "make it bigger."

"Yes," says Tiger, "we could do that."

"How?" asks Lucy. "With what?"

Edgar looks down at Thorne's weapon. "Good point. Even this gun can't do it, not to this rock. All we'd likely do is alert someone."

"We need a big blunt tool," says Jonathan.

"And other than you, we don't have one," says Lucy.

"One of us simply has to squeeze through it," says Edgar. He can smell an acrid stench coming from it now.

He has grown too large for this job, Jon is out of the question, and Lear could barely get through the opening if it were five times the size and just a few feet off the ground. There are only two candidates, Tiger and Lucy.

"I'll go," says Tiger.

"If anyone tries, it should be Lucy," says Lear decisively. Tiger's face falls.

But the rest of them know that Lucy is the one for the job, or at least, she's the one to attempt it. She is slimmer than Tiger and wearing a heavy blouse with a loose cotton skirt like a peasant girl's with no hoops or crinoline underneath.

Edgar turns to Lucy. "Will you?"

"O-of," she stammers, "of course."

No one says it out loud, but they are all thinking it is one thing to simply make it through the hole, another thing to be on the other side. What will she find there? If she succeeds, she'll be alone and perhaps in imminent peril, perhaps sealed off with the demon. Lucy is holding her mouth tightly closed.

"But I'm not sure—" begins her grandfather.

"It makes the most sense for me to go," she blurts out. "You can boost me up." The consequences of not trying could be deadly, for everyone.

"I'll get her up there," say Edgar and Tiger at the same time. And a moment later he has one of her feet, Tiger the other, and Jonathan's hands are near her rear end, down low on her back. They push her up. Her head comes even with the hole. She has her lantern in one hand and grabs the rough edge of the opening with the other.

"Look in first," whispers Lear. "Can you see anything?"

"It's pretty dark, hard to tell. It smells awful. I'll just have to chance it."

The other three glance at Lear, who pauses for a second and then nods.

"Toss the lantern in first. Don't worry if it extinguishes. You have matches in your dress pocket, don't you?"

"Yes, Grandfather."

They see the hole in the secret room dimly lit for an instant and hear the lantern crash on its floor and then the hole goes dark again. Silence.

"It went out."

Lear is solemn for a moment and then nods again. They boost her up higher. Her chin is now at the hole.

"Push me up farther!"

They shove upward again and she gets her arms, head, shoulders and the curve down to her waist through the hole, but her hips catch.

"Ladies and gentlemen, I think we have a woman up there. Imagine that, my little sister, a real, live woman," declares Jonathan.

A look of resolve comes over Lucy's face. She twists and turns and struggles, trying to force her way in. Her sides scrape against the rough rocks. But she breaks through and plunges forward and disappears like a big stone dropped down a well. They hear a loud thump on the other side.

"Lucy?" asks Jonathan.

There is silence for a second and then the sound of a match striking. The hole is dimly illuminated again.

"Oh, my God!" Lucy sounds like she has her hand over her nose.

"What is it?" asks Lear.

"Someone has been in here. There's . . . there's a table here like, like an operating table or something, and chairs and all sorts of tools."

"Tools?"

"They've been used recently. No cobwebs. Chisels and scalpels and knives and a sledgehammer and . . . wait a moment . . . there's something on the floor." They can hear her start to move but then she stops. "There . . . are . . . shadows on the wall. I think there's something in here!" She sounds terrified.

"You have to get out!" cries Lear.

"No. No, it may be just the lantern throwing shapes. I'm going to walk over now and see what that is on the floor."

Her footsteps echo as she crosses the room. They all hold their breath. She stops suddenly. Then her quick bloodcurdling cry pierces the air and there is silence.

"LUCY!" cries Jonathan, and he and Tiger attempt to scale the wall on their own, leaping for the hole, trying to scramble upward in desperation.

"I'm . . . I'm all right," says Lucy. "I'm sorry."

They all stop and listen, but she's stopped talking. They can hear her breathing loudly and rapidly.

"Lucy, try to breathe normally," says Lear in what is as close to calming tones as he can accomplish. "Take a breath or two and then tell me what you are seeing."

"It's . . . it's—"

"It's what?"

"A—"

"A what?"

"A skeleton."

"What kind?"

"It's human."

They hear her sob and then stifle it.

"It's not very big."

22

The Secret Room

Inside the sealed catacomb, Lucy is trying to hold herself together.

"Don't be afraid," says Edgar.

But the monster may be in there with her. She swirls around, flashing the lantern's light through the room.

"We have to get in!" says Lear.

"Lucy, pick up the sledgehammer and hold it up to the hole so we can reach through and get it," says Jonathan. "Can you lift it that high?"

"I think so."

"I'll get on your shoulders," says Tiger to Jon. "See if you can hand it to me, Lucy."

With a heave, Tiger is standing on Jonathan. They can hear Lucy groaning as she tries to lift the big hammer up to the hole.

"I—I can't."

Tiger peers down into the room. "Just a little higher; you can do it."

Lucy grunts. "Excuse me," she says and grunts again, good and loud, and gets the hammer even higher. "Perfect," says Tiger and reaches down into the hole and seizes it. The two girls work together to raise it all the way up and through the opening. "Beware!" cries Tiger as she drops it over her shoulder. It crashes to the cellar floor.

"Oh, don't worry about the NOISE!" says Jonathan. Tiger doesn't seem to care.

"We've already raised quite a ruckus," says Lear, "and no one has come. Let's proceed."

"I'll do it," says Edgar and grabs the hammer. But then they hear a sound behind them, this time like the shuffling of feet. They swing their lanterns around and examine the cellar as far as they can see, holding their breath.

"What's happening?" asks Lucy.

"Nothing," says Lear who nods to Brim. "Continue."

Edgar begins to pound on the wall above his head with the sledgehammer, working on the bottom of the hole, swinging from shoulder height and upward with as much strength as he can muster. Each blow sounds like a gun going off.

"If they haven't heard us yet, they've heard us now," says Tiger.

Ten blows knock a few inches off the hole and render Edgar spent.

"Hey, Goliath, let me have a chance," says Jonathan.

Edgar gladly hands over the hammer.

"Good work, Master Brim," says Lucy from the catacomb. Tiger puts her arm around his waist and gives him a hard squeeze.

Jonathan makes progress immediately. He swings the sledge like Hercules and powers it at the wall. After a few strikes, he wipes his brow and unbuttons his shirt, baring his muscular chest. Tiger stares at him, but when he notices, she turns her attention back to the hole. He begins again and soon the opening breaks down and enlarges.

"You must have loosened it up, mate," Jonathan grins at Edgar.

A half dozen more blows and the hole is crumbling: three feet across and five feet tall, the bottom edge now low enough to climb over. They can see Lucy standing on the other side, looking relieved.

Jonathan sets down the hammer and they all step through, Lear helped over by the boys. The acrid smell is stronger in the room.

It is an eerie scene. With all their lanterns brought to bear, they can see that the catacomb is about a dozen feet by a little more, with a grisly table at its center and tools lying about, some on it, some on the ground.

"There's dried blood here," says Lear, as they shine a lantern directly on the table's surface. "This looks like a human fingernail, a whole one, and . . . part of a nose."

"Wh-what do you think happened in this room?" asks Edgar.

"I don't know, but whoever—or whatever—was in here has been here more than once." Lear is pointing at the ground where footprints, large and clearly evident, mark the floor as if whoever came to this chamber carried grime on his footwear; some of the dirt is dry while other clumps are still damp. Someone has *recently* been inside this *sealed* room in this forbidding cellar and has been coming back and forth for a while. But how could that be? Did a phantom walk through the wall or squeeze through that tiny hole? All five hunters are quiet, but they are thinking the same thing.

The creature came here.

And there, in the corner as if tossed to the side, is the skeleton. Lear kneels at it while the others gather above him. He examines it, as if it were a specimen in his lab. "A boy's," he says, "about five feet tall, maybe thirteen years old, dead for decades." The professor's hands begin to shake. He has noticed the skeleton's foot.

They hear another sound outside the room. They all turn. They see a shadow looming on the wall, moving slowly but without hesitation directly toward them! Tiger had set Thorne's rifle against a wall. She picks it up and aims it at the opening. Jonathan pulls his pistol from his pocket. The shadow grows. Edgar steps in front of Lucy and turns to face it. Do not be afraid, he thinks.

The footsteps stop and they can hear breathing. It is close, just beyond the opening and slightly to the side. It moves again, dimming its lantern's light and then they can make out the shape of its head clearly in shadow, huge and round

"Wait until you can see it clearly," whispers Lear, who has risen next to the skeleton and is staring in the direction of the approaching creature. "I told you, Brim . . . it wants us."

Tiger and Jonathan cock their guns.

It reaches the opening and peers in at them. The lantern held to its chest below its chin casts a round face in a ghastly light.

Usher!

"Stop or I'll fire," says Tiger.

Edgar steps toward the menacing porter. He isn't wary of him now and is ready to fight him with his bare hands, to the death.

"Miss Tilley?" says Usher. "I heard you had returned."

His voice doesn't sound right. He seems frightened. Edgar stops.

"Why are you pointing those weapons at me?"

"Why are you here, Henry?" asks Lear.

"I was about to ask you the same question."

Lear nods to Tiger and Jonathan to lower their guns.

Usher steps into the opening and enters the room. "I've never had the courage to come past the wine cellar."

"You haven't?" asks Edgar. Why had he always assumed that Usher wouldn't be afraid of the depths of this cellar? He is just like the rest of them, afraid of demons.

"What is that?" Usher motions to the skeleton.

The bones are just behind Lear, whose hands are beginning to shake again. "It's a friend of mine," he says.

The four young people look at him with surprise. Edgar shines his lantern at the skeleton too, bringing it clearly into view. A foot seems deformed. He notices something else on its chest and it nearly causes him to gasp, but he keeps it to himself.

"A student of mine named Erasmus Scrivener."

"Scrivener?" says Usher. "Why, he drowned himself in the lake many years ago. It was very sad. He was a delightful lad. I know you cared for him, Lear. But this can't be him."

"I know how tall he was, his age, that club foot, and the skeleton is decades old."

"You were away having your arm mended when he died, weren't you, Lear?"

"That's a nice way to phrase it, Mr. Usher," says Jonathan, glancing at his grandfather's empty sleeve, "but I don't think they quite mended it."

"But Mr. Usher just said he committed suicide in a lake, sir."

Edgar is trying to sound hopeful. Maybe this skeleton is centuries old.

"They never found his body."

"Grandfather," says Lucy, taking his hand, "that doesn't mean this is him."

"Emeritus said it was murder."

"Yes, well, he's a lunatic," says Jonathan. "Based on what you've told us, he's a few slices short of a full fruitcake."

"Sometimes it's the lunatics who tell us the truth."

"And sometimes they are simply off their nuts. Listen, if he said it was murder and no one else thought so, then maybe *he* did it and left the body here. He was a right old sadist around the boys, wasn't he?"

"He wouldn't kill one of them. He was too careful. He knew when to stop."

"So why did he say it was murder?" asks Tiger.

"I think, sometimes, when you are losing your mind, you say things you have had suspicions about, things that are deep in the lower consciousness of your brain. They just come out. He must have wondered why they couldn't find the body in the water. They dove for it. That lake isn't very deep. Maybe there were particularly disturbing things going on that year here, eerie things, perhaps boys talking about seeing a figure walking the moors, strange sounds coming from the cellar."

Usher glances around, as if something might be coming out of the darkness.

"Well," sighs Lucy, "there were certainly disturbing things happening the year before."

"Yes, my dear." The old man puts his left arm up to his right shoulder and touches the empty socket. Then he motions down at the skeleton. "And maybe that was why *this* happened the next year." His face is gray.

"The monster came here, searching for you," says Edgar, not disguising the concern in his voice.

"The *monster*?" asks Usher. He sounds frightened again.

"I believe so," says Lear.

They don't speak for a moment as Usher gazes down at the skeleton and around at the room, his mouth open.

Edgar is still looking at Lear. "It killed your beloved student instead."

"And I was afraid." The old man seems ashamed. "So I concocted my plan to keep it away from me, to save my life."

"Look!" says Tiger. She has been examining the room with her lantern as the others talk. "There's another hole here, down low, a big one!"

They advance to where she stands at the far wall and gather round her. There, illuminated now and as obvious as the nose on Spartan Griswold's face, is the entrance to a tunnel.

"I'm going in," cries Tiger and jumps like a rabbit into the hole.

"Keep up," says Lear quickly. "Lights at front and rear. Use your eyes and ears and noses. If you suspect anything and I mean *anything*, come to a complete halt and remain absolutely still. Brim, you go second with the gun cocked."

"Stop!" cries Usher.

Tiger backs out of the tunnel. The others turn to the porter too.

"A *monster*?"

"We can't say more, Usher, not yet," says Edgar.

"And you cannot tell others about anything you are seeing tonight," adds Tiger.

"Tell them what? That I have seen all five of you sneaking in and out of the college ever since the day you returned? Had I wanted to tell *others* I could have done that long ago. The others you speak of are angry and unhappy old men who have their fun terrorizing and injuring boys while pretending that they are making men of them. They have not an ounce of kindness or decency in their souls. I wouldn't be surprised if one of *them* was this monster you seek!" Lucy reaches for Edgar's hand. "I have no desire to tell them anything that you have done. I have always admired you, Professor Lear, far above the others." He turns to Edgar. "I have had the utmost respect for you too, Master Brim, and always thought well of you, brave Miss Tilley, though you were, to say the least, not quite what I thought you were."

"All of this is for a most honorable purpose, Usher," says Lear.

The porter takes a few steps around the room. "Over the years, I have heard horrible sounds coming from here." He pauses. "You have my blessing. I shall not interfere. In fact, I shall be your ally."

"That is much appreciated," says Lear.

"Tell me one thing. Was the little boy, the one in the infirmary, murdered too?"

"We think so."

He nods. "I shall lock the cellar door for you at the top of the stairs; rap hard on it tonight or anytime you might need to come out. I shall hear you and make sure no one else attends. Carry on."

He turns and makes his way slowly back along the cellar toward the staircase up to the ground floor.

The other five soon vanish into the tunnel: Lear crawling on his knees like the others, Tiger in the lead, Jonathan bringing up the rear with his pistol. Edgar imagines the demon appearing in front or behind them in here, where they can't escape.

It seems that they crawl forever. Their knees ache. It defies belief that the tunnel could be this long: running out under the moors for a mile or more from the ghastly catacomb beneath the college. What is on the other side? Edgar wonders. Finally, the tunnel turns sharply upward. There are iron rungs here forming a vertical ladder. They climb.

Tiger peeks out at the surface. "There's brush or something up here," she says. "I'll clear it out."

They emerge into a starlit night. A wildcat yowls. A heavy wind is blowing, but the sky is miraculously clear, a big dark dome over the land at the end of the world.

"It's right here," says the old man in a quiet voice.

They all turn to see what he's referring to. It is directly in front of them now, the water almost as black as the night. *The lake.*

They stand looking out over the water for a while.

"We could wait for it here at night," says Edgar.

"And render it seriously dead!" says Jonathan.

"But are we *sure* we know how to do that?" asks Tiger.

"I don't think waiting for it is the best plan," says Lear. "It may have purposely drawn us to the college. It's likely watching us. It may *want* us to leave someone here." The others survey the moors. "Who knows how often it comes here anyway. It doesn't seem to be living in that room. It may be trying to control us, lead us places."

"There was an indentation on his breastbone too," says Edgar.

"A what?" asks Lucy. "What are you talking about?"

"Scrivener's remains," says Lear.

Edgar is trying not to think of what this thing may have done here long ago, using the student's boots to make the prints that lead to the lake, perhaps with the lad's feet still in them, attached or severed.

"There was a hole," says the professor, "in Scrivener's chest."

A few hundred yards away, out of sight in the darkness, a large figure in a cloak is watching them, gripping William Wilson by the harness.

23

Back in the Graveyard

"Where on the moors will you be?" Edgar asks Tiger as they part company at the lake. He can't imagine staying out there in the darkness.

"Nowhere."

"You're heading home?"

"Absolutely not. I'm going back down the tunnel."

"You're what?" asks Lucy.

"I'll stay the night in that room."

"No!" Jonathan blurts but then closes his mouth quickly.

"I've made up my mind. I'll find a way to lug the cannon down there. I can go in and out through the tunnel or Usher will get me in by the cellar door. I'll see this thing if it comes and I'll kill it if I can. I'll be well equipped."

"I don't think that is a wise idea," says Lear.

"It may not be, but I'm doing it."

"No, you're not," says Edgar.

"And who is going to stop me? I've faced awful things before, Edgar Brim." In an instant, she is gone.

"I'll go after her," says Jonathan.

"And do what?" asks Lear. "Try to bring her back kicking and screaming? I don't think that is wise either."

"She'd shoot you," says Edgar.

Jonathan smiles. "Yes, she would."

Edgar stares up at the ceiling of his dorm room listening for noises from the cellar but hearing only Jonathan's slow pacing in the hallway. It is the bigger boy's turn on watch, but instead of sleeping Edgar is thinking of Tiger. What would this creature do to his dear friend? He imagines himself down there with her, the thing approaching, attacking like lightning. He sees it breaking their necks, cracking holes in their chests. Why does it open its victims' bodies at the heart?

He has to distract himself. He turns his head and sees the novel on his bed table. Dare he read it at night? At first, he looks away, but when he closes his eyes, he hears and sees Tiger being brutally murdered in the cellar, so he lights his lantern, picks up the book and begins to read. Immediately, he is inside the story again.

The hero escapes from the European castle. Back in England, his fiancée awaits his return. Her beautiful best friend is having nightmares, sleepwalking, and something has been entering her bedroom through her window. She is seen in a graveyard at night talking with a tall, shadowy figure. Her nightmares grow worse. The frightening old man from the castle seems to be in England now, observed in the streets! Edgar stops reading and rises. He decides to go out into the hallway to keep company with Jonathan.

"Do you want me to take your place?" he asks Jon. "I can't sleep."

"No sugar plum fairies dancing through your dreams?"

"Go to bed. I'll get Lucy up at three."

Jonathan hesitates. But then he turns to his room, opens the door, retrieves the rifle and hands it to Edgar, who sets it inside his own door. When he turns back, Jonathan is still in the hallway. "Do you think Tiger is going to be all right?" It is a hard question for him to ask.

"I've known her a long time, Jonathan, and I think she will be fine," says Edgar.

Jon offers a slight smile and turns back to his room. "Just asking. Enjoy yourself, Brim!"

Edgar doesn't pace in the hallway, but stands still, listening. He hears the wind howling over the moors and thinks there are sounds coming up from the cellar again. What if he went down the stairs into the entrance hall and then into the cellar, down those long stairs to the secret room? What would he find there? Would he see Tiger's corpse, her eyes still open, a hole in her chest? Would the monster be waiting for him? *Do not be afraid.* He must help his friend.

He begins to walk toward the stairs.

He hesitates on the landing, unsure whether to continue. If he leaves, the rooms up here will be unguarded. If Lear is correct, their group is being observed, and this phantom might somehow know that he has left and murder Lucy and Jonathan in their beds, two unexplained deaths just like the boy's in the infirmary, swept under the rug by—he thinks about it—Griswold.

There's a window on the landing that looks out over the back grounds. Is that a light? He leans over the stone sill, the surface cold on the palms of his hands, and squints through the thick glass. There it is again. *Someone is out there!* He doesn't know what to do. Go downstairs to the cellar or sneak out to the graveyard or wake Lear?

He hits on a plan. He turns back and approaches Lucy's door and quietly opens it. There she is in bed, her lovely form wrapped tightly in her blanket, her arms bare. For a moment, he just stares at her: Lucy Lear, dreaming. The sensation of being in her bedroom with her as she sleeps mixes with the adrenaline already shooting through him and thrills him. He thinks of the young woman in the novel he's reading, attacked by a creature who craves females, attacked in her nightdress as she sleeps. He shakes it from his mind.

"Lucy!" he whispers.

She rouses and sits up, pulling the covers over herself.

"Edgar? Why are you in here?"

"There's someone in the graveyard," he says. "Get up. I'll wake Jonathan. We'll bring the rifle and pistol. We'll need you out there."

"Get my grandfather."

"No. It's too risky. We'd have to go down to the professors' chambers, past the others, and rouse him. We have to do this alone."

Ten minutes later, after sneaking out the big front doors, they turn the corner around the far side of the building and head toward the graveyard.

"Look!" says Jonathan.

There it is: a light, very still, near the back of the cemetery, past the disintegrating old granite crosses and stones, black from the unforgiving weather.

They approach carefully, Edgar with the rifle, Jonathan his pistol and Lucy with her senses alert in the night. As they get nearer, they can see a shadowy figure, vaguely human and down on its knees beside the little boy's grave. They stop and nod at each other. Edgar puts the weapon to his side but silently cocks it.

They move slower now. Edgar wonders why in the world they came without Lear. They should have chanced waking the other professors. But they can't turn around. The figure in the graveyard might hear them and they can't put their backs to it. They draw within ten feet and one of Jonathan's boots connects with a stone and kicks it across the yard. The thing turns. They halt. Edgar raises the gun, pointing it straight at the figure's head.

"Who's there?" it asks and rises to its feet, towering over them, some two heads taller than even Jonathan. They shrink back, but hold their weapons steady.

A pale face glares at them, lips scarlet, long teeth in a wet mouth. It is a remarkable transformation. Lovecraft is three feet taller than his normal height. An image from the yellow-covered novel flashes through Edgar's mind.

"I said, who's there!" The professor sounds angry.

"It's . . . it's me, Edgar Brim, and the Lears. What are you doing here?" He slides the gun back to his side but keeps his finger on the trigger.

"The grave looked as if it was disturbed," says the vampire, turning back toward the little boy's resting place again. "Or is it my imagination?" He holds his head as if it will burst and Edgar sees the skull's strange, almost inhuman shape. Is that its *real* shape? It certainly isn't Lovecraft's. He thinks of what the professor is impersonating and of the holes in the two young chests, right over their hearts . . . where the blood pumps from the body's vital organ.

"I—I doubt it's . . . it's been disturbed."

"Why are *you* here?" says the creature. "You should not have come!" It doesn't sound like Lovecraft. Maybe it *isn't* him? thinks Edgar. Maybe it never is.

Lucy moves behind Edgar, and Jonathan steps forward, trying to stand up straight as an arrow. His voice shaky, he calls out, "Why? Do you intend us harm?" His hand is on his pistol. "Because we will—"

"Harm? Why no, Master Lear." Lovecraft's voice is instantly sad. "Why would I mean any of you harm?"

"You sounded upset," says Edgar, pulling the gun behind him.

"I am."

"Why?"

Lovecraft sighs. "I suppose I must tell you."

"You will," responds Jonathan, "or I will force you."

"Jon, let him speak," says Lucy.

"It's about this little boy." He turns to the grave again and a sob erupts from him and when he turns back his eyes are filled with tears. Lucy goes to him and puts her hand on his arm. The other two stay put.

"Thank you, my sweet child. You are a true granddaughter of Hamish Lear, a dear man." Lucy can see now that Lovecraft has done something to his head with rags and bandages to create its unusual shape and painted it to make it whiter. "I was sure there were boys in the halls tonight whom I needed to shoo back to their rooms." He drops down onto his knees again and pulls up his cloak and starts unfastening something at his feet. He glances up at Edgar. "You were very kind."

"I was?"

"To my nephew."

"I don't know what—"

"I wouldn't tell any student but you, Master Brim, but I can trust you, I know." Lovecraft stops working on his feet and turns back to the grave. He starts to sob again. "The dead boy was my sister's son. He should never have been here. You yourself know it is not easy to gain admittance to the College on the Moors, but I arranged it at the insistence of my brother-in-law, the fool!" He looks down. "No one knew the child and I were related, not even Griswold. That sort of thing isn't allowed, so I couldn't say anything. It broke my heart when he died and I wept terribly at the funeral."

"That is nothing to be ashamed of, sir. You showed you cared."

The little professor tugs on his boots again and finally unfastens something. He stands up and has lost three feet in height! He pulls a handkerchief from his pocket, spits on it, and rubs his eyes and mouth. Gobs of white paint, makeup and lipstick come off on the cloth. He rips off some tape and takes down the bulbous shape from the top of his head. Reginald Lovecraft is not only the college's superb literature professor but also master of the Drama Club and director of the school plays, with access to all the greasepaint and costumes he can lay his hands upon.

"Your impersonation is extraordinary, sir," says Lucy. "But how—"

"This is how, Miss Lear." He holds up the two items he has

unhitched from his feet—stilts, each nearly a yard high. "I was a stilt walker as a boy, quite good at it; father said I should have been in the circus. I can practically glide on them!"

Edgar remembers him swooping down the halls like a ghost.

"I won't forget your kindness to my nephew, Master Brim, I won't." He is on the verge of tears again.

"It was nothing, sir." Edgar steps closer to Lovecraft. "I felt for him because I had struggled too. He did not deserve what happened to him. He was the victim of . . ." he pauses, wondering what Lovecraft might say.

"It was a rare heart condition, Brim."

Edgar doesn't respond.

"But you didn't answer my question," says Lovecraft. "Why are you here?" He examines them closely. "Is that a gun, Brim? A rifle? What sort of . . . Why are you . . ." He stares at Edgar. Again, the boy doesn't know what to say.

"We—"

"We couldn't sleep," says Lucy. "We saw a light down here from our hallway. We thought there was an intruder. The gun belongs to a friend of Jonathan's. I know it has an unusual appearance. It's for shooting . . . wildcats."

"Wildcats?"

"Yes, sir, wildcats and hares. It could kill a wolf too."

"There are no wolves on the moors."

"Shall we make our way back?"

They walk together: Edgar carrying the rifle out of sight; Jonathan holding the pistol in his pocket; and Lucy keeping Lovecraft talking, charming him with her smile.

Partway along their return Edgar sees that the light is on in the driver's stable. For an instant, it seems there are two figures in there, both cloaked, exactly the same size. Must be Driver's shadow, thinks Edgar.

24

Graduation

The Vampyre, the Frankenstein monster and the devil are walking the hallways of the College on the Moors the following evening. So are Captain Nemo, Scrooge and the Red Death, everyone heading downstairs to the Great Dining Hall where the tables have been pulled to the walls for the Moors Ball. It is the night before graduation. No one ever dances. An orchestra made up of several members of the dismal dozen, among them John the Baptist, Sir Walter Raleigh and Henry VIII, is playing what are supposed to be lovely tunes. Tasty treats of iced sweets, biscuits, chocolates and lemon drinks are in abundance.

But Professor Lear and his four young colleagues aren't enjoying themselves. In another day and a half, everyone will be gone from the college, and that may be all the time they have to find and kill their enemy, or for it to kill them. Tonight, it could come here in disguise.

Edgar isn't sure whom Lear is portraying and he doesn't ask. But the professor is disturbingly like the villain in his yellow book, dressed up in an evening suit, his face white as if he were undead. Edgar read more of the novel during the day, its old villain lurking in England, taking on different shapes, appearing and disappearing near the hero's wife and her beautiful friend. The friend has grown so pale and weak that they fear she is dying. Edgar knows it will happen soon. The old man, the demon, is somehow slowly killing her.

Tiger spent a wary, sleepless night in the cellar and is with them at the ball. She couldn't resist coming and they need her. She's here as the Invisible Man, the lead character in H.G. Wells's latest novel. She has wrapped her face in gauze, gloved her hands, tucked her hair up under her hat and is wearing men's clothing. In her characterization, the Invisible Man doesn't speak, so though several students and professors try to guess her identity, she simply waves them off.

Lucy is Cinderella, and Edgar thinks she makes a lovely one, especially with her wrist in the arm of Sherlock Holmes, Arthur Conan Doyle's ridiculously popular character. It didn't take much for Edgar to put that persona together, as hair dye, suits and pipes were easy to find in Lovecraft's Drama Club wardrobe. Vampires are all the rage in the hall tonight. Grendels, a Big Bad Wolf and even witches approach him to see how he will react. The legend of the younger frightened Edgar lingers at the college. But he merely glares at them, even shoves them away, though he may be sorely tested if a hag floats by.

The dashing Allan Quatermain, hero of thrilling African adventure novels, is keeping close to the Invisible Man. He is wearing his wide-brimmed hunter's hat, his billowing white shirt has several buttons undone, bullet belts cross his chest, and tight trousers and high boots grip his strong legs.

"We need to circulate," says Edgar. "Figure out who everyone is."

They move through the crowd and spot Fardle and his followers. Wearing a floppy hat and brandishing a sword, the large boy makes a beeline for Brim. His pencil-thin mustache curls upward as he grins, the sword in ready position. But Lucy begins to laugh and can't stop, and neither, inside her gauze, can Tiger. Maggett, Smith and Jones as the Three Musketeers are ridiculous enough, but Fardle as the romantic D'Artagnan is just too much for a girl to take. Embarrassed, Fardle backs off. He points his sword at the Invisible Man and hisses, "I'll find out who *that* is!"

"You can't stay long, Tiger," says Edgar, as soon as his old enemy disappears. "Someone is sure to figure out who you are."

Griswold doesn't seem to be in the room, though he may be ingeniously costumed. Some years he doesn't dress up at all. Where is he? Edgar wonders.

"It could be one of them," says Jonathan, eying several tall vampires clustering near the red punch decanter.

"Look," says Lear, motioning upward with his head.

In the gallery at one end of the Great Dining Hall, a lone figure has appeared—Driver. He jams his long frame into a seat a few rows back and begins observing, un-costumed, emotionless.

"*He's* the one always watching," says Edgar. "I'm going up there!"

"No," says Lucy, reaching out for him. But he is gone. The others follow through the Great Dining Hall to the door that leads to the balcony and pound up the creaking wooden stairs like an army. Jonathan has his hand on his pistol.

"Too fast!" says Lear partway up. "We need to be ready."

They slow and Edgar opens the door at the top cautiously. He slips through and sees the lone figure, now sitting in the front row, observing people below. They approach. The figure turns.

"Headmaster!" says Lear.

"What are you doing here?" asks Jonathan before he can stop himself.

"Well," says Griswold, "I am the headmaster of the College on the Moors and I'm allowed to attend our functions. This is quite a search party. What do you want?"

"Nothing."

He eyes them. He is wearing dark monk's robes, his head partially covered. His bone-colored, insect face peers at them under wisps of white hair, studying their expressions.

"I would prefer if all of you would confine yourselves to your rooms tonight," he says.

"Where else would we go?" asks Lear.

"Oh, I don't know—perhaps for another stroll on the moors to the farmhouse or an exploration of the graveyard?"

They don't respond.

"I could have sworn there were five of you."

Tiger, who was in the rear, has slipped away and already descended the stairs and will soon re-enter the cellar with Usher's help.

"No, only four," says Edgar. "Just came up to greet you, sir."

"You have changed, Master Brim."

"Thank you, sir."

Griswold fixes him with a stare. "But don't grow too bold. That wouldn't be wise." He jingles something in his pocket, a habit of his: the master keys to the college, which open every door, including the one to the infirmary.

"We shall be on our way, sir," announces Lear, shepherding the others away with his arm.

As they leave they notice Driver. He somehow sneaked unseen to the top of the gallery while they were ascending the stairs and is in the shadows, his head deep in his hood, only his mouth apparent. He points a long bony finger directly at Griswold's back.

They spend the night splitting the watch. Nothing happens, until sunrise. Edgar is on duty when he hears the scream. It comes not from the cellar but somewhere high in the college and is gone in an instant. It sounds like a man's voice. In fact, Edgar could swear it is Griswold's.

At breakfast they hear of Edward Emeritus's death in the night. But it is graduation day and the show must go on. There must be a ceremony and the boys must be readied to leave for their homes. Driver cleans the ancient headmaster's corpse and builds him a crude wooden coffin. While he works in the stable, the dismal dozen gather on a dais in front of their students on the back lawn, handing out certificates, the headmaster presiding. Tiger has made it through another night in the cellar and slipped out through the tunnel to the lake at dawn. Now she sits halfway across the moors, watching the ceremony with her binoculars. Edgar is observing Spartan Griswold closely as he takes his certificate from the headmaster's huge hand.

His imagination is racing. Could it really be *him*? He thinks about the fact that the headmaster is always the last to leave the college at the end of each year. Is he daring them to stay behind and confront him tomorrow when everyone else but the speech-less driver is on the train heading south?

Driver brings Emeritus's body down from the tower and places it in the coffin he has made. He sets the coffin on a table in the Great Dining Hall and opens it for viewing. Another night descends. Tiger crouches with her gun in the cellar. The other four lie awake or stand on watch, but no one comes.

The next morning, everyone files past the coffin to offer their respects. Griswold chooses Lear to help him bid farewell to the staff and students, and late that afternoon, the two of them stand on the front steps and watch the others depart. The cadaverous headmaster merely nods to his charges. Lear says good-bye to a few and shakes his colleagues' hands. He keeps his distance from Griswold. Down in the cellar, Tiger folds up the cannon. Edgar, Jonathan and Lucy are staying close together, ostensibly helping clean up the laboratory. They've made a vow to not let each other out of sight.

Every year, a remarkable scene occurs on the last day of school at the College on the Moors. Most of the students walk all the way from the dark building to the Altnabreac Station, more than one hundred and fifty of them, all but the youngest students, trekking miles across the moors on the rough gravel road, the professors and other school employees with them, trailing their possessions on ancient homemade carts that the students leave at the station for Driver to bring back. He also takes some of the smaller boys to the train in his black carriage.

The snaking procession is a quarter-mile long, observed

surreptitiously by the wildcats and moles, and by the hawks and vultures that hover up above.

In Lear's classroom, Edgar, Jonathan and Lucy put away test tubes and mortars and pestles, but their talk is of something else.

"We can't just kill him," says Lucy. "We have no proof it—"

"Sure we can," says Jonathan.

"What if we were merely murdering a man named Spartan Griswold?"

"Big loss."

"This would be a perfect place for an aberration to hide. He's been here forever. Maybe that's why Grendel came here," says Edgar. "It really could be him or he's somehow under its power. But Lucy's right. I can't imagine—"

"Blowing his head clean off," says Jonathan.

"Yes, that."

"I can imagine it. I'm imagining it right now. We can't let him attack us."

"He's out there with grandfather on the front steps, isn't he?" asks Lucy. "So he isn't in his office. It's empty, unguarded."

Edgar immediately understands what she is thinking.

Tiger can't sit still. Whatever might be happening is happening without her. She creeps out of the room in the cellar, wondering if she should chance sneaking up the stairs and into the entrance hall to take a look. In the darkness, she spots something at the foot of the stone staircase, a bag or a sack. It is blocking the way. She approaches . . . then freezes. *Usher!* She stares down at him. His bald head is bloodied and bashed in from behind. There's a dark pool under him near his chest. Tiger bends down and gently touches his pale face. It feels cool; he's been dead for a while. She turns and strides back toward the room and is soon rushing the cannon up the stairs to the cellar door, thudding it on each step, not caring about its heavy weight.

"Come with me to the headmaster's office," says Edgar to Lucy.

A slight wave of uncertainty crosses Jonathan's face. "We should stick together. I mean, I'm all right with being alone, of course, but grandfather said we shouldn't be apart, didn't he?"

"You have the rifle, don't you?" asks Lucy.

Edgar is getting excited. "Griswold's office is on this floor. We can be there in seconds. He doesn't lock his door. We can go through his files. If he's more than just the headmaster, it might be obvious quickly."

"I don't know," says Jonathan.

"Then we can shoot him," says Lucy, "without thinking twice."

"Well, if you put it that way," smiles Jon, turning to get the rifle from where it lies under his coat at the back of the room. Each classroom's door has a window in it. The lab is at a *T* in the hallways and from it Jonathan, gun out and ready, can see all the way to the headmaster's door. "I'll watch from here."

Almost instantly, Edgar (pistol concealed in his pocket) and Lucy are out in the hall and down to Griswold's office. They open the door and sneak inside.

Tiger moves quickly along the ground floor, rolling her weapon behind her. When she reaches the bottom of the staircase, she looks to her right to the open front doors and sees the headmaster's long back at the top of the steps, Lear just below him, the snaking procession of students in the distance winding through the moors. She heads up the staircase, her lean muscles straining, dragging the wheeled, boxed-up little cannon with her. She goes up to the third floor and finds Lear's classroom, not seeing Edgar and Lucy moving in the other direction toward Griswold's office. Jonathan is standing just inside the lab door, on guard at the window, rifle held at the ready. He smiles, lowers the weapon, and opens the entrance.

"Usher is dead—murdered," Tiger says grimly as she pushes past him. His smile fades. He turns away from the door, forgetting about Lucy and Edgar. "But I've brought this," she says, motioning to the cannon.

When the last student has left, Griswold turns to Lear.

"We are alone, Hamish, just you and I."

And I am unarmed, thinks the professor. Why did I put myself in this position?

"Oh, I'm sure the students could still hear us, sir, were we to shout."

"Yes, perhaps you are right. Well, almost alone." He offers a smile. "Staying long?" He takes a step toward his underling, his right hand thrust out.

"No . . . no need to say good-bye now, sir," says Lear. "I will take the evening train tonight. See you then?"

Griswold stops and seems disappointed. Then a thought appears to come to him. "Are your lot within earshot as well?" He glances toward the open door and then out to the disappearing students, as if calculating when they won't be able to hear them.

"I believe," says Lear, stepping around Griswold while he is turned and adroitly getting past him before he turns back, "they are upstairs, perhaps in the hallway watching for my return right now." He hopes that sounds believable. With his back to Griswold, he moves smartly up the steps and into the college.

"Wait for me?" asks Griswold.

"Ah, much work to do, sir. You know me, busy bee!"

He almost races the headmaster up the stairs. They ascend two flights before Lear turns around near his classroom. He can call out to his allies from here, and they have the rifle and pistol. Oh, that they had Thorne's cannon too!

He notices that Griswold's face is awfully red. He is heaving with the effort of climbing, not like him. Or is it something else?

Edgar and Lucy haven't gone through more than a few papers when they hear a noise in the hallway. It sounds like a door opening and closing.

"That doesn't make sense," she says, freezing.

"Jon is on the lookout. He'd do something if Griswold were coming. He has the rifle."

They turn back to the papers, but in a minute they hear another sound: two people, four feet, moving fast, reaching the top of the stairs in this very hallway!

"Two people?" asks Lucy. "Everyone is gone except—" She looks terrified.

We only have a pistol, thinks Edgar, but he doesn't say it.

"Are you all right, sir?" Lear asks Griswold.

"I . . . I am fine, just heading to my office." He barks it out with great effort.

Edgar, Lucy, Jonathan and Tiger all hear Griswold utter those words and for an instant they can't move. Lear smiles and bids farewell, but he checks over his shoulder as the old man walks toward his office. He doesn't want to be attacked from behind. Lear opens his classroom door and is shocked to see both Jonathan and Tiger moving toward him: he cocking the rifle, she reaching for the cannon to unfold it.

"They're in his office!" exclaims Jonathan under his breath.

Edgar pushes Lucy behind him and takes out the pistol. I'll be killed first, he thinks. It has to be me, that's the right thing to do, and maybe she can get away. Do not be afraid.

He puts his finger on the trigger.

Jonathan reaches the door first, though Tiger has the cannon unfolded in a flash. Fully confident in her ability to use it to the height of its deadly capability, she is ready to take off a skull. Jonathan can fire the rifle well. It has six expanding bullets. Every one to the head, he thinks. But as he is about to rush through the door into the hallway to get a clean shot, Lear pushes him back into the room, motioning for both Jonathan and Tiger to stay away from the door. Griswold has stopped just a few feet from his office.

Lear wonders if he can either steer his boss away or at least draw his attention until Edgar and Lucy can escape.

"Sir, may I be of assistance?"

Griswold turns to face him. "Not feeling well, Lear. I think I may descend to my chambers and lie down."

The professor has never heard Griswold say such a thing. The headmaster returns to the stairs and heads toward the ground floor.

Two minutes later, they are all in the lab, trying to take in the news about Usher. Lear tells them to stay calm and Edgar nods at him and draws a deep breath. Then Lear lets all his charges know how displeased he is that they disobeyed him, and quietly sets out instructions. He too wishes he could take Griswold by surprise and destroy him, but the old headmaster actually looks vulnerable now, ill and tired. Is he really the force that did all this, the creature they seek?

"Brim, you and Lucy go back to his office and see what you can find. Tear things apart if you must. If you can't discover anything in a few minutes, come back."

"What about me?" ask Tiger and Jon together.

"You two stay here with the cannon ready and the rifle cocked. I want you to be prepared to fire accurately at a moment's notice."

Jonathan and Tiger both smile.

"What about you?" asks Lucy.

"I'm going upstairs."

Lear ascends to the highest floor at as quick a pace as he can manage. From there, he'll climb to the turret formerly occupied by Edward Emeritus, and search the stacks of papers scattered around that room. Records, *private* records. Emeritus saw, heard and recorded everything that happened at the College on the Moors for most of the last eighty years. Lear thinks there may be a Griswold file with information about where he came from, or something else. Surely, there is a great deal to discover about the headmaster, easy to find in minutes. That, along with what Edgar and Lucy can uncover should tell them what they need to know. If not, they must simply act.

But before Lear reaches the top of the last flight, he glances behind and notices something moving up the stairs, a tall figure coming after him at a brisk pace.

Griswold!

The headmaster's face has turned purple, he is perspiring, the cords on his neck are standing out, and he is making horrific sounds, groaning and moaning as he glares up at Lear. His giant frame and skeletal head seem to be transforming!

"STOP!" Griswold shrieks. It is an almost inhuman sound.

Lear runs. He reaches the final little staircase up to the Emeritus turret. It ends right at the door, just a small landing in front of it. He is cornered!

"LEAR!" the demon bellows.

The professor looks back over his shoulder. The face is completely unlike Griswold's. Lear feels this is what has been watching him ever since he came to the moors. This is what *it* looks like. It isn't anything he recognizes, no villain from a novel. Or is it? Does it have the powers of something well known? Why did it make holes in its victims' chests?

The guns! But they are far away.

Down below, the others hear Lear shout and take off running. Tiger and Jonathan leave the heavier cannon behind but bring the rifle loaded with expanding bullets. All four meet at the stairs. They hear a loathsome sound up above. Griswold, the monster, is grunting and wheezing, thudding up the stairs at Lear.

The professor is right next to the door now. Opening it and going inside won't help. He turns to face his killer.

"LEAR! I WILL STOP YOU!"

Griswold staggers up the last three steps and towers over his enemy. Lear remembers how he fought another monster long ago. That was what made this one come after him. But Lear had a weapon then and was young and vigorous. He wishes now that he had never done it.

The headmaster's face turns gray.

"You can't . . . I don't want you to see . . ." His hand is on his chest, clutching at it. He is gasping for breath. He reaches for Lear.

"NO!" cries Lucy from below. Tiger rips the gun from Jonathan and trains it on Griswold's skull. Take off the head, she thinks. But the target disappears.

Griswold's left hand falls down at his side and quivers. He bends forward, swoons and collapses on the floor.

"Are you *him*?" asks Lear, standing back.

"H-him?" gasps Griswold up at him.

"Are you the monster?"

"I . . . I am ill . . . embarrassed . . . you cannot see our records . . . we did immoral . . ."

"Ill?"

"What are you after, Lear? . . . Why?" His eyes fill with tears. "Where is Usher?"

"You're dying!" exclaims the professor in shock.

"I am sorry," Griswold gasps. "It's bad . . . form."

Tiger lowers the gun and all four run up to the landing. Lear is bending over the headmaster now, his hand over his heart.

"He's dead," he says.

"He can't be," says Lucy.

"He's had a . . . heart attack?" Lear stares at Griswold in disbelief.

"It wasn't him," says Edgar. Supernatural creatures don't die of weak hearts. Edgar rips open the old man's shirt. There's no hole in the wrinkled skin on his chest over his heart. He's just an ancient human being, cruel at times and with secrets, but dead the way every other mortal will be, one day. All five of them sink to the floor.

As he sits there, Edgar thinks about a hooded man who never speaks, who pointed a finger at the headmaster, who they assumed was pitiful, helpless, perhaps used by the monster Griswold and afraid of him, wanting him dead. Edgar thinks of this man's bloodless face, the keys he *also* has to many rooms in the college, including the infirmary. He thinks of his lack of human emotion, how he is always watching . . . how he is now the only other living being at the college.

Lucy is trembling. "It's Driver," she says.

"But if that's so, why didn't it kill us all when it had us alone in the carriage the day we came back to the moors?" asks Tiger.

"Because it's smart," says Edgar. "There were others waiting for us at the college."

Lear's voice is low. "It wanted clean kills, incidents that seem like accidents."

"Like with Master Newman," adds Edgar.

"That don't have to be explained, my dear," says Lear.

"It has us alone again," says Lucy, "completely alone now." Her eyes are large.

They leave Griswold's body on the landing outside Emeritus's door and sneak down the stairs as though every one of their steps is being heard and are relieved to make it to the laboratory alive. "Bolt the door," commands Lear. They do, and then Edgar and Jonathan shove the professor's big desk in front of it. They don't hear a sound anywhere in the college. The building feels like a corpse, without a beating heart and no blood in its veins. The creature has them cornered.

25

Meanwhile

Far to the south, Bram Stoker is sitting in a front row seat at the Lyceum watching Henry Irving in the final dress rehearsal for *Faust*. The banners have been out for more than a week. It opens tomorrow. The master had tried *Richard III* last month and it had been one of his few failures, his portrayal too depraved for even the child-murdering hunchback king. They had stopped the production and substituted *Faust*—they still have the costumes and the black-and-white set from the long run that had electrified London in the 1880s. In rehearsals, Irving has been brilliant. They will do it for just a few weeks.

"You are a master in this role," Stoker says to him, lighting upon the stage as the scene ends. He gives Ellen Terry a wink. She smiles at him like a sister and offers Irving a different sort of look. Oh, that she would ever glow at him like that! He has Irving's dressing gown in hand, had been holding it ready in the seats, and drops it gently over Irving's shoulders. But the chief is barely paying attention.

"Yes, yes, Stoker. I am going to my rooms and don't want to be disturbed. Not even by Miss Terry. Please inform my lady, my good man." His face is drawn and white. It is angular, the chin long, the forehead high and sloping. He isn't really handsome, but there is something about him, something indeed.

"Yes, sir."

Stoker had hoped to ask his boss about his novel. He wonders if the master has read it by now. He had deposited a copy on Irving's dressing table, its lurid yellow cover and blood-red title looking perfect in the gaslight. It is his greatest work. He knows that like he knows he is living and breathing. He imagines them having a cigar and brandy in the wood-paneled Beefsteak Room and discussing it, Irving heaping it with praise, or talking it up during one of the dinners he convenes on the stage, attended by the glittering stars of London. There haven't been many of those lately.

"I don't dare even open your new book, Uncle Bram," says Ellen, approaching him. She likes to call him pet names. Her beautiful oval face and the gray eyes that entrance every man who sees them, smile at him. London has been at this woman's feet since she was a girl. Audiences sigh when she enters. Her voice is sweet and slightly husky.

Stoker shakes himself out of his reverie.

"Why ever not, dear one?"

"They say it is terrifying."

"It is my best."

"You say that with some conviction, not like you, uncle. But I've heard talk of it in my circles." She caresses his arm. "I am proud of you." Ellen is notorious—she flirts with everyone and they flirt back.

"I spent years on it."

"Not like you either."

"Yes, I am a hack, but I wasn't with this. It consumed me. Some sort of spirit ate me up." He stares off.

"Uncle?" she asks. "Are you in there somewhere?"

"Sorry, just thinking. I must run. I need to speak with him."

"Why don't you and I meet for a drink instead?"

It is a tempting proposition. But he knows she will only talk of Irving.

"He is a strange man," says Stoker, turning toward the floor Sir Henry had walked upon when he headed for his dressing room.

"Devilishly strange," says Terry with a smile. "He said not to disturb him. Are you sure you want to?" Long ago, Irving's wife had made a nasty comment about one of his performances and he had instantly left their carriage and walked out into the night and hadn't spoken to her or been near her since: a stretch of some twenty-six years.

"I shall take my life into my hands."

Irving, it seems to Stoker, has been growing even stranger and more disturbing lately. They had met long ago in Dublin when Bram was a theater critic. Irving had awed him. And lo and behold, the great man had liked him too. So much has happened since then. Stoker thinks of the chief's many riveting roles—his blood-soaked Macbeth while the Ripper stalked London, his unusual Hamlet, his shocking Shylock, his Beckett and King Arthur. He thinks of his knighting by the queen. An actor! Irving had said he would be the first and he was.

But Stoker also thinks of his master's sinister ways: their days in northern Scotland on the moors as he became Macbeth before his eyes; their visits to the dead houses in Paris to see corpses,

Irving grinning at them, learning for his art; their days on ships across the Atlantic when he won over America, standing on the deck in twenty-foot rolling waves, his arms crossed over his chest, smiling at God or the devil to have their way. Stoker thinks too of the conversations he has heard coming from Irving's dressing room . . . when the master was *alone* in there. Sir Henry could encounter someone for just a few minutes and then *become* him. That had to be what it was—he was speaking to himself in there, taking on other voices for conversation. But Stoker had heard one voice over and over again—an old man, and foreign.

Stoker had used the master in his novel. Irving was the villain. He wouldn't apologize for that. It just made sense. When he had first gone up to Cruden Bay on the Scottish coast three years ago to write it, the waves coming off the coast like cannonball shots, spooky Slains Castle nearby, a supernatural undead man had come to him like a dream, a nightmare, and he had begun to put a story down as if it had been handed to him by Satan. When he saw Irving's face in that character, the story deepened. Inventing that terrifying world had been an almost erotic experience. It was art—he was sure of it. He, Bram Stoker, had conjured up art! It was of the sort the master created on stage. It had seemed real to him. It told a truth about life, though he wasn't even sure what it was. He had written as if mesmerized, as entranced as when he watched Irving perform.

Stoker walks along the corridor behind the stage at the Royal Lyceum: *his* Lyceum and his master's. He needs to see him. As he approaches, he hears voices: Irving apparently conversing again, speaking with the old, foreign man. The character sounds alive!

———

Back on the moors, Edgar Brim plucks the novel out of his jacket pocket and enters its pages, in order to steel himself for what he must face. In the book, he is the hero again, home with his wife, traumatized by his terrifying experience in the eastern European castle. His wife's beautiful friend has died and the circumstances scare them. An old professor helps them investigate and develops a frightening theory. Now something is preying on the hero's own wife as she sleeps. She is fading and growing paler. One night, Edgar encounters someone in their bedroom, bent over his wife. There is blood on both of them. It is the freakish man from the castle in eastern Europe!

Edgar can't take any more. It is *so* vivid. But at least it is fantasy, while what is outside their door at the college is real. His nightmares have come to life.

A strange thought arises. What if the thing that is after them is like the creature in the book? But that is nonsense. Do not be afraid, he reminds himself.

Driver should be back from his trips to the train station by now, long since back.

"One of us should go into the hallway," says Lear. "We need to see if it is there or outside. We need to know what it is doing."

Jonathan and Tiger step forward.

"It should be me," says Lear.

"Grandfather, no," says Lucy.

"I'll do it." Edgar Brim walks up to the door.

"I think it is best that I—" begins Tiger.

"Professor Lear has made it clear," counters Edgar, "that this beast wants him and me more than any of you. It makes the most sense that I go. If it sees me perhaps it will do something rash and you all can act."

"All right," says Lear, "pull back the desk."

Lucy gives Edgar a longing look; Tiger walks away. But Edgar is focused on his task as they move the desk. Jonathan hands him his pistol and claps him on the back. The door creaks as Edgar opens it a crack. He puts his face close and searches the hallway.

"It doesn't seem like there's anyone about." Before the others can say anything else, he swings the door wide, darts out and closes it behind him. He hears the bolt snap back into place.

He stands still with all senses alert. Soon, he hears the winds blowing across the treeless grounds making the building creak here and there. It is still afternoon and the light is coming through the windows at either end of the hall. Thinking their enemy may approach from behind, he moves cautiously over to the big window at the back and looks down over the grounds. There are the playing fields where he had so many confrontations with Fardle, where Tiger was undressed; there is the graveyard, the ancient black stones sticking up, little Newman's grave toward the rear. It appears deserted.

Edgar turns and walks up the hall to the front window. He sees the stable near the gate on the lawn—Driver's domain, where he lives with the horse William Wilson. The sun will begin to set in an hour. He stays off to the side watching for a while. Nothing. Where is the creature?

He stands before the center of the window, easy to spot from the outside. Draw him out, wherever he is, Edgar thinks. Something is moving now in the bleak distance, coming toward the college at a steady pace. Edgar squints. Driver is just now returning from his last trip over the moors! Edgar examines him as he comes nearer: slim like a skeleton, his face, as usual, barely visible in his dirty red hood, the reins of his black horse held in his left hand. Edgar remembers the rumors about this man, this creature . . . found out on the moors, speechless and deaf. *Found.*

"Oh, my God," whispers Edgar. He shivers. Do not be afraid, he tells himself. He turns and walks forthrightly down the hall to the lab door and knocks. He hears the bolt being pulled back and enters.

"It's here," he says. Jonathan locks the door again, shoving the bolt back into place. "It's on the front grounds." No one speaks again for a while.

"I really wonder," says Lear finally, "what it can do." He puts his hand on the barrel of the cannon. "What if this can't kill it?"

Yes, thinks Edgar, what if the creature is almost unkillable, just like the one in his book? How did the man who wrote it conjure up such a monster? Did he have a model for it? Did he see it?

Bram Stoker is in the hallway behind the stage of the Lyceum Theatre in London at that very moment, pushing himself to stride right up to Irving's dressing room and knock on the door. He needs to confront him about the novel. Has he read *any* of it?

Stoker dares not stand too close to the door. Were he to put his ear to it and Irving were to find him there he would never forgive himself. The chief is not a violent man, but he is sometimes given to violent words, and one does not want his disapproval.

Stoker hears the sound of the other man's voice again, speaking in hushed tones to Sir Henry, his accent foreign, eastern European. Stoker smiles. Irving is known for being absolutely dedicated to his art. At age fifty-nine, knighted and renowned, he still practices in his dressing room. Stoker can only make out a few words. The two voices seem to be speaking of history, mesmerism and art.

Stoker knocks gently. The voices stop.

"Who is there?" asks Irving.

"Stoker, sir."

"Give me a minute, my good man." But it is more than that before the door swings open. In it stands Sir Henry, a little makeup on his face: his brows darkened and his lips glossy red. "What do you want?"

"Might I come in?"

Irving hesitates. "All right, but not for long."

This sort of attitude makes Stoker sad. Gone are the days when they stayed up all night talking. He enters the room and glances around. It is dim, just the gaslights around the dressing table and mirror glowing. Irving still paints his face with watercolors, not greasepaint, producing an eerie look. The great man stands near him, declining to sit. The novel is nowhere in sight, though Stoker had left it right on the table.

"Have you had a chance to read it yet, sir?"

"Read what?"

"My novel?"

"You have another one, do you, Bram? They haven't done well, have they? Though, I dare say, it is a nice sideline for you."

Stoker feels like shouting at him, but controls himself: "This one may do better. It has been published for more than a week or two. I left a copy on your dressing table the day it appeared. You were in the building when we did a reading on the stage to copyright it and I believe you heard some of it peripherally."

"I don't recall. What is it about?"

"One would term it a sensation novel, rather frightening."

"Ah, like Le Fanu or Wilkie Collins or that monstrous Drood thing The Inimitable was working on when he died? Collins was mad, you know. He thought there was two of him. He is known to have held long conversations with himself and feared the other Wilkie."

"Like you, sir?"

"I beg your pardon?" Irving fixes him with a glare. "Whatever do you mean?"

"Well, there is certainly more than one of you."

Irving smiles. "I see, quite right."

"Where is it?"

"Where is what?" Irving is impatient. He walks to the door and puts a hand on it, as if to begin ushering his assistant out.

"My novel."

"Must be here somewhere."

"You may recognize things in it."

"Oh?" Irving is trying to stifle a yawn. Stoker notices the painting hanging on the wall just behind him. The master used to have several of his own portraits here: all the artists want to paint him. But now he has just this. Stoker's favorite paintings are of Ellen Terry as Lady Macbeth and one he has just seen this week, inspired by his new novel, both of beautiful women in erotic poses, strong and enticing, yet somehow vulnerable. But he wishes Irving wouldn't hang the one he has on his wall now. It both draws and disturbs him.

"You are keeping that picture, sir?"

Irving turns to it. "Yes. Why do you ask?" He looks a little guilty. He had first placed it here about a decade ago. It depicts Vlad Tepes, the ruler of Wallachia near Transylvania in the Carpathian Mountains in the fifteenth century. The face is frightening, almost sallow, and the smile cruel. The subject was known as Vlad the Impaler. Irving had long since told Stoker the whole story.

"He was the most brutal ruler the world has ever known," he had said with a strange smile. "He is a portrait in evil. He impaled his enemies upon stakes, you know. Were you to cross him or were he to simply not feel the best about you, he would spit you upon a stake outside his castle. There are accounts of hundreds of writhing people on his grounds, not just men, but women and children too. It is historical fact. I shall share further details someday, if you like!" He had laughed. "Lovely man!" Irving had leaned closer to Stoker and added: "Someone has informed me that he is a distant relative of mine, maybe a direct forebear. Can you imagine? Perhaps that is where I get my reserves for dark characters, my good fellow. I find it fascinating! One must do what one must for art! When I need inspiration for a little evil, there it is!" He had directed a finger at the portrait and fixed Stoker with an expression that caused him to step back.

Irving revels in his ability to take his work where other actors are frightened to go. He once played a villain murdering a child while patting a horse.

"Well, sir, perhaps you might find the time to read the novel soon? I should like to discuss it with you."

"Yes, yes, of course, Stoker, I shall give it my undivided attention at the first opportunity." Irving motions for his assistant to leave. As Stoker walks back along the hallway, he hears the two voices again.

26

His Father's Son

"We must confront this thing. Gather up the guns." Lear grips Edgar by the arm. "I need a moment with Master Brim before we leave."

The two of them step aside.

"We are facing death today, my boy."

"Yes, sir."

"I have something to tell you. I promised you earlier." Lear pauses and gathers himself. "About thirty years ago, I had another remarkable student who was as remarkable as Erasmus Scrivener and almost as extraordinary as you."

"Thank you, sir."

"He was here not long after Scrivener and stayed for just part of a year. His parents wanted to toughen him for the world, but much to their credit, soon saw that this college was too hard on some children. They were good people. The other professors have forgotten this boy, but I have not." Edgar wonders why he is telling him this at this desperate moment. "As you know, I taught litera-ture in those days. He was an excellent student, imbued with an artistic nature that was unique. I admired him deeply. And so, I told him—" He stopped for a moment.

"Told him what?" Edgar is beginning to feel anxious.

"I . . . I asked him, more than once, if he thought the demons in the stories we studied might be based on something real. I said I had a theory about it. I told him about my paper. I should not have done so." He is talking faster now, glancing at the door. "It was a dangerous thing!" he says in a raised voice. "You *know* that, Edgar." The professor has never used his Christian name. "This sensitive boy, I think he may have believed it. He asked me about it several more times, but thinking better of it, I said no more." He glances at the door again. "The monster was about, my boy! We know that now. It was here on the moors watching whom I befriended, listening to things I said, and to whom I said it!"

"Who, sir, was that student?"

"His name was Allen Brim."

Edgar freezes—*his father had been in these halls!*

"But the monster didn't get him, sir. He left the moors healthy. He must have. He met my dear mother. They had me and he raised me. You need not feel badly."

"No, I should."

"Why, sir?"

"Need I tell you?" Lear seems like he may weep.

Edgar thinks back to that horrible day at Raven House seven years ago, the day after his father attended the theater to see that Henry Irving play. He remembers waking in the morning to a deathly quiet house. He walked up the stairs from his room to his parents' where Allen Brim had read those stories that came down through the pipe. He saw his father lying on his mother's side of the bed, absolutely still, eyes wide open.

"It was a mysterious death," whispers Lear.

My father! Edgar had known it deep down. *His heart!* "It killed him!" he shouts. Tiger and Jonathan look over.

Lear lowers his head. "I fear so, my boy. I am sorry."

Without warning, the hag grips Edgar Brim and tries to knock him to the floor. He staggers and drops into the chair behind him. She climbs on top of him and presses her legs into his chest, pinning him down. He can't breathe. He hears his father's voice. *I am with you. Do not be afraid.* Edgar has had enough. He swings at her and knocks her flying.

"I'll destroy it myself!" he shouts, heading for the door.

"Edgar?" asks Lucy. "Don't!"

"He's fine," spits Tiger.

Lear lifts his head and smiles. "What do you have in mind, my young friend?"

"My bare hands!" Edgar cries out.

Now, even Tiger is alarmed. Her friend's face has become very red. "Eddie," she says, "calm and calculated."

Jonathan seizes him by the arm. "Brim," he says, and there is admiration in his voice, "we must do this together."

"But we need to go *now*, out this door and down those stairs with the weapons, no more waiting."

"So what exactly are you suggesting we do, my hero?" asks Jonathan.

But Lear intervenes. "We will not be rash. Something doesn't make sense to me about Driver being our target. He doesn't seem to have the wits to do what has been done here over the years."

"But he is the last one!" cries Edgar. "It can't be anyone else!"

"Or our enemy is just making us think that. Driver wasn't here when Erasmus died."

"So you believe, sir," says Jonathan. "Perhaps he was living down in the cellar and then showed himself later, dressed up as the driver. When did he first appear here? He was found on the moors, wasn't he?"

"Alone and starving. I believe it was the year after Scrivener—" This fact, suddenly apparent to Lear, stops him in his tracks.

"Died!" says Lucy.

"It IS him," says Tiger.

Lear stands in front of them at the door, still barring them from a reckless departure. "But I keep thinking this dumb and deaf creature cannot be it."

"He is acting," says Edgar.

"Or he is someone's weapon," says Lucy.

"We will go out cautiously," insists Lear, "with all our guns loaded. Tiger, Lucy and I will stand guard, while Jonathan and Edgar go upstairs and see if Griswold's body is still there. If it is, bring it to us. We will then move downstairs and open the front doors. Jonathan, you will stay there and train the cannon on Driver, but keep it out of his sight. The rest of us will carry the corpse out onto the lawn for him to see. We shall observe his reaction. It may tell us something. Two of us will approach him face-to-face: Edgar with the rifle and Tiger with the pistol. I have my big blade. If he does not attack us, we will ask him to bury the body. We shall see what he does with his back to us, working. If he still hasn't come at us, we will indicate to him that we want to go to the train. We will stay alert, weapons ready, Driver in front of us on the cart, the cannon stowed but available."

His young colleagues are staring intently at him, Edgar with a hand on the doorknob.

"We will see what transpires."

Bram Stoker walks out of the Royal Lyceum's entrance and stops beneath the cream-colored stone pillars. He sees the bonnets and top hats passing by, no one even glancing his way, colors moving about in London's brown and yellow world. He hears the rattle of the harnesses, a sound some say will soon be gone, the cries of hawkers, the usual din of the London streets. Amidst it, a voice comes to him: the one Irving imitates in his dressing room, eastern European. Stoker realizes for the very first time that he has heard it somewhere else!

It was at Cruden Bay in northern Scotland on the coast of the North Sea, more than a year ago, the second time he went up there to write. He took the room in the Kilmarnock Arms he'd had before, looking out over the village and the water. He wrote well there. He could see Slains Castle again, just a ten-minute walk away, a perfect home for monsters. That vision of the undead man kept unfolding for him, looking like the master: elegant, brilliant and deadly. Irving as a villain brought to life, intent on sucking blood to stay undead, cornering a young hero in a castle in the Carpathians, as evil as Vlad the Impaler, with elements of him too. Stoker remembers how he tried to frighten the hell out of his readers, incite the horror that lurks in all of us, tell dark truths and deal in human fears, explore the unsaid things, emotions we all hide—how women arouse men, and men excite women, and some men . . . other men. His face grew red at the memory. Then that voice came back to him. He had heard it as he sat at his desk in his room at Cruden Bay, booming while it asked for directions in the lobby downstairs.

"I have had a nautical accident," it said. "My conveyance was wrecked." A deep, foreign voice!

The night before, a ship had gone aground on the rocks nearby in a storm—Stoker had written through the gale, energized. He had heard there was just a crew aboard, no passengers, and that one or two had been swept into the waves.

"I like to holiday on the moors," the voice had said, "but I usually dock at Inverness. Is there transportation that can take me there so I may board a train north to Altnabreac?"

Afterward, Stoker had peeked out his window and saw this man from behind. He was dressed in black, remarkably tall. Stoker had watched him make his way down the village road in the rain. He had seen his face in profile. The nose had been like Irving's.

Stoker shakes his head. "What nonsense, what imaginings."

They lug Griswold's body down the stairs, while Lucy stands at the window watching Driver carrying the students' little carts from the wagon into the stable. The headmaster's corpse is so heavy even Jonathan can't lift it, a dead weight. It thuds on each step as they pull it along. They have the weapons at hand. Lucy watches Driver emerge out onto the grounds one last time and then joins her friends. At the big front doors, they ready the cannon. Jonathan is behind it and has it sighted. Edgar has the rifle loaded and ready, Tiger the pistol. Lucy puts her ear to the entrance.

"I can't hear anything close."

"All right," says Lear to Edgar, "open the doors."

27

The Novel

D river is standing beside the black horse near the stable. Only his prominent nose is visible inside the dirty red cloak, but it is certain that he is watching them.

Edgar and Tiger take Griswold's hands and drag him forward. Lear and Lucy follow a few paces back from them. She's as alert as a meerkat. They drop the corpse halfway across the lawn.

"Uh!" says the headmaster when his back strikes the ground. They all start and stand back. But it is just air being released from the dead body's lungs.

"I'll take the lead," insists Edgar. He has the rifle. Tiger pulls the pistol from a pocket.

Edgar walks directly toward the demon, his gun cocked but not pointed at its target, not yet. Tiger is just behind and ready to strike, hiding the pistol.

The creature doesn't move. He just watches. They trudge forward. They're within ten feet and he still hasn't budged. Now they can see his eyes deep in the hood, almost violet colored in that scarred face.

"I can't believe he's capable of so many well-executed murders," whispers Lear.

"I can," says Tiger.

Edgar says nothing. He holds up his hand so they all halt, and then he looks back toward the corpse, lying on the ground halfway between them and the college. He can see the glint of the cannon in the slightly open doorway, Jonathan ready to fire.

"We want you to bury him," says Lucy.

Driver doesn't move.

"You have to show him," says Edgar.

"That's what he wants you to think," adds Tiger.

But Lucy shows him, miming carrying the body and digging a hole. Driver turns and walks into his stable. William Wilson neighs and seems to eye them.

"What's he doing?" asks Tiger.

"I don't know," says Lear. "Ready your guns." They point them at the two big swinging doors. After a while, Driver comes out. Tilley cocks her pistol. Driver looks at her and then Edgar, registering no reaction. He is carrying a rough wooden coffin, a spade shovel on top of it.

"He keeps coffins in there?" asks Tiger.

They all step back and let him walk past, towering over them. His hands aren't usually visible, often gloved or covered by the sleeves of his dirty cloak. But they're apparent now, huge mitts with fingers the size of the iron spokes on a locomotive's wheel. Edgar hears wheezing in his throat as he passes. They keep the guns trained on him. But the monster never turns, and when he reaches the body, drops the coffin and picks up the giant headmaster as if he were a small sack of potatoes and throws him over his shoulders. Edgar and Tiger had barely been able to drag him partway across the grounds!

Driver bends down with Griswold still over his shoulders and picks up the coffin and the spade. He trudges toward the graveyard, casting a look over his shoulder at them. The expression makes the back of Edgar's neck tingle.

"We need to leave," says Lucy, "now!"

"It won't matter if we run," says Edgar. "If this is him then he will either kill us or we will kill him." Lear motions for Jonathan to come out of the college. He emerges with the cannon and moves it forward on its wheels.

They all follow Driver around the college to the graveyard in the back grounds, keeping their distance. Then they watch him dig the grave. He grunts as he works, but he never removes his hood; in fact, he grabs it once or twice when it begins to fall back off his head. Twenty minutes later he has a deep hole dug. He creaks open the coffin, picks up the body and throws it in with a thud.

"He doesn't like the old man," says Lear.

It only takes Driver a short while to lower the coffin and pile the dirt back into the grave. He doesn't bother replacing the sod, and when he's finished, the spot is marked by black muck. The driver turns and stares at them.

"What is he doing?" asks Edgar.

"Waiting," says Lear.

"For what?" asks Tiger.

"An instruction."

Lear points to himself and his friends, then to William Wilson and the carriage, and then out over the moors in the direction of Altnabreac Station. The train for London will arrive in about an hour. There are always two on Fridays, about five hours apart.

They step back again and let the creature pass. Edgar thinks he sees sadness in his eyes and wonders what is going on.

A short while later they have their bags on the ground next to the carriage. Driver loads them on to the racks beneath it. He motions for them to get in, but Lear insists that he board first. The hooded man does as he is told, mounts the driver's box and takes the reins in his hands, his back to them. They get in. Jonathan has folded up the cannon: they can't have it ready to fire. He wants the rifle, but Edgar keeps it. Jon will have to use his hands if a confrontation comes. Lear and Lucy sit on the rear bench and the other three at the front, directly behind Driver, Edgar in the middle, rifle pointed straight at the back of the creature's head. Tiger's pistol is pointed at his heart. Driver doesn't seem to care. Edgar isn't sure if that should calm or terrify him.

They move out, the black horse ambling forward, the wheels turning slowly. The black wooden benches creak and the black harness jingles in a slow and steady rhythm as they move.

The sun is going down, bright in their eyes, blinding them when they face it. Perhaps this is part of the creature's plan. Were he to turn and lunge, they couldn't see him.

Edgar shifts in his seat and knocks his book out of his pocket. It falls onto Lucy's lap. She picks it up and sees the title.

"*Dracula.*"

"What is this about?"

"It's, uh . . ." Edgar is trying to talk to her and keep his eye on Driver. "It's a sensation novel, very frightening."

She reads the author's name. "Bram Stoker."

Lear turns around. "Bram Stoker?" But then he shifts back, keeping his eyes ahead.

"I'll read some," she says. "Make us brave." She pulls out the bookmark and begins in a quivering voice as they move across the desolate land under the setting sun.

Edgar wants to keep his mind here on the moors in this carriage, on Driver. But his surroundings fade and he finds himself drawn seductively into the novel by the sweet sound of Lucy's voice. The hero, the professor and their friends are searching for Count Dracula, the old man who imprisoned him in his castle and killed his wife's young friend and is now infecting her, secretly sucking on her, mingling his blood with hers. She is growing ever paler and having evil thoughts, dreams of dying! They must find the elusive count. They discover coffins inside his home near the docks just east of London and fill them with garlic and crosses, and pursue his ship over the English Channel back to eastern Europe. He lies in his coffin during the day, undead. They are equipped with stakes and knives and a huge sword.

Driver stops the carriage. The station is still a hundred yards away. Edgar shoves the gun into the back of the thing's head, his finger pressing the trigger. Jonathan stands up, fists balled, Tiger with the pistol in the creature's back now too. Driver gently turns around to regard them, appearing perplexed. He gets down and points to a little bridge over a stream. Two rotten boards have fallen through. He motions for them to get out. They descend slowly, Edgar keeping Lucy behind him.

Driver indicates that they cannot go any farther. He motions for them to get their bags out of the carriage.

"No one move!" cries Lear. "We can't put our backs to him!"

The creature still looks perplexed. He motions again.

Lear's face grows red with anger. Perhaps he is thinking of his wife, his son, or of Scrivener and little Newman. "Keep the weapons on him!" He advances toward a startled Driver and seizes him. The creature does nothing. Lear grabs the hood and pulls it back. They gasp.

His face is horribly scarred. The wounds run across his visage and shaved head, as if various features have been sewed onto him. An ear appears torn. He looks at the ground. He seems ashamed.

Edgar thinks of the room in the cellar.

"What are you?" asks Lear. "Who did this to you?" He seizes him again, shakes him, and grabs the front of his cloak and rips it off, tearing the loosely tied knots down the chest. Underneath, Driver is wearing old trousers and his chest is bare. Lucy screams. Four words are carved into his skin. They are still red, only just beginning to heal.

COME

AND

GET ME

They all stand still under the dimming sky. They hear the locomotive approaching in the distance, steaming along from the north, heading toward London. The freakish man, shirtless and shivering, drops his head. Jonathan steps forward and gently takes Driver's face in his hands, gripping him on either side of the jaw and by opening his own mouth gets him to open his. Inside, he can see a severed tongue, long since cut out.

"Oh, God," says Lear, dropping the cloak to the ground.

"The demon did this," says Edgar. "It was here." He looks around the moors. "But it's gone."

"We've been searching in the wrong place." Lear lowers his head. "It knew we would come to the college. It drew us."

"But why didn't it just kill us there?" asks Edgar.

"Because it didn't make sense," says Lear. "I've been a fool!" He cocks an ear toward the sound of the approaching train. "It saw how many of us were here. If five people died in a week at the College on the Moors, attention would be brought here and a cause for the deaths would be sought."

"So," says Tiger, "where is it?"

Edgar picks up Driver's cloak and searches the pockets. He pulls out a piece of paper. *I drove you to the college* is written in an old-fashioned hand.

Five mouths drop open. They all think back. The monster had been under the cloak in the place of Driver the day they arrived, right with them in the carriage!

"It must look something like him," says Tiger, staring at Driver.

Edgar thinks of the room in the cellar with Scrivener's skeleton, its operating table, its pieces of human flesh—the blood, the fingernail and part of a nose. "It was operating on Driver."

"Remaking him!" says Lucy.

"To look enough like him so he could walk about in the college under that hood," says Lear, "watching, listening, entering the rooms and doing as he pleased!"

Edgar thinks he is going to vomit. He brings the cloak up toward his face to cover his mouth but when he does he notices a label inside. **Royal Lyceum Theatre, London** it reads. "It's a costume," he says. He looks closer. *Abraham Stoker, manager.* An image of Sir Henry Irving in the street flashes through Edgar's brain, and of the man who was there with him.

"Bram Stoker," says Lucy. She glances at the novel now lying on the ground at their feet. Edgar is staring at it too.

"Our enemy," says Lear, "drew us up here where it last struck to get us to kill someone at the college in its place and think the job done!"

It was genius, thinks Edgar. It was the *monster* sitting there under the cloak in the balcony, *pointing at the giant headmaster, nodding his head!* It has all been orchestrated. But the creature's first plan had failed, so now it was calling them south to finish them, even telling them where to find it.

COME
AND
GET ME.

ROYAL LYCEUM THEATRE, LONDON.

It was daring them.

"It can kill us down there," says Lear, "one after the other, amidst the great metropolis where our deaths won't be suspicious."

Edgar remembers buying the novel in Euston Railway Station. As they run for the train, the whole scene is suddenly clear in his mind and it sends a shiver down his spine.

III

Last Pursuit

There is no such thing as a moral or an immoral book.
Books are well written, or badly written. That is all.

∞

Preface to *The Picture of Dorian Gray*,
Oscar Wilde (1891)

28

The Creature in the Book

"**W**hat did he look like?" asks Lear, leaning forward in his seat on the Far North Line's southbound train for Edinburgh and London. He is still sweating and puffing from the run over the moors to catch the train. But the excitement in his eyes has little to do with that.

"I told you, I don't know," says Edgar. "He had his back to me." Through the window, he sees Driver standing in the distance on the moors, his black horse at his side, staring after them. He grows smaller.

"But he was tall?"

"Very."

"Complexion?"

"I didn't see his face, though I remember seeing the tip of a long, aquiline nose."

"That could be anyone," says Jonathan. "It could be Henry Irving, for God's sake!"

"Do you think he knocked the novel off the bookstand on purpose?" asks Lucy.

"He doesn't know," snaps Tiger. "He already said that."

"Give me the book!" says Lear. He opens it and starts reading at top speed, scanning the first page, flipping to the next. "It wanted you to read this."

"The villain in it is undead," says Edgar.

"Male or female?" asks Lear.

"The main one is male."

"Main one?"

All five of them are avid readers. They all know the stories about these creatures, from *The Vampyre* novel to Varney in the penny dreadfuls and Sheridan Le Fanu's creepy tale of a female fiend. Edgar knew how these monsters were often depicted— frightening figures with manners and wealth, foreign with blood-less faces and fang-like teeth, who live in crypts during the day and come out at night to suck the essence from the living, turning them into fellow demons. But there had never been one like the thing in this book. Edgar can see him now: wide awake in his coffin.

"The boy, Newman!" exclaims Lear. "The way he died!"

"Thank God you severed the head," says Tiger.

"But there were no marks on his neck," says Lucy.

Edgar's mind is racing. "The creature in the novel is from the Carpathian Mountains in eastern Europe. This one can't be seen in a mirror."

"Really?" asks Jonathan, leaning forward.

"And he is somehow connected to a ruler from the fifteenth century in Wallachia near Transylvania, someone named Vlad the Impaler from the Draculesti family."

Lear swallows. "He was one of the cruelest human beings in history. He liked to drive stakes through people while they were still alive—women and children as well as men—and watch them writhe on the grounds of his castle." Lucy turns away.

"There are all sorts of victims in the novel—Count Dracula gives a child in a sack to female vampires to drain and kill."

"That's enough, Edgar," says Lucy.

"No, tell us," demands Tiger. "We need to know this."

Lucy puts her fingers in her ears.

"Dracula imprisons the hero in his castle at first and wants to suck his blood, but needs him for other things. Three females try to go at him at once, their mouths on his neck as he sleeps."

"Really?" asks Tiger.

"But the Count preys on women . . . young ladies." Edgar tries not to look at the girls.

Lucy glances at Tiger. "I think we've heard enough," she says.

"I thought you weren't listening," says Tiger.

"Is there garlic and stakes through the heart and head severing and that sort of thing?" asks Jonathan.

"In spades: a man drives a huge stake right into his wife-to-be in a crypt."

"Really?" says Tiger again.

"Because she's been infected by this thing—they actually saw it, on top of her, attacking her in bed before they chased it off. She sucked on *his* chest too."

"What is going on in Mr. Stoker's head?" asks Jonathan.

Lear gazes out the window. "These creatures are really just fantasies that people have brought to life because of human fears. All this stuff that Polidori and Le Fanu came up with, and I suppose Stoker now, that's the modern version. But the undead is an ancient idea. Human beings have always been frightened about what happens after death. That's why we still have bells on coffins with a string going inside to the corpse, in case we aren't *truly* dead. What if some of us come back to feed on others? That's what all this comes from. It was there in the Dark Ages, in the days of the Goths and the Huns, though they used to call them *revenants*. They used to dig up unusual people and kill them again with stakes through the heart or some other gruesome method. Skeletons have been found with objects driven through the chest."

"They're just creatures we've made up," says Lucy, as if trying to convince herself.

"They come from the same anxiety that gives us ghosts and witches," says Lear, "and people with evil powers. But now the revenants in stories have black cloaks and canine teeth; they used to have ruddy faces, full of blood from sucking others."

"It's just fear," says Edgar firmly.

"But what if someone," asks Tiger, "just once, just one single, solitary time *actually* didn't die? And then maybe needed blood to survive? Could that happen?"

"And maybe such a being isn't what these fantasies say," says Edgar. "Maybe it has been seen once or twice and the legends have expanded from those glimpses? What if what it really does is suck blood through a hole in the chest directly from the heart?"

"A vampire," whispers Lucy.

"Now we're sounding *worse* than Shakespeare," says Tiger, trying to smile.

"But something abnormal killed our father," says Lucy, "and something strange killed Scrivener and Newman, and both had chest wounds. They all died of unexplained heart failure." Edgar thinks of his father. He still can't believe it. Lucy's eyes well up. "It must have been hideous!"

"And now," says Lear, "it is daring us to come to London."

"It threw the novel on the floor in front of me," says Edgar quietly, "told us where to find it." He pauses. "But it wouldn't draw us to London if it thought we had any chance of destroying it." Fear is rising inside him.

"No, it wouldn't," says Lear. "It is certain it will kill us."

The rest of the trip to Edinburgh is quiet. No one says that they should stop their pursuit, though they all think it more than once. When they reach the great Scottish metropolis, the sun has long since set. They get out and sit on an old wooden bench in the clammy station, leaning against each other, falling asleep. When they hear the first locomotive's whistle in the wee hours of the morning, they rouse and buy breakfast at an all-night tea room in the station and take an early train south.

When they arrive in London it is past noon hour, and as they walk through Euston Railway Station toward the street, they pass the W.H. Smith bookstand: a stack of *Dracula* sits there, yellow and blood red, the sign still advertising it.

They head south down Gower Street past the university and the British Museum under a cloudy sky. Edgar regards the beautiful stone building, remembering those long-gone days in the library and his father searching for the truth about stories.

Their first stop is in Drury Lane, number 173, J. Sainsbury's grocery shop, with its tall glass windows and fruit and vegetables in baskets right out on the footpath. Rows of plucked chickens and geese hang head-down on hooks from the ceiling. Lear is sure this place will have what they need. Not all shopkeepers in London would stock such a thing, some think it foreign. But sure enough, upon request, one of the gentlemen servers, dressed in the company white shirt and tie with a long blood-stained apron, fetches what they need.

The five friends leave with a small brown sack filled with heads of garlic on strings.

Next they move farther down Drury Lane to the office of the Crypto-Anthropology Society. They find Shakespeare engrossed in his studies, of course, but sitting beside him is a new book, well-thumbed already. *Dracula.*

"A little light reading?" asks Jonathan.

"It is disturbing," says Shakespeare.

Lear nods at it. "That's what we may be after."

Shakespeare stands up and staggers back. "Lear, I'm not sure you should. I talk about such things, but if it were actually real, then my God!"

"We have reason to believe it is."

"There will be others! They will come after you!" The madness is rising in him.

Jonathan smirks. "Not that again."

"Lear, you killed Grendel!"

"I killed something, my dear old friend."

"No, you killed Grendel, and now this," he points at the book, "has come for you."

"We don't know that's how these things work," says Lear, but his voice is low and he sounds worried.

"If you kill this one, and there is little chance you will, and if he is the vampire . . . then what will—"

"Not THE, my good man, just A—" says Jonathan.

"THE vampire!" shouts Shakespeare. "You have not so much brain as earwax! I have always believed that if there is one of *that* kind of creature, then there is *only* one. If it multiplied the way the fantasies claim, we'd all be infected by now!" William sits down with a bang in his chair.

Jonathan smirks again and rotates a finger in a circle near his temple.

"We need money," says Lear.

Shakespeare nods toward a painting of the three witches in *Macbeth*. The professor goes to it and takes it off the wall, revealing a safe with a combination lock. He opens it quickly, obviously knowing the numbers. He pulls out a stack of bills and stuffs them into the pockets of his greatcoat. Shakespeare appears to be in another world, staring off into the distance. Lear closes the safe, replaces the painting and motions for them all to leave. But part-way over to the stairs he turns and takes several crucifixes from a chest of drawers, putting them into his big pockets too.

They head out into the street and find another place to buy a quick meal. Pickled herring on bread, some roasted fowl and a little ale will have to do for their late-afternoon repast. They take it to Lincoln's Inn Fields and eat outdoors, sitting on a wrought iron bench. The gray sky is darkening. After they have finished, Lear leads them to the Liberty department store on Regent Street to get them properly attired—ready-made silk dresses for the girls at more than twenty pounds each and evening dress for himself and the boys at nearly the same steep price. They take their new clothes to the Langham where they get rooms and prepare. The girls should feel like princesses preening for a ball, the boys their beaus, but it seems more like the day before a hanging or going off to war. Lear hands out the crosses. Edgar writes a note to the Thornes, saying he is at the Langham for a few days with friends. He has to let them know why he hasn't arrived at their Mayfair home. It seems like a farewell.

There is a sort of electricity in the air outside the Royal Lyceum that night, as there is every night the master is upon the stage. Every performance of *Faust* has been sold out and tonight's is no exception, another reason Lear needed so much money. They find the five poorest-dressed theater-goers—in threadbare suits and dresses and wearing rented top hats and bonnets, pretending they have not paid a month's wages for their passes—and give them sums that are twice the value of the tickets.

And then they are in.

Despite his deep concerns, Edgar can barely contain the thrills that run through him. At first, he even forgets to keep an eye out for Bram Stoker. The sight of the huge staircase ascending to the fabled auditorium takes Edgar's breath away. Up all five of them go, way up to seats in the highest levels against the wall. Edgar wonders if he is sitting near where his father was the night before he died. The scene below nearly makes him faint. The theater shines in blue and green colors like a peacock, the ceiling turquoise and gold, the cavernous room lit by candles in red shades, the stage with its shimmering golden curtain otherworldly in the shelled footlights. And up rise the seats in every direction, nearly 2,000 of them, the balconies hanging above. And there Edgar is, dressed in a black evening suit and cravat, Lucy on his arm, casting admiring glances his way. She's in a glowing white gown that makes her look, to him, almost perfect.

He scans the crowd. Jewelry glints from this far away. The men with their mustachios and broad shoulders in tight suits and the beauty of the women in their low-cut gowns is dazzling too. Edgar takes out their pocket binoculars and surveys the people in the front rows and in the grand boxes that hang almost over the stage. Imagine sitting there, that close to Irving on the prowl! One young lady draws his attention. He doubts he has ever seen a more beautiful girl. She is perhaps eighteen, dark hair and snow-white skin, her lips glistening red, her eyes flashing when she turns to look up to the balconies. Edgar watches her for a while, feeling guilty but unable to turn away, noticing her lovely mouth move as she talks to her handsome young gentleman. Then the orchestra begins. The lights go down. There is a hush.

It opens on a black-and-white background but soon something red appears, materializing in Faust's study from a puff of smoke. *Irving!* He moves like a freak across the stage, dragging a leg, in ghoulish makeup, the devil. Mephistopheles! A mysterious blue light moves with him. His voice is electric too, pronouncing words in strange but musical ways. Edgar believes every evil word he says. He is mesmerizing. Time slips by. Edgar forgets they are there to search for signs of the demon. He feels as if he is in a dream world. Soon, it seems Irving is talking directly to him. Then he knows he is really dreaming for he sees the beautiful girl actually on the stage beside the great actor! He thinks he sees a man there too, tall and strange, with a nose like Irving's and Driver's, looking down upon the girl, who is lying helpless at his feet. He sees the man rip her dress open at the chest and descend upon her. The excitement is overpowering. But then the hag appears! She is coming over the balcony and up the steps toward his seat. Her red eyes are glued on him and he feels his heart pulsing fast, too fast, as if it will kill him. He can't breathe! She stops at his row and steps over others, who seem to notice nothing, her talon hands tearing at the seats, about to climb onto his chest. He resists, and suddenly, as if emerging from a deep lake into cold air, awakens from his visions.

The applause comes as a shock to him. Relieved and thrilled, he stands and whoops with the others. Beside him, Lucy, Jonathan and Tiger are ecstatic. He cannot believe he has just passed two hours in the Lyceum Theatre under the master's spell.

Edgar wishes he could stay and enjoy the atmosphere. He is worried that he may never come again, but he is whisked from his seat by Professor Lear. He looks down toward the front rows and sees the beautiful young woman staggering out of her seat looking pale and ill, leaning on the arm of her young man, who seems concerned. Edgar smiles. Irving has deeply affected her. What surpassing art!

"Come, Edgar!" cries Lucy.

They move down the big stairs to the vestibule and quickly out into the street. Lear wants them to see Irving in the flesh and out of character, and Bram Stoker too. He hopes it will tell them something.

The monster must be near. The two girls have their crosses tucked into their dresses; the boys have them in their pockets.

There is a little crowd attending at the side stage door, excited and breathless.

An hour later, most are still waiting. Finally, a hansom cab comes out of the night and Henry Irving is suddenly among them. He emerges from the side door briskly, top hat on, walking stick in hand and wearing a cape, noticing no one. Stoker and two other men have slipped through the door with Irving and are shielding him from onlookers. A few women seem like they may swoon and a young man cries out, "Irving is God!" Edgar and his friends watch closely. They search for marks on Irving's and Stoker's necks, but their collars are high and tight. The great actor appears pale and tired, his black eyes dull as if he were drugged, vacant in his famous stretched and angular face, marked with thick brows and long center-parted hair with streaks of gray, a cruel slit for a mouth. Stoker, in contrast, is energized, as if still moved by what he has just witnessed.

Edgar is nearest the carriage. Irving approaches. Edgar could touch him if he wanted, smell him too, but there is no scent. He searches for sweat on the brow, but there is none. Up close, Irving is white and pasty; he looks ill. *Undead.* A woman puts her hand on his arm. He moves past without acknowledging her and up into the carriage. "Can't you control these people, you fool!" he mutters at Stoker. But when he sits in the cab, he motions for his manager to come to him. Edgar can hear Irving's hiss. "I am him again! I am the devil, Stoker!"

His manager nods and steps back with a smile. The hansom cab pulls out. Everyone disperses, except the five friends and Stoker, who stands there watching Irving's carriage move away.

"A great man," says Lear to Stoker.

The gray eyes that light on Lear's contrast with the red hair and beard. He is burly and ruddy faced, full of blood it seems, yet so ordinary, so able to fade into a crowd. There is something in his expression, though—wariness, anger or resentment—something.

"He is a bastard sometimes," says Stoker, a hint of Irish in his voice, "but God, what talent, what art! Sometimes I wonder if he's really done it—sold his soul to the devil!" He turns to go.

"Mr. Stoker," says Edgar, "may we have a moment?"

He regards them, as if surprised that someone knows who he is.

"We need to speak with you," says Lear.

29

Stoker's Art

S toker looks as though he will send them away.

"I am an admirer of your novel," says Edgar quickly.

The big man's eyes soften. "You are?"

"We all are," says Lucy.

"I would be honored if you would consent to discuss it," says Lear. "I am a professor of English literature at a highly respected school for boys." It is only a slight lie.

Stoker's eyes are smiling now. "But, of course."

"It is hard to believe we are meeting you," says Tiger, affecting a gush.

Stoker bows slightly to her and then turns back to Lear. "Would you and your party like to come in?" He holds out his right arm and motions toward the door. "Hawkins," he says to one of the Lyceum's young attendants dressed in a crisp evening suit, "the door, please."

Hawkins opens the entrance and they all file in. As they do, Stoker whispers something to the young man. He departs.

Inside, they introduce themselves and then all move along a

dark corridor, Stoker in the lead. It is tight and brick walled and clammy. They hear a thumping sound.

"We have ghosts, you know," says Stoker over his shoulder, "many of them. The most popular is an elderly lady who is often seen with a severed head in her lap, stroking it." He laughs.

The dark corridor twists and turns. The thumps sound ominous, but after a while, Edgar realizes they are simply behind the stage and hearing stagehands moving props.

They keep walking, descending and then rising up a stone staircase. This would be a perfect place to kill someone, thinks Edgar. But moments later, he is filled with wonder. As they emerge through a door, the stage is right there! He could take a few steps and be upon it, the very boards on which Irving and Ellen Terry have just trod. It is lit softly now. The workers have moved off and there is a strange silence: awaiting the great artist and the world he will conjure.

Several strides farther, Stoker leads them up a tight staircase to a large, ornately carved wooden door at the top. He opens it and ushers them in. They enter a wood-paneled room with a low ceiling, full of busts of actors, authors and royalty and beautiful paintings. Flames crackle in a fireplace. A long dining table sits in the center, attended by more than a dozen empty chairs that appear as though they were made for King Arthur and his knights.

"Welcome to the dining room of the Sublime Society," crows Stoker.

Edgar has read about this fabled place—the Beefsteak Room. All of London wants to be invited here where Irving holds dinner parties, sometimes after performances, entertaining the greatest stars of the realm. Prime ministers have sat here, Oscar Wilde, the immortal Dickens and the Prince of Wales. Edgar imagines the bright talk that has flowed in this room. He envisions Irving, the most spectacular of them all, making his entrance fresh from the stage and still in makeup, as if from another reality, ferocious past the witching hour. It is said that he seldom sleeps at night: consumed by his performances, he cannot return to earth for hours.

"Please sit down," says Stoker, aware of the awe he has aroused.

Edgar descends gently into his chair, wondering who may have been in it before him. Stoker pours a glass of port for everyone and then pulls back a seat at the head of the table and takes it, his attitude open and inviting, a hand hanging over one of the arms and the other elegantly holding his glass.

"You know," he says to Lear, "some silver-tongued talker who was here said that there was no such thing as an immoral work of art. I liked that. It gave me courage. It allowed me to write *Dracula*." Stoker stares off for an instant and then comes around. "What would you like to know?"

"First, let me offer my compliments upon a remarkable achievement. Your novel strikes me as a groundbreaking work."

"Why, thank you, sir."

"I would not be surprised if the name of Dracula is still discussed decades from now."

"You are too kind."

"But how did you conceive of such an idea? A monster, yes, I can understand that, Polidori's work and *Varney the Vampire* and all that stuff, but this is truly different. It affects one, how should one say—"

"Viscerally?"

"Why, yes, an excellent word. There are currents in it, under the text, that give one startling sensations."

"It is the truth!" Stoker's eyes glaze over when he says it. Edgar tries not to sit forward.

"I beg your pardon, Mr. Stoker? It is all true? Surely, you can't mean that—"

"I didn't say it was all true, my good man. I said it was the truth. There is a very great difference."

"How so?"

"It is, may I be so bold as to say, art, and of the sort I was not sure I was capable. Some force guided me as I toiled over it for six long years." He seems entranced again.

"Why so long to create it?"

Stoker turns his eyes on Lear, but they gaze right through him. "It was because it took possession of me and I wrote and re-wrote! I knew that in a way, like I said of Mr. Irving this evening, I was selling my soul to the devil. One shouldn't write such horrible things. But I couldn't stop. I could *see* this revenant, this Count Dracula, this *undead* man! He was old and foreign and he was trapping me in a dark European castle . . . and I could see him coming through young women's windows in England, undressing them and . . ."

Lucy shifts uncomfortably in her chair.

Stoker notices and turns to her. "I must apologize, my dear. It is not something fit for a lady to hear. But sometimes, I realize now, artists must tell dark truths. They are deep in that book. I am not sure I was in control as they came from me!" He stares into the fire.

"Was there a model," asks Jonathan, "for your villain?"

"A model?" Stoker comes out of his reverie.

"Yes," says Lear, "did you base your Dracula on a living human being?"

Their host hesitates. "How could I possibly do that? We are speaking of a despicable creature here, a demon who murders and defiles, someone who feeds children to his female undead!" He shouts the last few words.

"Of course," says Lear, "a rather silly thought on my part."

"Indeed."

"But," says Edgar, "have you never felt that some of the creatures you have read of, like the Frankenstein monster or Mr. Hyde, might in some way be real?"

"No, I have not. That is madness."

There is a knock on the door.

"Enter!"

Hawkins comes in bearing a silver plate with something on it.

"Oh yes, hand them out, my boy."

The handsome young attendant, broad shouldered in his snug-fitting suit and sporting an admirable and manly black mustache, walks around the table handing something to each guest. He pauses slightly at both Tiger and Lucy, glancing down over their shoulders at their bare necks. Miss Lear knows he is doing it and blushes; Miss Tilley fixes him with a steely gaze.

Edgar looks at what he has been given.

"Stoker, this is too kind of you," says Lear.

"They are in the stalls."

Edgar can't believe it. "Tickets in the front row!" he exclaims.

"Yes, my young friend," says Stoker, "for tomorrow night. Now, *there*, on that stage, you shall experience a *real* demon!"

Stoker gets to his feet, indicating that the others are to rise. He walks to the door and returns with them along the shadowy corridor to the backstage exit on Burleigh Street. They bid farewell and are about to make their way toward Wellington Street when they hear his voice in the mist behind them.

"Come early, about four, and I shall give you a private tour of the Lyceum."

30

The Night Before

They make their way back to the Langham Hotel. They have two rooms, one for the females and another for the males. The professor feels it is best that no one is alone.

They have a late supper in the restaurant, a circular room with big windows that face the street. It should be a special occasion for Edgar (and Tiger) but his mind isn't on the lovely cream-colored room, the finely dressed waiters who tend to their every need or even the roast duck with pigeon pie and potatoes—and stewed fruit for afters.

"Stay in your rooms," says the professor, "with the doors locked and bolted. Girls, I want your beds covered with garlic strings, placed on either side of you, above your heads and below your feet, and keep a crucifix in hand under your pillows. It may be nonsense, but if he should come, hold it toward him. Latch all your windows and pull the curtains. Leave your lights on through the night. You will have the rifle, Tilley."

"Cry out and I'll be there in a second!" says Jonathan. Tiger rolls her eyes.

"I want you three to take every precaution too," Lucy says, looking at Edgar.

"We shall, my dear," says Lear, "but I am not sure anymore if it is Brim and I who are in most danger, not initially. Remember that in *Dracula*, the creature wants females."

"When you fight a man," says Tiger to Lucy, "hit him where it matters and hit him hard."

"This isn't a man, Tilley," says Lear.

They say their farewells in the hallway, trying not to linger. Edgar feels for Lucy, who seems terribly frightened. Their rooms are beside each other and high on the sixth floor at the top of the building; Lear insisted on that.

Tiger and Lucy undress one at a time, each taking a turn on watch, holding a crucifix. They've placed a string of garlic along the door frame so it hangs down over the entrance. Then they get into bed and lie still, lights blazing, Tiger with the rifle at her side, her hand near the trigger, ready to blast anything that appears in their room, no questions asked. They have agreed to keep talk to a minimum. They need to hear any suspicious sound, and they need to hear each other, even through the walls.

Edgar, Jonathan and Lear don't bother to undress separately. Their manliness doesn't allow them. The professor shows his concerns, but Jonathan pretends it is all good fun. Edgar puts on a tough front, but he is churning inside. When they go to bed, they turn off the lights.

"Best to draw it to us first, anyway," says Lear.

If it wants us, thinks Edgar lying awake in the dark, it will come no matter what.

The others seem to go off to sleep, but Edgar can't. He gets up and puts on a hotel dressing gown, goes to a wooden desk near the window and lights a small candle. He wants to find out how *Dracula* ends. The instant he opens the novel, he is back in the Carpathian Mountains in Transylvania, this time with a gang of men equipped with Winchester rifles, knives and a sword, racing up a winding road through the forests in pursuit of Count Dracula. The monster is in his coffin on a wagon driven by menacing men, fleeing toward his castle. The sun is setting in the wintry day, and when it is fully down, the creature will arise from that coffin up ahead. Edgar and his friends are urging their horses forward, his wife with the professor near the castle, converging on the beast from there. She is infected, fighting her desire for the demon, hoping they can destroy him. Edgar races his horse around a bend. The wagon comes into view!

Edgar rises to his feet.

He thinks he should go back to bed, get his sleep, but he knows he won't be able to. How can old Lear snore like that? He begins to pace in the darkness. As he walks, he hears sounds from the streets, perhaps as far away as Oxford Street and Regent—drunks crying out, the chime of women's voices, men calling for hansom cabs, the odd neigh of a horse, a train whistle and a crash or two of unknown origin. It sounds like a regular London night. He returns to the little desk and the yellow book with the red title. He has just a few pages left. He takes a deep breath.

He opens it and returns to the winding road leading up to Castle Dracula. Snow is falling. They are closing in on the wagon racing ahead of them. But the sun is setting! They reach the vehicle and attack, but the armed men transporting the coffin fight back. One of Edgar's allies is wounded, sliced open with a knife. Edgar forces his way forward and manages to get onto the wagon and knock the coffin to the ground. They leap upon it and force the lid off. The demon is awakening! It lies there waxen and pale but its eyes are opening.

Edgar hears the door to the hotel room open and when he turns the hag is there. He bangs the book shut and she vanishes.

"What? What?" Jonathan mumbles from his bed, then settles.

Edgar opens the book again. He is armed with a big kukri, a sword-like Nepalese knife as deadly as a machete. Though Dracula is stirring, Edgar doesn't crumble. He slashes at the monster's face with the sword and opens a gaping wound across the throat! The blood oozes out, but the villain doesn't die. It is about to kill Edgar Brim! But his friend leaps forward with a bowie knife and plunges it hard and deep into the demon's chest, right into its heart. It falls back in the coffin and disintegrates into dust before their eyes. The castle looms above them against the red sky amidst the falling snow. Wolves howl.

Edgar closes the book. There is still a page or two left. But he knows what it will be like. It won't be the truth. It will be a happy ending, and the hero will embark upon an idyllic married life, the monster far behind them. Life isn't like that.

But why, thinks Edgar, did Stoker not have his characters put a *real* stake through the beast's heart? And why did it vanish? Does that mean something? Is Stoker saying the demon is still alive?

He spends a sleepless night, but nothing comes for them. As soon as the sun rises, he and Jonathan make their way to the girls' room and are relieved to find them well. They breakfast in the Palm Court room in the hotel, famous for its afternoon teas. There are scones, kippers, sausages and lots of coffee and fruit juice. They are so relieved that the talk is light and there is even laughter. Tiger begins mimicking Numb and Lovecraft, though her imitation of Griswold falls flat, the image of his corpse still in their minds. But they eat well and laugh more as the meal goes on, perhaps because they are tired. Then Lear, who has been somber throughout, steers them to more pressing matters.

"We shall spend the day out in the crowds. I believe there will be safety there. We will visit the National Gallery at Trafalgar Square, perhaps the South Kensington Museum in Knightsbridge; we don't have time for the Crystal Palace. It is best to stay in the city anyway, among greater numbers."

"I agree," says Edgar. "It's unlikely to appear in the streets or among the tourists. It's the Lyceum—that's where it wants us."

"But why?" ask Lucy. "And how? That's a public place too, very public: there are nearly two thousand people there every night."

"Perhaps it wants to draw us to some particular place within the building?" says Tiger. "Maybe down that dark hallway Stoker lead us through?" Her voice grows softer. "Take us one at a time."

"During a private tour?" Lear lets that thought linger over the table.

"Just say it," says Jonathan. "Do you think Stoker is drawing us into a trap?"

"I don't know. But we will be alone with him and perhaps with someone else."

"We just have to be vigilant," says Edgar. "We must be available to whatever is after us, so we can attack it, but not vulnerable. We need to bring whatever weapons we can conceal—the pistol, the big knife and our crucifixes."

"And we must never let Lucy and Tiger from our sight," says Jonathan.

Tiger looks like she wants to protest, but says nothing. They hear the tinkling of utensils on plates, of teaspoons stirred in cups and gentle talk.

"Thank you for adding to our terror, dear brother."

"Not at all, Lu."

"He is just stating the obvious," says Tiger. "If it wants young women, like Dracula, then we must face that. I see it as an opportunity. Perhaps the creature will be drawn to one of us and we can use its weakness for our blood to make it somehow vulnerable. Women must use all the power at their hands. It is a power the rest of you do not have."

Edgar realizes at that moment how deeply he admires his old friend. He looks at her and smiles. She catches his expression and actually colors a little as she turns away.

"Well," says Jonathan, getting to his feet and seizing Tiger by the arm and steering her away from the table and Edgar, "it is time to go out on the town. Museums and art galleries and all of London await us!" She pulls away from him but they head toward the lobby together, Jon, big and bold, actually making her laugh.

The other three sit silently at the table, Lucy watching Edgar staring at her brother and Tiger Tilley.

"Just to change the subject," she says and waits until Edgar turns back to them. "Grandfather, why do you think little Shakespeare is *so* certain that there are more aberrations about than just this one?"

"It is something he has gotten into his head. He believes it fervently."

"Well, then it is likely nonsense. There's no proof of any others, is there?"

"I have no idea. Sometimes I think he is mad like a fox. But mostly, I just think he is mad."

"And yet," says Edgar, "it seems this thing we are pursuing now is real, which means he was right that something would come after you if you killed the Grendel creature. If we kill this one, then why couldn't another come too?"

"I think we should be on our way," says Lear, getting to his feet. "We can't let those two have all the fun."

They spend a glorious day in London at the museum and the National Gallery, slipping back for a while on an omnibus to the Langham to eat at the Palm Court. They forget their troubles for stretches and couple into different combinations, each pair on their own at times—Edgar with Lucy on his arm, Edgar with Tiger, and Jonathan with the combative Miss Tilley.

But one moment thrills them more than any other, and it isn't necessarily because they enjoy it. It happens at the gallery. At the top of the marble stairs leading into the first viewing room, the sun shining in from glorious Trafalgar Square through the windows, a painting sits on an easel for the public to examine. It is new and arousing a good deal of controversy. It is by an artist named Philip Burne-Jones and called *The Vampire*. It depicts a full-figured woman clad in loosened undergarments, her beautiful dark hair unleashed and cascading down her back and naked arms, black eyes shining, lips blood red, her teeth showing, leaning over a man in bed, smiling while he lies sleeping or unconscious under her, his shirt ripped open, his chest bared, prey for his gorgeous conqueror.

"It should be removed!" shouts an old woman as they come up the stairs.

"It is said," snarls another, "that the artist adores an actress, and it is her, his fantasy come to life, who is upon this poor man in this bed. He should be arrested!"

"It is influenced by that novel, I've heard," says a stern man. "That hideous sensation trash by Henry Irving's manager, Stooker or some such name. Sir Henry should dismiss him and all copies should be burned!"

Edgar and Lucy are close to each other as they approach the painting, but she sees it first. He shuffles nearer her as she looks at it, her face slightly reddening. He can feel the heat of her arm next to his. But when he turns and gazes at it too, he is almost instantly inside it: on the bed, a woman over him and smiling down on him, her thigh pressed against his torso. He looks up and sees that the woman isn't Lucy. Tiger Tilley has him in her grip, alarmingly alluring. He turns away and walks into the gallery, his heart rate accelerated. Jonathan lingers. He makes a joke as he looks at the canvas, but glances back several times when they leave. Tiger stares at it too, for a long while.

They reach the Lyceum at four o'clock and make their way to the side door. As they near, Tiger, Lucy and Jonathan join arms and walk quickly, teasing Edgar that they are running away together. There is something forced about their attitude, as if they are trying to stave off their fears.

The building's shadow looms over them.

The side door of the Lyceum opens with a bang. Bram Stoker is standing there. He smiles at them.

"Welcome," he intones.

31

The Devil's Set

Stoker shows them the lobby and the ticket office first, and then takes them back to the hallway under the stage. He suggests that the "young ladies" go first, but Tiger demurs, saying she is frightened and wants to be near Jonathan, and Lucy says the same about Edgar. So Stoker takes the lead. Halfway along, deep in the theater at the darkest point in the hall, he stops and turns to them.

"I have a confession to make." He pauses. "I am not what I seem."

Jonathan, who is in front of his friends, makes himself large in the tight space and puts his hand into his pocket to find his pistol. Lear, who is wearing his greatcoat, has his huge knife concealed inside it. Tiger has stolen two small carving knives from the Langham's restaurant and given one to Edgar: hers is in her purse, his up a sleeve. They all bear crucifixes on little chains around their necks, hidden under their clothing. Tonight—if they make it that far—the girls will be sure theirs can be seen, displayed on their chests.

"What are you then, sir?" asks Jonathan.

"I have powers," says Stoker. No one responds. His left hand moves toward his coat pocket. "I am not merely the manager." He pulls something out. Tiger quietly unsnaps her purse and puts her hand inside. "I have the run of the place." Stoker jingles what is in his hands, and it's hard to make out in the dimly lit corridor, but when he holds it higher, they can see it is a ring of keys. "Follow me," he says.

They ascend the stone stairs again, pass the wing to the stage and move by the staircase that leads up to the Beefsteak Room. Then they descend a few steps and turn down another hallway, this one wider and wood paneled. They pass more doors, going deeper into the basement of the theater.

"These are the dressing rooms of the lesser lights, but here," he pauses and mentions an actor who often plays opposite Irving, "is one that might interest you." He unlocks the door, flips on an electric light and ushers them inside. It is small but cozy, smells of greasepaint and has a desk with a chair and mirror, lit up with lamps. There's makeup in canisters and a rack of costumes along a wall. Among them is Faust's clothing.

"Won't he mind?" asks Lucy.

"It is my choice to show you," says Stoker, "and he will not dare confront me." There is a hint of anger in his voice, a dictator's tone they haven't heard before. But then he smiles. "Shall I leave you alone in here for a while?" he asks and begins to close the door on them, but Lear puts his big arm against it. They slip quickly back into the hall.

"One more," says their guide. There is a long gap before they reach the next door. Stoker is about to use his key when he sees a line of light along the crack at the floor. "Ah, the great artist is in." He knocks. There is silence but the door opens on its own. It hadn't seemed that anyone had approached. In the entrance is Ellen Terry. Lucy and Tiger gasp.

"Uncle Bram!" Miss Terry exclaims and smiles at them all, her mouth large and sensual on a flawless face glowing without a stroke of makeup, her gray eyes bright with spirit. Her shining hair is tossed about on her head, not yet attended to but somehow perfect. She is fifty years old and ageless, as beautiful as the day she made her debut. The greatest actress in the world stands before them.

"Miss Terry, I thought I might acquaint you with some friends, readers of my novel."

"Oh! I have begun it, though I don't know if I can go on!"

Stoker grins and introduces his guests. The young ladies offer slight curtsies and the men actually lower their heads. Lear is speechless and extends a shaking hand, which the great lady takes gently and squeezes. She gives him a flirty look. Edgar wonders if he should stand near the old man to keep him upright. She is wearing a red dressing gown. It is done up to her chin and they cannot see her neck.

"Why are you here so early, dear one?" asks Stoker. "This isn't like you."

"I thought I might see him for a few moments, but he is not seeing anyone now. So I am glad to have visitors. Won't you come in?"

They survey the room in awe. Her mirror, the pictures of her two children and her costumes seem to sparkle. As the five visitors leave, she gives them each a flower from a vase on her desk.

In the hallway, they turn in the direction from which they have come. Lear stops. He looks the other way toward a door down the hall, a good fifty feet from them, closed and in shadows, a light coming from under it too. "Can we not . . ." He pauses.

"Can you not what?"

"See his room?" asks Edgar.

Stoker glares at him. "The master's? Have you taken leave of your senses, boy?"

"No, sir, but we saw Miss Terry's and—"

"He is NOT Miss Terry! I shall show you the stage and then we must end the tour."

Stoker is in much better spirits when they emerge onto the stage. He takes them out through the wing near the Beefsteak Room. The theater is still dark, just a few footlights are lit, but the dim lighting creates a spooky effect. They are in the realm of the devil.

Stoker is going on about a scenery detail, his chest puffed out and proud, but Edgar can barely listen. He cannot believe where he is. The seats rise before him like a sea of possibilities—he can see thousands of mesmerized eyes, hear the rapturous applause. He notices marks on the boards. One near the edge of the stage says Mephistopheles. It's Irving's mark! He goes to it and stands on it. For an instant, he is Sir Henry Irving! He becomes Satan. But he shakes himself out of it. He knows he needs to be respectful and listen to Stoker, and turns back to the others. The stage tour is in full swing. Stoker writes some of Irving's public speeches and has a way with words: he loves to hear himself speak.

"There are, of course, many special effects in our production of *Faust*: from the opening in heaven to the devil materializing from smoke when he comes to tempt Dr. Faust, and so on. But the ultimate moment occurs on the Brocken, the fearful German mountain top where, on Walpurgis Night, the witches and other evil ones meet and dance in a horrific display." Stoker smiles at the thought. "In order to create such scenes, we move parts of the set on and off the stage, but some things are permanent. All of the Walpurgis Night set remains in place throughout, here at the back."

Stoker takes them toward the rear of the stage. Upon it they see mounds of what appears to be black earth. Edgar reaches down and touches it.

"Yes, it is real," says their host. "Sir Henry demands nothing less. And how, you might ask, did we get so much soil on stage? It is ingenious yet simple. Directly below, at the most removed part of the stage, is a deep basement with an earthen floor. We opened up the stage and, using a pulley system, raised tons of soil. When we are done, we will remove the boards again and let it fall back from whence it came!"

The huge mounds have a scattering of gravestones, a guillotine and five-foot wooden stakes for grave markers, sharpened to deadly points. Edgar remembers the Walpurgis Night scene. It was during that presentation of flying beasts and evil that he imagined he saw the beautiful young woman thrown upon the boards at the feet of Irving and the tall man.

"There isn't a graveyard or a guillotine in Goethe's original play, but we added them for effect."

Edgar recalls, with a shiver, the gravediggers excavating one of the plots as Mephistopheles spun tales of depravity and temptation for Faust.

"Do they fill it back in after every show?"

"That was what you heard last night when we walked down the hallway—stagehands shoveling soil into a grave—though it may have been our ghost, as well." Stoker grins.

Edgar approaches the guillotine. He remembers the animals' heads being put into it during the scene, the sound of the blade falling, the blood oozing, the thunder cracking through the building, the orchestra playing frightening music. The animals seemed real and so did the blood. They had cried out as they were being taken to their deaths.

"Is this real too?" asks Edgar, reaching out for the killing machine.

"DON'T!" cries Stoker.

But it is too late. Edgar puts his hand on the guillotine, right where a victim's head would go, and the blade is unleashed. The heavy steel shoots down in a flash.

"No!" cries Lucy.

At the last second, Edgar gets his fingers out of the way, leaving the flower Miss Terry gave him behind. The blade slices through it, sending its red petals spraying across the soil like drops of blood on black.

They all stand still.

"The . . ." says Stoker finally, "the mechanism is tripped by placing something in the head hole. Sir Henry insisted it be real. All the stagehands have been warned."

Half an hour later, Bram Stoker walks alone down the hallway toward the door at the far end. He can hear Irving talking to himself again, imitating the old man with the eastern European accent. Stoker hears just snippets. "Tonight is the night," he thinks he hears the old man say. "Yes," replies Irving in his own voice, "tonight."

Stoker raps on the door. There is a long silence and then it opens. Looking gaunt and strange in the full makeup of Mephistopheles, a ghoulish green tinge on his face, his lips blood red and eyebrows thick and as black as brimstone, Irving stands before him. That face, put into the red hood of the character, presents an unnerving appearance each night. He wears red tights and shoes, red from head to foot, a new color for the devil on stage.

"Yes, Stoker, what do you want? You know I do not like to be disturbed this close to a performance."

"Might I come in?"

"For seconds."

The room is dark, only the mirror lit. Irving likes it this way. It feels evil to him and he is summoning that feeling tonight.

Stoker eyes the painting of the Impaler again.

"What did you want?" asks Irving.

"It's about my novel."

"Did we not speak of it before?"

"I would like to turn it into a play."

Irving grins. "An admirable idea, I am sure, though transforming your sort of work into a production that makes the money we demand would not be easy, you know."

"I think this one would suffice."

"Oh, really?" He smiles indulgently again.

"It is much different. And I would, of course, like you to play the lead role, sir."

"Yes, I would have guessed that, dear Stoker. And what *is* the role?"

"Count Dracula."

"A count? I see. Well, that in itself has possibilities. What sort of man is this chap?"

"He is not a man, sir."

"Not a man? Then what, pray tell, is he?"

"He is a vampire."

Irving's green-tinged face seems to turn white.

"Nonsense!" he says. "Leave me. I must prepare!"

32

Walpurgis Night

T hey return to the theater early and are in the stalls in front row seats, armed and excited, long before the orchestra even begins. Lucy and Tiger, though wearing the same gowns as the previous night, seem even more beautiful to Edgar. Perhaps it is the thrill of being so close to the stage or of what might transpire afterward—when they plan to sneak back into the theater and explore its hidden chambers—that makes their complexions glow and their eyes shimmer. They both wear silk lilac gloves that go up past their elbows, their polished crosses displayed on their chests. They seem especially enamored with their escorts tonight too. Edgar has Lucy on his arm, of course, and Jonathan guides a reluctant Tiger. Handsome in black again, Edgar has tried to calm his unruly hair, but it sweeps about on his head, flaming red above his blue eyes and dark complexion.

He stands until the last minute, gazing around, the seats behind him filled with excited people. The music swells from the pit near them and he feels as though he is already being transported into the world of the great play. But he knows that when

Irving appears, electric and nearly within touching distance, the effect will be even greater.

The lights begin to go down and he turns and gives one final, sweeping glance toward the anxious crowd. A tall man with an aquiline nose and a black bowler hat pulled down almost around the ears enters the auditorium at the last moment. Edgar squints in the dimming illumination, thinking the man looks familiar. For an instant, he feels he is under the gray skies on the moors again, on the front lawn near the stable. But darkness in the theater swallows the man and Edgar turns back to the stage.

When Irving enters, Edgar feels as though he is pinned to his seat. The great man is like a specter up close: the pale face, red lips, the mesmerizing black eyes, all framed by scarlet. He comes to the edge of the stage and peers down on the first row and his gaze lights on Edgar. There are no irises in his eyes! They are all black pupils! Irving stares right into Edgar Brim and the boy feels as though the great man touches his soul, as if a clammy cold hand has gripped his heart.

Edgar soon drifts completely into Irving's world. He senses that this artist is talking directly to him again, telling him to listen to the sound of his voice. The Walpurgis Night scene on the Brocken nears. As it opens, a movement off to Edgar's right and behind him catches his attention. The tall man he had seen entering the auditorium late is rising from his seat. He moves to the aisle and begins approaching the stage! Edgar can't believe it. He glances around and sees that no one else has noticed. They are fixated on the spectacle in front of them.

The tall man stops before he reaches the stage and turns down Edgar's row, stepping over spectators with his long legs, nearing them! Edgar realizes that he is not looking directly at the man, nor had he turned his head to see the audience. He is observing everything peripherally. In fact, he cannot move. He is entranced! Paralyzed! He can only move his eyes. He looks up and sees the hag on the stage beside Irving. The great man is talking but the hideous old woman doesn't care. She leers at Edgar Brim. She is coming for him.

The tall man stands directly over him for a moment, long legs on either side of him, huge thin hands on his shoulders, pressing down on him. The odor of something burnt and metallic, like blood, fills Edgar's nostrils. It almost makes him retch. The man has taken his hat off and Edgar sees him clearly. But the gaunt face is staring past him. It glares down at the girls as if it wants to possess them, a terrifying, rapacious expression.

Then it seizes Lucy! . . . And then Jonathan!

They rise with him, enthralled. Edgar tries to move. But the hag intervenes. She has leapt down from the stage, clambered into the crowd and is climbing on top of him. His arms and legs are now useless weights. The tall man has one of each of his friends' hands in his and is elegantly guiding them past the other rigid spectators in the row and out into the aisle. As Edgar sits there horrified and straining to see past the dirty, clotted hair of the hag, the man sets Lucy and Jonathan on the stage, placing them so they sit facing out. He leaps onto the boards and lands behind them. He lifts them, one in each arm, as easily as if they were lambs, and carries them across the stage!

"NO!" Edgar shouts inside his mind. No sound comes out. Fear engulfs him. The hag is going to act now. She leans down, her fanged teeth bared, and begins to bite his neck.

The tall man drops Edgar's friends at Irving's feet—as he did with the beautiful young lady last night. Brim wonders if she is still alive.

Irving continues to emote, spinning his evil lines in the Walpurgis Night scene, but he is slowing down, his words beginning to slur. The tall man regards the audience and bends down and takes Lucy in his arms, his face close to hers. He opens her dress and slides it down, baring her to just below the collarbone. Edgar squirms inside his rigid body. The man undoes her copper hair and lets it fall over her shoulders. She lies there below, gazing up at him. Edgar screams. But there is still no sound. The big man lays Lucy on the stage and moves to Jonathan, unbuttoning his shirt and laying him out at Irving's feet. The man turns to Edgar and opens his mouth. Edgar doesn't know what terrifies him most: that he will watch the vampire—THE vampire, not a fantasy—defile Lucy and Jon before his eyes, or that it will then return for Tiger, Lear and him.

The demon keeps its attention on Edgar Brim as it bends over Lucy. She waits for him, ecstasy in her vacant eyes. Jonathan will soon be next, strong and powerful yet meekly yielding at his conqueror's feet.

Do not be afraid.

Edgar turns to the hag and stares into its eyes. "No," he says to it. He understands what is happening. The demon on the stage is somehow working with the great actor to mesmerize the audience.

The two of them are conspirators in evil. The creature likely does this any night it pleases. There, before it, every evening Irving is at work, is a vast banquet of blood in the audience. It can have its pick! And they have no idea! It can drain whomever it wants. They soon die in their homes, just as his father did, an anonymous victim in the world's greatest metropolis. But why had it taken Allen Brim? Edgar thinks again of what Lear said—Lear sitting there unaware and transfixed—about making the mistake of telling his father that he suspected some demons were real, about being close to him, about his belief that the creature was somewhere in or near the college, listening, ever ready to remove anyone who might be a threat. It had let his father go . . . but then it had seen him years later in this very theater, and in recognition and hunger, had descended!

"No," Edgar says again to the hag, and she begins to fade. She tries to cling to him, but the weight has been removed. Up above, the monster has his hands on Lucy's bared shoulders, his mouth moving toward her chest.

A hole in the heart! thinks Edgar. This thing will puncture her and suck blood straight from the source! The best blood, the purest. Why would it bother with a neck? That's just a story.

At that moment, Edgar becomes fully aware of his powers. Though everyone else is helpless, he is different. Edgar Brim can be in an imagined world and also be aware of it. He *knows* he is being hypnotized. So he can step out of it! He has always had the ability to understand stories, enter them and watch and mine them as he reads or listens. He is aware of *both* stories being played out on the stage. The demon doesn't know that. It cannot entrance Edgar like it does the others.

Edgar rises to his feet. He scrambles over the seats to the aisle.

Up above, the tall man spots him out of the corner of his eye and pulls back from Lucy's chest, utter surprise on his face.

Edgar seizes the edge of the stage and leaps onto it. He turns for an instant and looks back at the crowd. Every face stares at a now-frozen Irving!

Edgar turns to the demon. It takes a step away, almost frightened. But then it leans down and again picks up Lucy and Jonathan. They droop over his long spidery limbs.

"Let them be," says Edgar. His voice is strong but quiet. "Or—"

"Or what?" says the man. It is a deep, foreign voice. He is late in his middle years with dark eyes and brows, a shaved head with a long nose like an eagle's. He is dressed in black, his white shirt almost startling amidst his long dark coat.

"I will shout," says Edgar and motions to the audience, "and all this will end." He scans the crowd. "They will awaken!" He hopes this is true.

The revenant pauses. "So we have a standoff, Master Brim. I believe, however, I have the advantage upon you."

"And how is that?"

"Should you shout and break the spell, I shall kill one of your lovely friends here instantaneously. Examine them, so delectable! You can watch." He smiles and Edgar can see the long teeth inside his red mouth. They aren't fangs, but they are big and long and powerful, perhaps grown sturdy over the centuries, beyond human teeth. He sees that one has been sharpened to a point. Edgar imagines this beast penetrating Lucy's or Jonathan's chest, driving down right through the breastbone, cracking it, the blood sucked from the heart.

"I used to take from the jugular vein but I was still weak afterward. I needed purer sustenance. I learned to bore into the heart, crush through the protective bone for the best wine! I'm sure I was seen sucking on necks! It gave rise to such silly, romantic twaddle!"

Edgar isn't sure what to do. But he must do something. He considers attacking his opponent. But a better idea comes to him.

"I shall let you go," he says, "if you let them be."

The revenant ponders this for a moment. "No one can know," he finally says, stepping back. His eyes glisten. "And I shall come for you again, very soon."

"And I for you."

"Please do."

"Let them be."

"I shall set them down and walk up the aisle within inches of hundreds of people. Should you shout at any moment, I will kill someone, perhaps more than one."

He keeps his red eyes fixed on Edgar as he sets Lucy and Jon onto the boards. Then he leaps down into the aisle and turns to observe his enemy. He walks slowly backward, his face toward the stage, his long fingers caressing one spectator after another. And then, in the blink of an eye, he is out the door.

Edgar feels like he should weep. But he doesn't and neither does he shout. If he cries out, how will he explain all this, standing here alone on the stage with the Lears at his feet, their clothes disheveled and undone? He looks around in this frozen work of art. Irving stands just a few feet away. Edgar walks toward him.

He brings his face up within inches of his. He looks into the black eyes. Are they truly evil? What, really, is his role in this darkness? Edgar turns toward Lucy and Jonathan, spread out below him on the floor. They had been at the monster's mercy and he had saved them.

He advances and stands over Lucy. Her beautiful copper hair hangs down over the top of her opened dress, her red mouth open, her eyes still caught in a look of desire. She is truly magnificent. He kneels down between the two siblings. He is remembering what Mephistopheles says to Faust about women: that they were there for his pleasure.

He reaches for Lucy, quickly re-fastens her dress, fixes her hair back into place and does up the buttons on Jonathan's shirt. He drags the bigger boy to the edge of the stage, gets down, then hoists him up on his shoulders with a grunt and somehow gets him to his seat. He does the same with Lucy, carrying her in his arms. Then, he returns to his own place.

He shouts.

There is a different sort of silence in the theater as the spell is broken. The actors, including Irving, come out of their freeze but are still. But then the great stage veteran declaims his next line and the play resumes.

Lucy and Jonathan are staring up at Sir Henry, alive and intrigued. She finds a hair out of place and absentmindedly puts it back. She notices Edgar looking at her and smiles at him. He smiles back. Did he dream what just happened?

He feels a couple of marks on his throat, just slight ones, already fading.

At the play's end, they head up the aisle and retrieve their coats from the cloakroom.

"Nothing remarkable in the production," says Lear. "We must sneak back in once the crowd disperses. We know the innards of the theater well now."

"No," says Edgar firmly.

"I beg your pardon?"

The boy has never spoken like this to the professor.

"Our plans have changed."

Outside, Edgar explains. He sees faces grow white, even Lear's. He takes Lucy's hand as he speaks and feels her tremble. Tiger looks angry. Only Jonathan is unaffected. He offers a smirk and shakes his head in disbelief.

Edgar is thinking of two other things as he speaks. The first is that the crosses on their chests did nothing. The second is what the demon said to him when they were locked in their duel upon the stage.

"I shall come for you again," it had said, "very soon."

33

After the Master

"The creature isn't here now," says Edgar as they all stand in a circle outside the theater. "He has fled the building."

Lucy, who had pulled her coat about herself as Edgar spoke, now feels Tiger's arm go around her too. They stand close.

"Eddie," says Jonathan, "you can't expect us to believe this. These things you dreamed this phantom did to me? Not possible."

"Jon," says Lucy, "he saw—"

"I suppose it didn't say where it went?" asks Jonathan. "Perhaps out for a spot of tea?"

"I don't know," replies Edgar. "I saw what I saw. You can believe as you wish."

"It is said that hypnotism is a power these creatures possess," says Lear.

"Where? In the handbook for vampires?"

"Why would Brim make this up?"

"I didn't say that. He fell asleep. He was dreaming. He's good at that."

"We cannot take the chance that he wasn't."

"I think we should proceed as if it was real," adds Lucy. Tiger says nothing.

"Sis, I believe you are biased. We should re-enter and search inside, trap this thing." He puts his hand on the pistol in his coat. "I'm ready!"

"That would be useless," says Edgar matter-of-factly. "It has gone. We need to seek it somewhere else."

"Perhaps in your fantasies?"

"If this is happening," asks Lear, as much to himself as the others, "then what, exactly, is Irving's role?" He addresses Edgar. "Is he making you see this man? Is *he* the monster?"

"I can't say for sure."

"What of Stoker?"

Even Jonathan is grim at that.

"We need to see Irving in person again, examine him closer this time, speak to him and draw him out."

Edgar realizes that when Sir Henry was frozen and within inches of his face, he had been so intrigued by his eyes that he hadn't bothered to examine the rest of him. He should have looked closely at his throat and unbuttoned his costume and searched his chest. He worries that Jonathan is right—perhaps he dreamed everything. Standing outside in the cool London night now, it all seems a fantasy.

"We must speak to Stoker more forthrightly too," says Lear. "Corner him. Make him answer!" He turns to Jonathan. "For now, let us believe what Brim is telling us and move forward. If we are wrong, we will know soon enough!"

Moments later they are at the back door on Burleigh Street. Another little crowd has gathered. They wait for a long while. A drizzle begins to fall. The sounds of the city—the harnesses, drunken shouts, distant conversations—lessen as the night lengthens.

Then the door opens with a bang. Hawkins pushes the crowd back. Out comes Irving, appearing more exhausted this time, his eyes dead under his top hat, his walking stick hanging limply from his side, Stoker behind him and concerned, his arms reaching out but not touching him, as if trying to guide him toward the hansom cab that is now rolling up. Edgar steps directly in front of Irving, checking his neck, ready with a question.

"Are you—"

"Stand back!" cries Stoker. "You should know better! Step away!"

There are no puncture marks or healing wounds anywhere that Edgar can see, but he is aghast at how drained the face is. Then again, Irving is nearly sixty years old and at the end of another exhausting, soul-stirring turn. Edgar again wishes he could see his bare chest.

Alarmed by the boy, Irving steps quickly up into the carriage and it is sent away before another word is said. Stoker turns back to them, eyes on fire.

"What can you possibly be thinking?"

Lear moves close to him. "We believe that the fiend in your novel may be *real*. And it may have something to do with Mr. Irving."

Several of the other hangers-on hear what he says and turn back from watching the carriage slip into the night. They step away from the business manager of the Royal Lyceum Theatre and the one-armed man who is confronting him.

"I shall call the police," says Stoker. "You are mad."

"I do not mean that you saw a demon exactly like that or even that it exists in that form. But you saw or heard something. Some force caused you to write *Dracula*, something deep and meaning-ful, more than you have told us, something somehow real!"

The onlookers start to walk away. Hawkins stands near his boss, unsure what to do.

Stoker steps back from them. He thinks of the second voice he has so often heard in Irving's dressing room. He thinks of the cruel deeds of Vlad the Impaler, of Irving's fascination with the long-dead tyrant, of what he learned when he researched his life, imag-ining human beings impaled right through their bodies from their trunks up through their throats. He thinks of the man with the foreign voice in Scotland that seemed to match the one in Irving's room, walking away in the rain in the direction of the Highlands and its desolate moors. He thinks of Irving in the morgues of Paris, on ship decks in storms on the Atlantic, and of the power Irving has over people, the way he connects to evil. Stoker won-ders about a vampire, not a fantasy, not something fended off with garlic and crosses and feared only between the pages of a sensation novel. What if one were real?

"Did you," asks Edgar, "model your demon after Irving?"

Hawkins walks away and re-enters the theater. Only Stoker remains near the five friends, though a young woman, who was here the previous night, is listening carefully a carriage length away.

"Did you?" repeats Lear.

"That is nonsense," says Stoker, swallowing. He walks toward the door and then is gone.

"We must pursue Irving," says Edgar.

"But we have no idea where he has gone," says Lucy.

"I do," says a voice behind them. The young woman steps forward. "I come 'ere every night to see 'im walk by, though I've only seen 'im once upon the stage. Can't afford more." Her eyes glow. "I've followed 'im, sirs, and I know where 'e lives. Takes Miss Terry with 'im some evenings." She smiles. "I 'ave sat outside 'is place all night, many times, until the bobbies 'ave moved me on."

Tiger walks up to her. "Tell us where he lives," she demands. Jonathan advances too.

But the woman barely hears. Perhaps forty years younger than the legendary master of the Lyceum stage, her mind is soaring and in his thrall. "You are right about 'im! Powers, 'e 'as!" Her eyes are huge now. "I love 'im. But 'e's a demon!"

They hail two hansom cabs and tell the drivers the address the woman gave them: 17 Stratton Street off Piccadilly. It takes them less than fifteen minutes to get there. They head west down The Strand through the south end of Trafalgar Square and then along the north side of Green Park, its wrought iron fence between them and Buckingham Palace, lit wonderfully in the distance. They tell the cabbies to stop on the corner. Number seventeen is a cricket bowl away, up this short, canyon-like road of four- and five- story buildings, most made of stone or brick and set tightly together like walls.

"Let's go right in, surprise him," says Edgar.

"That would be best, weapons out," says Jonathan.

They had decided not to take the time to return to the hotel, so they don't have Thorne's guns, but they have the pistol, the kitchen knives, and Lear has his sword-like blade. They have their crucifixes and strings of garlic in the pockets of their out-of-door coats. They have a measure of deadly force.

"We may find only Irving," says Lear, "not the creature."

"Perhaps one and the same," says Tiger.

Edgar is looking out into the night. "We may have to kill both."

Jonathan turns to his grandfather. "Your blade goes through his heart."

"We shall knock and I'll send up my card," says Lear. "We want to speak with him first. Our journey will either end here or come very close." His voice falters a little on the last word. "Be prepared for anything, all of you."

They walk up the street and find number seventeen, a five-story red brick building at the end with little iron balconies, extensive flats on each floor. The young woman had said that Irving's was at the top. They can see a light up there and a shadow pacing back and forth.

There is no footman at the main door. It creaks when they open it. They begin walking up the stairs.

34

In the Demon's Nest

Lear puts a finger to his lips and they ascend the stairs as slowly and quietly as possible. But the girls are in evening dresses and coats and have to hold them up as they walk, setting the narrow heels of their boots carefully on each step. Tiger's face is filled with frustration; Lucy is patient. The stairs are wooden and the five intruders go rigid with each creak, even as they pass the first few stories. Once they get to the fourth, they slow even more, hearing footsteps pacing on the floor above, and as they light upon the first step going to the fifth, they hear voices and halt. The dominant voice is not Irving's. It is deeper, foreign. Edgar cups his hands over his mouth and whispers to the others. "It's the demon I saw on the stage!" Fear flickers across Jonathan's eyes, as if for the first time he is facing the possibility that the scene in the theater was not a dream.

Edgar thinks of his father. He pulls his knife from his coat and advances up the stairs.

"Edgar!" cries Tiger as loudly as she dares. But he doesn't stop and she follows. Just as she did against the coward Fardle long ago, she will defend him tonight to the death.

The others have no choice but to go with them. Up on the top floor there is only one door. They sneak down the polished wooden boards of the hallway toward it. When they arrive, Edgar motions to Tiger. She pulls a wire from the underclothing inside her dress. In less than a minute, she has sprung the lock.

As the door swings slowly inward, they can hear the deep voice much clearer. In fact, that voice is now all they hear. It is moving about, its owner pacing. They get inside and gently close the entrance, crouching down in the vestibule. The voice is coming through a partially open door, emotionless.

"I cannot die. I am undead. You are related. You are a genius. You can be irresistible. You can be evil for your art. Listen to me. Listen to me."

Lucy puts her jewelry into her coat pocket, slips the coat off and drops it onto the floor, then unlaces her high-heeled boots and removes them. The others watch in silence. They know what she is doing. She is the stealthiest of them all. Edgar wants to stop her but understands he shouldn't. "You see," mouths Lear to the others, "a woman!"

But then Lucy does something that startles them even more. She takes off the cross. Jonathan reaches out to pull her back, but she is gone.

Lucy crawls on her hands and knees into the drawing room. She catches a glimpse of the pacing man, but doesn't pause because she's exposed between a chair and a sofa. She darts behind the bigger piece of furniture.

"I must sleep. I must sleep," says the man. "It will be light before I know it."

Lucy peeks around the end of the sofa. The man is walking directly toward her. *It's Henry Irving. And he sees her!* She scurries away, back toward her friends, knocking a lamp over as she flees. Edgar reaches out and catches it, but it still smacks into his hands.

Jonathan leaps to his feet, pulling his pistol out. Tiger grabs her knife in one hand, holding out her cross in the other, and Edgar is instantly on his feet too, standing directly in front of Lucy, with his own knife out in a flash.

Henry Irving stalks toward them.

"I can do as I please!" he intones in the voice of the monster. His eyes are on fire, red in the dim electric light. His long face seems lit from within and very white.

Jonathan raises the pistol and trains it at his head. Six shots. They must all hit the mark and then the five of them must fall on the demon together. Lear must drive the knife-sword deep into his heart.

But then Irving turns away. He had almost reached one end of the room as he neared them but then pivoted and is pacing toward the other, still speaking.

"Better and better every night. Tell the truth! Be the devil!"

"He didn't see us?" whispers Jonathan.

Irving turns at the far end of the room and comes at them again. They raise their weapons again. But before he reaches them, he pivots once more and turns around!

"He's in some sort of trance," says Lear, lowering his sword. "He can't see us."

"No fantasy," says the great actor, "just me."

"But that voice," says Edgar. "I am certain it's the one the creature used on stage! He is speaking in *his* voice."

"He speaks in many voices," says Lear. "He has for years."

They hear the creak of a door. Someone, something, that has remained absolutely silent until now, is entering from another room! All five of them dart behind the big sofa again. They barely fit but are out of the way just as the intruder nears.

"To bed, mon cher!" says a deep, foreign voice, even more resonant than the one Irving had employed.

The demon—in the flesh!

"Heed me once more," he says to Henry Irving. "You are my vessel. You must sleep." He sounds upset, thinks Edgar. "There is much to do tonight!"

The creature swoops across the floor and picks up the gaunt, aging artist in his arms and carries him, not through one of the doors to the bedroom, but to a sofa that sits directly across the room from the other one, no more than ten strides away. There, he sets him down, sweeps a blanket from a nearby love seat with a flourish, puffs up a few pillows, sets Irving's head on them and covers him up. "Sleep well, my comrade. I may have need of you soon."

Between the spaces in the curling designs on the furniture's wood frame, Edgar can see the revenant's mouth in profile. It curls into a cruel smile. The lips are scarlet. Then the villain turns and bends down toward Irving and lingers there, the great man helpless beneath him. They hear the creature removing Sir Henry's clothes, then some sort of sound, perhaps a long kiss, perhaps a slight sucking. The villain's head is below the actor's, on his lips or his neck or his chest. Then he rises and sighs, and pauses before turning toward the room he had come from, loosening his cravat as he goes, closing the door behind him.

The five hunters don't move for the longest time. No sounds come from the bedroom.

"We cannot leave," whispers Edgar finally. "It might hear us. We must use what we have with us now to kill it." The others nod.

"It is still dark out," says Lear. "I do not know if the vampire myths are correct, but I will not take any chances—we will wait until the sun rises and assume that is the best time to act. We will try the crosses again too—we won't be entranced this time. At the first crack of dawn, we enter that bedroom. We should be able to take him by surprise. Lucy and Jonathan go first, Lucy with both crucifixes held out and Jon shooting at point-blank range at the head, all the bullets. The rest of us will fall upon him: Brim's knife to the neck, Tilley's to the abdomen and mine will go into the heart. If I cannot penetrate deeply enough, someone may have to help me, putting more weight down upon the big blade. If we are successful, we instantly sever the head. You all must have a string of garlic around your neck."

They nod again, looking grim. "We have just a few hours. At least one of us must remain awake at all times."

But none of them really sleep. They stay behind the sofa leaning against each other, coats wrapped around them, trying. The bedroom remains quiet. Jonathan pretends that he has drifted peacefully away, but his eyes keep opening.

"Now," says Lucy, as the first rays of light come through the drawing room windows.

They get to their feet and walk silently toward the bedroom door, exchanging anxious glances. They line up in the right order,

Lear's hand gently on the knob. Lucy holds the two crosses, arms straight out and trembling, and Jonathan cocks his pistol. Tiger is in her bare feet, her heeled boots left by the sofa, her eyes lit up. By her side, Edgar is determined, his mouth set tightly.

"Ready?" asks Lear.

They all nod.

He opens the door.

35

The Real One

The creature isn't lying down with his head on the pillow in a darkened room, as they hoped. The curtains are open and he is sitting up on the bed, fully clothed in the growing sunlight, unaffected by it, awaiting them. He has a vase in his hand, which he hurls at Jonathan just as he is about to pull the trigger, sending the gun flying. It hits the floor with a crash.

We needed the cannon, thinks Edgar, as guilt mixes with the fear that invades him. It should have been ready in the other room, waiting to unload an expanding steel ball that would take off this thing's head.

But that isn't possible now.

The creature leaps to his feet and comes at them. Edgar, Tiger and Jonathan all reach for Lucy and pull her to them. But the revenant doesn't touch them. Instead, he picks up the pistol and throws it through an open window into the backyard. Then he steps back and lies down on the bed.

"Do what you will," he says. "My time has come." He unbuttons his shirt and reveals his chest, a white breastbone over the heart. They stand together near the door, unsure what to do. Then Edgar thinks of his father. He turns and takes the big blade from Lear's hand and advances to the bed.

"You murdered my father," says Edgar Brim.

"And mine," says Lucy, advancing too.

"Scrivener," says Lear quietly.

"But this," cries Edgar with fire in his eyes, "is for the little boy!"

He drives the big knife down into the demon's chest. It enters the breastbone with a scraping thud and goes deep into his vital organ. Jonathan stands helpless without a weapon, but Tiger flies onto the bed, both her hands around the sword, putting her full weight onto it, penetrating him up to the hilt. The demon gasps and quivers.

And then he smiles.

With one long spidery arm, almost as long as Tiger, he grips Edgar by the scruff of his neck and sends him sailing across the room. The boy smacks against a bureau and his back smashes the mirror, which shatters into a thousand pieces. He slides down to the floor, his smaller knife still in hand.

With the big blade sticking from his chest, blood oozing from it, the demon rolls Tiger off and pins her with an arm. When she kicks, he grinds his forearm into her neck. He looks at her and licks his lips. "Ah, this one!" He regards the others. "You can watch. Remember, Brim? This is better, since she is awake!" Edgar gazes at his dear friend, her black hair disheveled around her angry face, her twice-broken nose the emblem of her bravery, still kicking beneath the creature. "Afterward, I shall choose which one of you will be next." Tiger's kicking fades as the revenant's big arm drives into her windpipe.

"B-but the knife," stammers Lear, "in your *heart!*"

"Oh this?" asks the demon and pulls it from his body, slicked red with dark blood, and licks it clean with a long tongue. He tosses it at the old man's feet. "Surely you don't believe in fairy tales. Been reading Stoker's novel? Polidori's? The penny dreadfuls? A *vampire*, that's the word, isn't it? Isn't that what I'm supposed to be?" He sees the cross Tiger dropped on the bed and picks it up. "Oh, so terrifying!" he says in an effeminate voice. He tosses it across the room at Edgar, where it lands on his lap. "I am undead!" he declares. "That is all. I do not know why I live on, but I do. I cannot be killed. And you *cannot* know about me!"

"Where did you come from?" asks Lear.

The creature glares at him. "You erred when you killed the beast on the moors. You erred! You were going down a path I could not let you remain upon. Had you let it be, I might have let you be." He directs his hand to the gaping red wound on his chest. "Do you think you should interfere with ME?" Edgar tries to rise to face him, but the demon turns his gaze on him. The boy stays on his knees. "I learned terror from the best. Perhaps I'll put the lot of you on stakes when I am finished and then throw you into the Thames. It will be a good lesson to others who might find my trail."

"You beast," says Lear.

"You all smell! Garlic?" he sneers. "Human beings make up such nonsense!" He meets Edgar's stare again. "Yes, I am real. People want to think the likes of me only exist in stories or paintings or upon a stage. I love that. It keeps them afraid. They don't know the truth is in their art. Henry knows!"

He knocks a limp Tiger to the floor, rises and advances on them all. She staggers to her feet behind him, refusing to stay down.

"Take me first!" shouts Edgar. Perhaps the others can escape.

There is a sound from the next room.

"Count?" says a groggy voice. Irving is waking up. "Are you there?"

"Henry? Go back to sleep."

"Count? What are you doing?"

It strides past them into the other room and speaks to Irving in a soothing voice. "You are going to sleep," it says. "Listen to the sound of my voice. We are related, you and I. We have powers together. You are going to sleep."

"Come!" cries Lear. He reaches down and picks up his big blade and rushes into the drawing room. Irving is on the sofa with the creature, staring at him, and begins to turn his head toward the other five but the demon shouts at him.

"Look at me!"

Irving's face goes back to him. The group races to the door, into the hall and toward the stairs.

"He needs Irving!" cries Lear. "He provides him with a sea of blood every night. If he has to choose between him and us, he'll choose him."

"For now!" says Edgar.

They are in the street in a minute. It is a crisp summer morning. Out on Piccadilly, a few hundred yards away, they see pedestrians passing, and carriages beyond them. They run.

When they reach the thoroughfare, they turn back and see the revenant coming out of Irving's building. He eyes them. But he doesn't run. He cannot betray his presence in public. He has put Irving down and put on a clean shirt, all in a flash. He wants them. They have his secret.

"Oh God!" cries Lucy. "We need help!"

"From whom?" asks Jonathan. "Shall I stroll up to a bobbie and tell him a vampire is after us?"

"We could do that," says Lear, struggling forward, searching up and down the street for a carriage heading east. "And they might put us in a cell where this thing can't get at us. But it would only be temporary. It will come for us until it destroys us."

"We must confront it!" says Edgar. *Do not be afraid*, he tells himself, but it seems unkillable.

Lear flags down a cab.

"I will take Lucy with me to the theater. Lead it there, I hope, where we can corner it. You three return to the hotel and get the weapons. Both Thorne's rifle and cannon! Meet us. RUN!"

Lear and Lucy get into the cab. "Lyceum Theatre, fast!" he cries. The driver snaps his whip and they are off. Jonathan, Edgar and Tiger run with all they have along Piccadilly. She is still in bare feet, a strange sight on the street: a woman in an evening dress, holding it around her knees, running full out and keeping pace with two sprinting young men. It won't take them long. They will turn north at Regent Street and make good time in the early morning on its wide foot pavements. It should be less than five minutes from there up to Oxford Street, and less than that to reach the hotel.

The creature is coming east along Piccadilly now, toward them in the bright early sun, looking calm, his head nearly a foot above the rest of the crowd, that bowler hat pulled down, his aquiline nose, so like Driver's and Irving's, peeking out. They keep glancing back as they run up Regent Street. He doesn't follow. Instead, he turns in the direction the hansom cab went.

While Tiger changes her dress, Jonathan and Edgar get the rifle and cannon in hand quickly. They also wipe off the knives. They will not be able to entirely disguise what they have. Edgar brings the rifle, holding it down almost like a walking stick and Jon rolls the cannon, folded up into Thorne's ingenious box on wheels. Once they are out onto Portland Street, they rush down Regent, and then back toward the West End and the theater.

When they reach it, Lear and Lucy are nowhere in sight. But they see someone strolling along Wellington Street toward them.

It's Bram Stoker.

36

Confrontation

Stoker stops at the sight of them. As he does, Lear and Lucy emerge from hiding in a recessed doorway and the two parties stand some ten feet from each other. Jonathan is in front of the box he has been rolling along and Edgar turns slightly sideways, hiding the rifle as much as possible.

"We must apologize for our recent conduct, sir," says Lear finally. "We did not repay your kindness as we should have."

Stoker doesn't respond at first. Then he smiles. "Not at all. You have been in the grip of the master's spell. I remember the first time I saw Mr. Irving, upon a stage in Dublin when I was a young man. He was mesmerizing. It made me think all sorts of things. I saw the possibilities of art before me. I have gone on quite a journey with him since. I could not have written *Dracula* without him."

"Oh?"

"But enough of that; I understand your excitement."

"I wonder," asks Lear, surveying the street, "if we might view the auditorium once more. It was marvelous."

"I am sorry, but I am not at liberty to allow that, especially on your own. I was not entering the theater myself just now. I am on my way for breakfast nearby."

"A pity. I had more thoughts about your wonderful novel. I was thinking of how it is theatrical in a way, a deep way, and it filled me with ideas. The subtext in your work is remarkable. Surely this majestic place here influenced you. I wanted to see the stage again. And I wanted to speak with you in more depth. I am considering teaching *Dracula* next year, though I know that will be daring."

"You are?"

"Why, yes, of course. It deserves attention. There is more than one great artist at the Lyceum now, more than two including Miss Terry."

Stoker's eyes glint. "He never appreciates me, you know." He reaches into his pocket for his keys. "I suppose there is no harm in allowing you in for a while. I shall be round in about an hour or so. We can chat then."

He walks toward the doors and opens one. They step through, thanking him. He starts to close it and then opens it again.

"You know, I suppose I did see Dracula in real life."

"You did?" asks Edgar.

"I often hear Irving talking to someone in his room. But he isn't. It's just him rehearsing, putting on voices. There is one persona that sounds like the devil. I gave that voice to Dracula. Sir Henry has a painting of Vlad the Impaler on his wall, a sadistic ruler in eastern Europe long ago. He claims to be related to him." Stoker chuckles. "That's just him sinking himself into character, pretending that he has the mind of a wild artist who is above morality. I gave that voice to the man in the painting and I put it all together with the master's black eyes and his long porcelain face. Then . . ." He pauses. "I saw the demon."

"You saw it?"

"I . . . I saw someone walking away in the rain. From behind, he looked like Irving. He filled me with dread and excitement. It was just a coincidence, of course, but the image of that strange man helped me imagine my villain, make my story real. I believed in it even more." Stoker is staring off as if contemplating something only he can see. Then he remembers himself. "Nonsense!" he says and laughs. He closes the door after them and locks it from the outside.

A few minutes later, they are huddled in the lobby, making plans. The theater is quiet. Lucy has torn the bottom few inches off her dress so she can move about better, and taken off her shoes again. Somehow, she doesn't appear disheveled. Lear has dropped his coat and taken off his cravat. Stoker had either not noticed or not been concerned about the item that Jonathan was rolling behind him or the strange walking stick held slightly behind Edgar's back. They are inside the theater equipped with Thorne's powerful weapons.

"We need to stay together," says Tiger. "But we need to spread out to find this thing and draw it."

"How do we do that?" asks Jonathan.

"It will come searching for us," says Lear. "Here is what I suggest. We set up the cannon on the stage at the back, fully primed and loaded. We leave one person with it, back to the wall with no chance of being surprised. The other four stay together, bearing the knives and the rifle."

"I'm on the stage with the cannon," says Tiger immediately.

"But I—" begins Jonathan.

"No," says Lear, "I want it to be Brim."

Edgar wants that too. His eyes are shining. "All right," he says.

Ten minutes later, while the other four search the bowels of the theater, knives out and rifle trained, Edgar stands at the rear of the stage near the grave and the guillotine, adrenaline pumping through him. The weapon is ready, cannonballs loaded in the chambers of Thorne's ingenious barrel. It is light and moveable. He can swing it around and fire it quickly. He has it trained at exactly the right height to hit the revenant where the neck meets his head.

There is something magical about the silent auditorium. The seats are waiting. It strikes him that life is like this: an empty theater before we come into it, then there is a show, then we fade and the theater is quiet again.

"Where is he?" says Edgar into the scene. "*He* was the other man in the dressing room. *He* is using the great artist to mesmerize the crowds. But if he is really Irving's friend or master he knows this building intimately. Perhaps he is—"

A cold, skeletal hand covers Edgar's mouth.

"Good day, Master Brim," says the vampire. "So glad to see you alone upon the stage of life." Edgar turns his eyes upward and stares into the creature's, smiling down on him below those black brows and above that nose and red wet lips. The skin stretched over the skull is pale. He looks like a monstrous Irving with a shaved head. "A lovely soliloquy, but alas, it must end. I am going to remove my hand from your mouth now. If you cry out, I will kill you instantly."

Edgar doesn't say a word. He is trying to keep his lip from trembling, gazing into the revenant's eyes.

"*Do not be afraid.* Can you do it now?"

Edgar swallows. "I do not fear you."

"Oh yes, you do! Or you are a fool." He points behind him. "Observe." Edgar sees a door there, now open, disguised as part of the wall. "Mr. Henry Irving has shown me many things in this building, many passages." He turns to the auditorium. "I first saw him here long ago when he had his first great success in *The Bells*, which electrified London. *The Bells*! The *horror* of the bells!" The creature grins. "I was struck by the way he held the audience in his thrall. I had never seen anything like it. There seemed to be an opportunity there. But I had other things to do, another life on the continent. I had been coming to Britain for more than a decade . . . since your mentor made his kill on the moors." The demon is growing angry. He turns toward the boy. Edgar shrinks back, putting his spine against the wall. "I was born in Europe well before *Beowulf* was conceived, but we Visigoths had roots in Scandinavia. I knew of this so-called Grendel."

"How could . . . who are you, really?"

"I began as a mere traveling musician and soothsayer with a talent for mesmerizing. That's what they call it now, don't they, on the English stage in this century? My people sacked Rome in 410, you know, but I was never really one of them. I am an artist! I *believe* in art. I was an outcast, a minstrel playing upon my harp!

I went from village to village and performed for people. And I told them about their futures, about life after death, and made them believe it: me, a strangely tall Goth with magic in his eyes. I stole from them when I had them in my power. But at one place they found me out and attacked me! They chased me through a forest and brought me down, murdered me with axes and buried me in a shallow grave." He stares off. "But somehow . . . I awoke!"

Edgar knows he must keep the creature talking. It's his only hope. And it seems that this beast *wants* to talk. Perhaps he is lonely. He constantly spoke to Irving about his life, having found a vessel he could fill. Now he walks about the stage, as if he were a star performer, emoting, telling his tale.

"I didn't die, Master Brim! I don't know if the devil did this for me or to me." He pauses theatrically. "I am the one from whom the legend comes, but I cannot be killed with a stake to the chest. How ridiculous. I need blood to live, but I take it directly from the heart! This neck-sucking is pure invention." He looks out at the empty seats. "I did my deeds and ran: to Bohemia and the Balkans during the Dark Ages. I couldn't stay anywhere because I didn't age. I grew tired of hunting and craved easier opportunities to drink the sustenance I needed. And when I was being held in a Budapest jail by the Hungarians in the 1400s, biding my time, I met their great prisoner, a man called Vlad of the House of Draculesti."

Edgar's mouth drops open.

"You are astonished that I met the Impaler. I more than met him, my young friend, I *became* him! He was the Voivode, the prince of Wallachia on the Transylvanian border, a tall man with

318

dark eyes and hair like mine. So I took his blood and his life and escaped back to his country to rule!

"It was long before photography and realistic paintings and no one knew a great deal about Vlad's true appearance. He had been away for a long while. I saw an opportunity. I could reign in his castle and take the blood I needed by using his methods. I could make people fear me and do what I must! I killed many thousands, Master Brim, impaled them alive. I did it out of need, but I found it thrilled me too! When you cannot die, when God means nothing to you, you experiment." He turns to Edgar. "Now, what shall I do with you? You, who threaten to reveal my existence!"

He takes a stride and is instantly upon the boy, ripping his shirt open from neck to belt. Then he places a frigid hand on Edgar's chest and violently shoves him to the ground. Edgar's neck snaps back as he lands in the dirt, but he glares up at his enemy. He tries to tell himself that fear is of no use.

The demon regards him for a moment. "Dig!" he finally says.

"I beg . . . I beg your pardon?"

"I have several options," says the demon as he clenches his fists. "I could take your blood . . . or do something else." The shoulder-high wooden stakes are behind him on the graves, their points sharp. He bends over and caresses Edgar's chest with his cold fingertips. The boy knocks his hand away. "Or perhaps," says the monster, smiling, "I will have it all. I want you to dig."

A *grave*, thinks Edgar struggling to his feet, hesitating. He picks up a shovel left behind by the stagehands but stands still, shaking.

"BEGIN! Or I shall rip you open *now*!"

Edgar starts excavating a plot beside the one that is unearthed each night.

"No one can know I exist."

Edgar pivots and swings the shovel at the revenant's head. The creature catches the blade with his hand, though it slices into his palm. A glob of black blood plops out. He snatches the shovel from Edgar and smacks him across the head with the back of the blade. There's a dull sound as it strikes bone. Edgar staggers and falls. He sees stars.

"DIG!" cries the creature, throwing down the shovel and slurping on his wound. Edgar rolls over and climbs to his feet. He shovels, listening for sounds at the door between stabs at the soil.

"What about Stoker? He knows, doesn't he?"

"He is a problem with which I will deal. He does *not* know, but he has somehow learned bits and written this tract that puts the finger upon me, tells a sort of truth. I am not sure how I feel about it. It gives me a certain fame!" He puffs out his chest. "But it is *Irving* who fascinates me. In fourteen hundred years I have noticed few people who resemble me. Vlad was slightly comparable and one other had a distant similarity."

Driver, thinks Edgar.

"But Henry—his nose, sloping forehead, black brows and those eyes—that first night it was as if they were all cheering for me! I had been coming to the British Isles to keep Lear at bay. He should have let the Scandinavian beast be!"

"It killed his wife!"

The villain ignores him. "I knew the creature had vanished from its home and was being pursued. I tracked it to the moors and found its corpse, picked to pieces by crows. I discovered who had done it: the man with the grievous wound. He knew about us!" The demon stares out to the seats. "I know of one other. It would come for you should you kill me. But that *will not* happen!" He stamps his foot. "Lear became afraid. I listened to him begging God, worried about the things the lunatic Shakespeare said. Lear was a formidable opponent with his threat to reveal my existence. So I couldn't kill him, but I watched him. I snatched a German peasant about my height and skull size and worked on him. I cut out his tongue." Edgar swallows. "I adjusted his features—it wasn't hard to find the pieces I needed. I deeply entranced him. He is terrified of me! And so he should be."

Edgar doesn't interrupt. Keep him talking, he thinks. The demon turns to the audience and addresses the empty seats with feeling.

"I eliminated the driver who had been at the college and left the mute freak on the moors, dressed in a hooded garment. The fools at the college kept him to replace their man, just as I hoped. And then, I sometimes traveled up there and exchanged places with him, keeping him in the cellar room when I was in residence, adjusting him. I could move about as I pleased, listen and keep an eye on Lear." There are still no sounds outside the auditorium doors. "The imbecile! Even after I killed his student to warn him, he still spoke to Allen Brim about demons."

"You murdered him!" Edgar quivers.

"Lear couldn't resist you when you came! He told you! So I took his son too. The power to expose me was being passed on. And then *you* spoke to the child! *You* spoke of us while I was in the very room, listening! So I took little Newman. I put mouthfuls of my saliva into him when I drained him, so he would live in his grave, so I could excavate him and have more sustenance. I was on the moors a long while and needed it. But then *you and Lear* dug up the child and took off his head! How dare you!"

Edgar sees real passion in the creature's face. Then his voice turns softer, more dramatic in the empty theater.

"Irving loved his secret, sinister friend, a man of manners from eastern Europe, an aristocrat, related to the Impaler! I gave him the painting. He and I, we like our art deep and dark; the ingredient of evil in his work makes it frightening and real! I hinted I had killed people, that I might have known or been the Ripper."

"Were you?"

The monster merely smiles. "Irving gave me the costume he first wore as Mephistopheles as a token of friendship. He was aroused by the idea that he might be Vlad's descendant! He could see we had similar profiles. I began to entrance him. And so, he unknowingly mesmerizes crowds for me every night! Crowds of blood! I could never have done it alone, not safely." He pauses again. "But Irving has great powers. I do not suck his blood! He is my artist! My twin! He is almost too much for me. I must keep him entranced."

Edgar, filled with adrenaline, had worked quickly, and the grave is four feet deep.

"Get in!" says the revenant.

Edgar's heart leaps in his chest.

"In?"

"I am going to bury you alive, sir, and when your friends arrive, I will show them what I have done. They will hear you moaning. I shall deal with at least one of them too. Unfortunately, more than that would be suspicious." He turns to the wooden stakes behind him and grips one. "Yes, just you and one more today," he sighs. His huge left hand caresses the sharp end of the stake. "But believe me, once they have seen how you and your friend die, the others will never bother me again."

37

Buried Alive

E dgar stands on the edge of his grave. He is inside one of his nightmares: inside a story by Poe. He can no longer help himself or his friends. He pulls open his shirt, fully exposing his bare chest, the breastbone over the heart.

"I would rather—"

The monster waves it off. "I have made up my mind."

"How will—"

"Your death be explained? Your friends will be forced to say, if they say anything, that you have disappeared, another death like many others that happen in London every day, dead like those who just happen to expire after being overly excited at the theater."

"But . . . but my body."

"Now, now, Master Brim, you are not thinking. I know you did the tour with Mr. Stoker. In fact, I was flitting about here when he was showing you around and droning on. He is such a tearfully boring man, not my choice for a biographer! Recall, sir, what he said. This mound of earth was brought up from below. When they finish the play's short run, they shall open up the stage boards and let it fall back to the basement where no one goes. You shall vanish, as will the contents of one more grave. But look at it this way: you will rest forever in the Royal Lyceum Theatre with the ghosts. GET IN!"

Edgar is shaking. He feels as though he will retch. But he has no choice. He drops into the grave and lies in it. He is almost unconscious. Perhaps it is the blow to the head or maybe the mind-bending fear. A face appears at the edge of the plot, peering down at him. *The hag!* Then the first shovelful of earth hits him in the chest. Edgar sees the creature smiling as he works. He tries to imagine his mother. He can't see her, so he thinks of his father, of Annabel Thorne, of Lucy and Tiger. It calms him somewhat as the weight of the dirt gets heavier. His arms are at his sides. The vampire is keeping the soil from his face, as if he wants to watch his expression as he dies. Edgar remembers little Newman and tries to have courage. The weight is getting oppressive. He is having trouble breathing. He tries to move his arms and legs but can't. The grave is filled almost to the top from his neck to his feet.

The demon begins to drop the dirt onto Edgar's face. "I wonder," he says, "if I can infuse Irving with my blood, like in the story books, and make him my follower forever!"

Jonathan takes his first shot from just inside the doors. It hits the demon in the shoulder near the neck, Thorne's exploding bullet so powerful that it knocks the beast down. The girls shout in approval. The creature is stunned. But he rises to his feet, black blood in his gaping wound. He sees Jonathan standing in front of Lear and the girls, aiming the gun once more, and drops to his knees, just before the trigger is pulled. The bullet rips over him and hits the mountain of earth, disappearing deep into it. The revenant rises and swoops across the stage and leaps into the aisle. Lucy screams.

Edgar struggles in the grave, but the hag has jumped down, right on top of him!

He hears another shot. The bullet zings through the air and thwacks into the earth. Edgar can hear the others running, attempting to get away and crying out. He tries to move under the dirt, the hag with her face in his. "No!" he screams at her.

Jonathan fires another shot and curses. Four shots, thinks Edgar. He has only six. Two more shots ring loud in rapid succession, the demon cries out at the sound of one. Then Edgar hears Jon cursing their enemy. He can hear them grappling.

He hears the vampire dragging Jonathan down the aisle toward the stage, his friend making a gurgling sound. They come into Edgar's view, over the hag's shoulder. The demon has another bloody black wound, this one in the abdomen, but it doesn't seem to be bothering him. His face is flushed with anger and he has Jonathan by the throat. His fingernails are long and sharp. He's dragging his captive toward one of the tall wooden stakes.

"Let him be!" he hears Lucy cry out, and then Lear too, begging the monster to put his grandson down, to take him instead. They all seem to be on the stage now, though Edgar can't hear Tiger. *Where is she?* he thinks. Is his dear friend dead? *Tiger!* Terror engulfs him and he fights, spitting in the hag's face, frantically twisting and turning beneath the earth.

"I shall kill him as you watch," says the demon. "I will show you, Lear, what your curiosity has done! You will see true pain administered to the strongest of you all, and then I will suck him dry while he writhes. You are turning away, old man! Watch!" Edgar sees the villain take a swing at someone with Lear's big knife in hand! The professor cries out and Edgar hears a thud. Lucy screams again. *Where's Tiger?*

Edgar makes one last twist, using a strength that seems to him to come not from his mortal powers but somewhere else. He hears another shot. *Seven?*

The vampire groans and falls from view, just as Edgar rises inside the grave. Drops of black blood splatter across his face. He scrambles out and gets shakily to his feet. The revenant has a hole in the side of his neck, a third of it ripped away, and lies on the ground, gasping, struggling to get up, his white shirt soaking up his blood. Looking across the auditorium, Edgar sees Tiger standing rigid with her mouth set, the rifle still aimed this way. A seventh bullet! He remembers now that she had taken an extra one from Alfred Thorne's lab. *Tiger! The one and only!* She had been re-loading. She has made a nearly direct hit! But now all the bullets are gone.

"Help me!" cries Edgar to Lucy as he rushes toward the demon. Lear is groaning on the ground, holding his head. Jonathan is groggy too and Tiger is across the auditorium by the doors. The creature has taken all their knives and thrown them out into the seats. He is trying to get to his feet, struggling, but his strength is returning. Edgar bears down on him. Lucy moves toward them.

"Help me pull him!" cries Edgar.

"Pull him where? We need to take off his head!"

Their enemy gets onto his knees.

"Pull him!"

Then she sees what Edgar is planning.

The *guillotine*!

Edgar kicks the vampire in the temple and knocks him down and they both seize a shoulder, pulling him toward the razor-sharp killing machine. The demon's eyes look like an animal's being led to slaughter. There is fear in them!

He tries to resist them. "Another will come after you!" he cries.

They lug him closer, up the little mound toward the guillotine, Lucy summoning all her strength.

The creature pushes against them, succeeds in shoving them off and staggering to his feet. Edgar thinks of little Newman wanting to be the hero in the life that he never got to live. He rushes at the demon as if he were against Fardle again on the rugby field. He bends down as he approaches and hits his target low at the knees, sending him flying backward. The creature falls and his neck hits the guillotine right in the head hole and the blade rockets down.

"Another will—"

The revenant's head strikes the soil with a thud. It rolls several feet away and stops, the eyes staring up.

38

Another?

They help Lear and Jonathan to their feet. They move as quickly as they can, Lear sitting in a seat, still groggy. There is a wound just below his rib cage, that he is staunching with his suit coat. They bury the creature in the grave that was meant for Edgar, his head placed at his feet. They find the knives and clean them with handkerchiefs and put the exploded bullets in the box with the cannon on wheels. When they are done, they rush up the aisle toward the doors. One suddenly opens.

It's Bram Stoker.

His face looks ruddy from his meal and walk, and he is smiling. "Ah, there you are! Shall we adjourn to the Beefsteak Room for our discussion?"

"Uh," says Edgar, "as you can see, Professor Lear is not feeling well."

Lear has his hand on his coat, hiding his wound. He offers a slight smile. "I am so sorry, Stoker. Can we arrange this for another time?"

The red-haired man's face falls a little. "I suppose we can."

They nod at him and make their way toward the door. He doesn't seem to have noticed Edgar's dirty clothes, Lucy's bare feet, that they are all disheveled. His mind appears to be on something else.

"I doubt," he says behind them, "that I shall ever write another book like *Dracula*. I doubt that I can revisit such truths. It is too much. I had my moment and now it has passed. But, we shall talk."

"Most assuredly," says Lear.

Jonathan takes the old man back to the Langham in a cab. The others follow on foot, Edgar saying little, keeping most of his story so Lear can hear it later on. He says nothing of the demon's warning about another creature coming, but he looks behind several times as they walk. Lucy heard the vampire's threat, but in all the excitement, she seems to have forgotten. Once, Edgar thinks he sees something, big and freakish, staring out at them from the corner of an alleyway. But it vanishes.

Lear had seemed to be recovering by the time they got him into the cab, so Tiger and Lucy are happy as they walk by Edgar's side.

"We have destroyed the menace," says Tiger, her face beaming.

"And grandfather seems to have survived," says Lucy. "It is almost too much to ask for!" They can barely believe that everything is coming to a happy ending.

Edgar tries not to show his concern.

When they reach Lear's room, the old professor is much better. Jonathan has put him in bed and his wound appears to be slight. The hotel has supplied some iodine and a bandage and he's sitting up, talking. But he doesn't like everything Brim has to say.

Edgar recounts the history of the revenant as told to him by the hideous man himself. He had no minions, it seems.

"Shakespeare is right," says Lear. "If his kind could make undead followers like the books say, and they in turn could make more, we would all be such creatures by now."

"Perhaps we are," says Jonathan. "Brim has rather long teeth, think you not?"

They all laugh, except Edgar.

"Master Brim, what are you thinking?" Lear looks as if he knows.

"He spoke of another."

The room goes silent.

"You mean," says Jonathan finally, "just like the little lunatic said?"

"Yes."

"So you are going to take the word of an aberration who was attempting to frighten you and a mad old man who talks to ghosts? If something were after us, wouldn't it be in pursuit immediately?" He turns to Lucy. "Seen any monsters in the hallway?" He gets down on his hands and knees and checks under Lear's bed. "None in there!"

"We must remain vigilant," says the professor.

And so they do. But nothing comes. There's no sign of any sort. The four friends grow progressively bolder and lighter, taking a few chances, splitting up for little trips together in the city—Edgar with Tiger, Edgar with Lucy, Jonathan with Tiger. They take Thorne's weapons to Drury Lane and leave them with Shakespeare, just in case they should need them soon. The little man almost collapses with excitement. Lear remains in his room recovering, though they are sure to never leave him alone. But on the third day, he convinces them to enjoy dinner together in the Palm Court, without him. He wants to sleep.

The four young people are anxious to turn from bad tidings, to enjoy themselves. The boys sit on one side of the marble table with the spotless white tablecloth and gleaming china and cutlery, the girls on the other, engaging in lively conversation. They speak of Lear's improving health and their great triumph. They discuss the terrible news in the papers about Henry Irving. He has fallen on the stairs at his flat and injured his legs and has cancelled the last day of *Faust* and other performances for an indefinite period. The great man has never missed a single day of an engagement in his career.

"Perhaps we can put to rest our concerns about more demons?" asks Jonathan.

"I hope so," says Edgar.

"Well, it is taking its time, if it is about!"

"If something did come," asks Lucy, a little tentatively, "it would come for all of us, wouldn't it?"

"It would know that we all know," says Edgar.

"Well, Brim," says Jonathan, "you are such a cheery chap! Look around you. No monsters, no demons, only piles of food, beautiful girls and one grump!"

They all laugh.

"Anyway, I shall be at Sandhurst in no time," cries Jonathan, "learning to shoot better than I do now!"

"One can only hope!" exclaims Edgar and then receives a kick in the shins.

"And I will soon be the toughest man in the bank business in London!" adds Tiger.

They laugh again.

"Perhaps Lu could marry you?" says Jon. "She's looking for a gentleman with earning power."

"Oh, be quiet!" says Lucy. "You never know what I might do!"

Edgar smiles at her. "And what about you, Edgar?"

A note had arrived from Alfred Thorne that morning. "Dear Brim," it had said, "I await your return." That was all.

"I don't know. I shall go back to Thorne House first, of course."

"Become chief assistant to the weapons man?" asks Jonathan. "Ah, I can see it now. Edgar Brim, vanquisher of millions."

"I doubt that."

"Then what, old boy?"

"I think I should like to write."

Tiger smiles.

"Write what?" asks Lucy.

"Novels. I think they will be frightening tales."

39

Not the End

They climb the stairs back to the top floor of the Langham, laughing and teasing each other, their stomachs full.

"I think I need to loosen my stays!" says Tiger.

But they freeze when they come to the end of the hall. Lear's door is open. There is a hole in it, a big one, as if made by a sledgehammer, or an enormous fist.

Inside, the room is silent. And so is Lear.

He lies in his bed with his eyes staring wide and hardly breathing.

Lucy runs to her grandfather, shaking. She takes his head in both her hands.

"Monster," he says, barely above a whisper.

"Another!" says Jonathan, his face white, coming up to the bedside with Tiger.

"Worse," says Lear, "worse."

"Don't talk!" cries Lucy. "We'll get a doctor."

The old professor lifts his head and looks toward Edgar Brim. "It is coming for you all," he gasps. And the light goes out in his eyes.

Acknowledgments

The Dark Missions of Edgar Brim was many years in the making
and many people contributed to its creation. First there were
Alison Morgan and Tara Walker at Tundra Books, who loved the
idea and encouraged me to pursue it. Tara, a kindred spirit and
believer in my work, then stuck with Brim and with me through
thick and thin, through complex and changing story structures
and editing rounds, all the way to the end. I feel lucky to have her
on my side. Lara Hinchberger entered fearlessly into the creative
process about halfway through, providing new perspectives and a
steady editing hand, bringing her passion and understanding to
what we were building. Her work was invaluable. And Shana Hayes
helped us near the end, undoing final knots and setting the story
properly in history whenever it unintentionally strayed. Jennifer
Lum, who created such a striking look for The Boy Sherlock
Holmes novels, has done the same for our first Edgar Brim cover.
This project was most assuredly a collaborative effort.

There are authors to thank as well, each of whose works I
mined for information and inspiration. Bram Stoker, creator of the

immortal *Dracula* is, of course, at the front of the line. I also read deeply in the works of Mary Shelley, John Polidori, Wilkie Collins, Sheridan Le Fanu, James Malcolm Rymer, Johann Wolfgang von Goethe and the one and only Edgar Allan Poe, that triple threat of American letters and one of history's most sensitive and artistic souls. Also of particular guidance were Michael Holroyd's *A Strange Eventful History: The Dramatic Lives of Ellen Terry, Henry Irving, and Their Remarkable Families*, Barbara Belford's *Bram Stoker and the Man Who Was Dracula* and *The New Annotated Dracula,* put together by the big-brained Leslie S. Klinger, who seems to have similar tastes to mine, being one of the world's foremost experts about a chap named Sherlock Holmes.

Henry Irving and his extraordinary art were also inspirations. I have long wanted to write about him, wish with all my heart I had seen him in action and greatly enjoyed putting him back on the stage, at least in my mind. My apologies go to him, Mr. Stoker, Miss Terry and other historical figures for sometimes slightly adjusting their lives and the dates of their endeavors to fit my story. I am in possession of a hard-earned artistic license, as they all (thankfully!) were too, and I occasionally used it.

Final thanks go to the people who are and always will be the constants in my life: my amazing wife, Sophie, and our maturing and brilliant kids, Johanna, Hadley and Sam.

Novels can have very different starting points. Mine usually begin not with characters or even a scene or a plot, but with my story's meaning. *Edgar Brim* began with a desire to write about fear. We all fear too much and today many people, often our young people, are debilitated with fears they sometimes cannot even articulate: fear and anxiety that can lead to depression, other mental illnesses and, occasionally, to suicide. It is due to them and to my concerns about those problems, more than anything else, that *Brim* came about. I made Edgar a fighter, a hunter and vanquisher of his fears, and I wish that for others who struggle as well.

Do not be afraid . . . unless you are reading this novel!

Be sure to read all six books in Shane Peacock's
award-winning Boy Sherlock Holmes series.

EYE OF THE CROW

It is the spring of 1867, and a yellow fog hangs over London. In the dead of night, a woman is brutally stabbed and left to die in a pool of blood. No one sees the terrible crime. Or so it seems.

Nearby, a brilliant, bitter boy dreams of a better life. He is the son of a Jewish intellectual and a highborn lady – social outcasts – impoverishment the price of their mixed marriage. The boy's name is Sherlock Holmes.

Strangely compelled to visit the scene, Sherlock comes face to face with the young Arab wrongly accused of the crime. By degrees, he is drawn to the center of the mystery, until he, too, is a suspect.

Danger runs high in this desperate quest for justice. As the clues mount, Sherlock sees the murder through the eye of its only witness. But a fatal mistake and its shocking consequence change everything and put him squarely on a path to becoming a complex man with a dark past – and the world's greatest detective.

DEATH IN THE AIR

till reeling from his mother's death, brought about by his involvement in solving London's brutal East End murder, young Sherlock Holmes commits himself to fighting crime . . . and is soon immersed in another case.

While visiting his father at work, Sherlock stops to watch a dangerous high-trapeze performance, framed by the magnificent glass ceiling of the legendary Crystal Palace. But without warning, the aerialist drops, screaming and flailing to the floor. He lands with a sickening thud, just feet away and rolls almost onto the boy's boots. He is bleeding profusely and his body is grotesquely twisted. Leaning over, Sherlock brings his ear up close. "Silence me . . ." the man gasps and then lies still. In the mayhem that follows, the boy notices something amiss that no one else sees – and he knows that foul play is afoot. What he doesn't know is that his discovery will set him on a trail that leads to an entire gang of notorious and utterly ruthless criminals.

VANISHING GIRL

When a wealthy young socialite mysteriously
vanishes in Hyde Park, young Sherlock Holmes
is compelled to prove himself once more.
There is much at stake: the kidnap victim, an
innocent child's survival, the fragile relationship between himself
and the beautiful Irene Doyle. Sherlock must act quickly if he is to
avoid the growing menace of his enemy, Malefactor, and further
humiliation at the hands of Scotland Yard.

As twisted and dangerous as the backstreets of Victorian
London, this third case in The Boy Sherlock Holmes series takes
the youth on a heart-stopping race against time to the countryside,
the coast, and into the haunted lair of exotic – and deadly – night
creatures.

Despite the cold, the loneliness, the danger, and the memories of his shattered family, one thought keeps Sherlock going;
soon, very soon, the world will come to know him as the master
detective of all time.

THE SECRET FIEND

In 1868, Benjamin Disraeli becomes England's first Jewish-born prime minister. Sherlock Holmes welcomes the event – but others fear it. The upper classes worry that the black-haired Hebrew cannot be good for the empire. The wealthy hear rumblings as the poor hunger for sweeping improvements to their lot in life. The winds of change are blowing.

Late one night, Sherlock's admirer and former schoolmate, Beatrice, arrives at his door, terrified. She claims a maniacal, bat-like man has leapt upon her and her friend on Westminster Bridge. The fiend she describes is the Spring Heeled Jack, a fictional character from the old Penny Dreadful thrillers. Moreover, Beatrice declares the Jack has made off with her friend. She begs Holmes to help, but he finds the story incredible. Reluctant to return to detective work, he pays little heed – until the attacks increase, and Spring Heeled Jacks seem to be everywhere. Now, all of London has more to worry about than politics. Before he knows it, the unwilling boy detective is thrust, once more, into the heart of a deadly mystery, in which everyone, even his closest friend and mentor, is suspect.

THE DRAGON TURN

herlock Holmes and Irene Doyle are as riveted as the rest of the audience. They are celebrating Irene's sixteenth birthday at The Egyptian Hall as Alistair Hemsworth produces a real and very deadly dragon before their eyes. This single, fantastic illusion elevates the previously unheralded magician to star status, making him the talk of London. He even outshines the Wizard of Nottingham, his rival on and off the stage.

Sherlock and Irene rush backstage after the show to meet the great man, only to witness Inspector Lestrade and his son arrest the performer. It seems one-upmanship has not been as satisfying to Hemsworth as the notion of murder. The Wizard is missing; his spectacles and chunks of flesh have been discovered in pools of blood in Hemsworth's secret workshop. That, plus the fact that Nottingham has stolen Hemsworth's wife away, speak of foul play *and* motive. There is no body, but there has certainly been a grisly death.

In this spine-tingling case, lust for fame and thirst for blood draw Sherlock Holmes one giant step closer to his destiny – master detective of all time.

BECOMING HOLMES

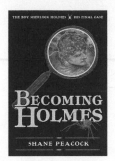

t is the summer of 1870 in London, and death seems to be everywhere; at least it feels that way to Sherlock Holmes. Almost seventeen now, he cannot shake the blackness that has descended upon him. And somewhere in the darkness, Sherlock's great enemy, the villainous Malefactor, is spinning his web of evil, planning who knows what.

Only one thing can rouse the young detective from the depths of despair: the possibility of justice. Holmes uncovers a new and terrible plot unleashed by his nemesis. Prepared to do anything to stop Malefactor, Sherlock sets out to destroy his rival, bringing him and his henchmen down, once and for all. Everything in the brilliant boy's life changes as death knocks again. . . . In this shocking and spine-tingling conclusion to the award-winning series, Sherlock Holmes transforms, becoming the immortal master of criminal detection.